following LOVE

CELESTE O. NORFLEET

following LOVE

FOLLOWING LOVE

An Arabesque novel

ISBN-13: 978-0-373-83020-6
ISBN-10: 0-373-83020-3

www.kimanipress.com

Printed in U.S.A.

To Fate & Fortune

Acknowledgment

To all the readers who stay up late at night reading to the last page. Thank you.

To all the readers who write me with comments, suggestions and praise. Thank you.

To all the readers who patiently, faithfully wait for my next book to be released. Thank you.

Prologue

The scent of fresh flowers punctuated the air in the small room with a heavenly bouquet. Beautifully adorned, the Mayfield Plains Plantation was the perfect setting for their little soiree. Within the lavishly decorated mansion, set aside from the formal dining hall, was the ladies' afternoon tea-room, which was occupied by a small party.

It was the final day of celebration and the last formal flower show of the season. Although it was only the middle of summer, the winter would soon come and a well-earned hibernation was due for all of them.

The ladies, Louise, Ellen, Pearl, May, Julia and Grace, called themselves the Little Girls Flowers Club. Since they'd met while in a ladies' room line at the regional flower show nearly forty-five years ago, the name seemed humorously appropriate. Originally six, only five remained. One, Grace, had moved back to her home in London, England, a year ago.

This afternoon the grouping of five had together celebrated eight first-place blue ribbons, four second-prize ribbons, two best-in-show ribbons and one unprecedented grand-prize ribbon. Now, disbanding in a scattered array—a flight to Colorado, a flight to Boston, and a train ride to Florida—they parted ways. There were two left seated at the large table in the center of the room.

The lunch dishes long since cleared, along with the celebratory champagne, the two sat sipping tea reminiscing the good old days and plans for the coming weeks. Then a moment of silence passed between them.

Ellen Peyton smiled her satisfaction. It had been a good week. A blue-ribbon win for her orchids and begonias; they were the best she'd grown in years. Decidedly it was the new soil mix she been trying out and the new terrace bed she'd had built inside her greenhouse pagoda.

She picked up the ribbon and ran her finger along the gently embossed lettering. Louise looked on, knowing the look on her friend's face. Never bothering with formalities, their friendship was the closest. "If you're not careful you're going to rub the lettering right off that ribbon." Ellen looked up, seeing her friend of so many years smiling at her. "You want to tell me what's going on? You've been distracted all week."

Ellen knew that hiding anything from Louise was really impossible. She smiled then sighed heavily. "You remember me telling you that my great-niece, Dena, came to stay with me a few months ago to help me out when I sprained my wrist."

"Yes, of course," Louise said, already knowing Dena's tragic circumstances. "It was a perfect idea, her being there helped you with your wrist and hopefully got her out and back to living her life again."

"I had hoped so but it looks like she's still hiding behind her self-imposed guilt. She never leaves the house, barely eats, and heaven knows when she's going to get herself a social life and meet someone. She's been at the house for three months and not a soul even knows she's even there."

"The death of her husband still pains her," Louise said sympathetically.

"She's just about martyred the man. Mind you, I'd be the last to speak ill of the dead, but Forester Graham was a lazy, two-timing, philandering momma's boy with a trust fund, a serious drinking habit and not enough sense to appreciate what he had."

Louise chuckled softly at the stark honesty as Ellen was well-known for speaking her mind and letting the chips fall as they may. She reached over and took Ellen's hand. They were more than friends, they were family. When one of them hurt, they all did. "She's made the first step, she's left the house and now she's back with you. That's a good thing. And as for Forester, she'll learn to let go."

"Not until she sees him for what he really was."

"That, too, will come, in time," Louise added.

"It's been almost five years," Ellen said impatiently. "She stayed in that house of theirs and stewed about his memory for too long. It took me almost six months and a sprained wrist just to talk her into getting out of that house and staying with me awhile. Now she wants to get rid of the house and move halfway across the country to start a new life with her son. She needs to be here with her family."

"Did she sell it?" Louise asked.

"No, not yet. I know it's probably the best thing for her. She just doesn't need to move so far away."

"How's Dillon?" Louise asked.

"The little scamp gets more handsome as the days go by. He's such a sweet child, fun, loving, nothing like his father, thank heaven. And Adel, that grandmother of his, has near 'bout destroyed everything with her vindictive selfishness. Do you know that she still won't release Forester's life insurance policy or his trust fund to Dillon? It's been held up in her legal mumbo-jumbo law firm for years. Dena's just about worn out fighting with her."

"We can't change other people, you know that. We can only change ourselves."

"I know," Ellen conceded. "I just wish there was something more I could do to help her heal her heart and move on emotionally."

"Being there with you is exactly what she needs."

"But I can't be there if she moves away."

"When exactly does she intend to move?"

"She mentioned the end of the summer. But thankfully the real-estate market is slow right now, so interest in a large, expensive house is sporadic at best. And thanks to Adel, she won't move until she's finished with the legal battle. She doesn't need the money to move or get on with her life. She just wants all this behind her and to walk away from all this without looking back. She's given herself until the end of summer, that's less than three months."

"I'm sure that's best, and at least she'll be around until then, that's something."

Ellen nodded, knowing that Louise was right. She would

always be there for her only great-niece but she still refused to sit by and do nothing. There had to be something else she could do to help Dena through her sorrow. Moments later she smiled, remembering. "You still make love matches, don't you?"

Louise nodded.

Ellen smiled. "I've been thinking, there's a nice young man…"

"Only when they're ready, Ellen, you know that. The heart can't find love if it's not open to it," Louise said. Then seeing her friend's disappointment added, "But when she's ready, love will come to her. There'll be no stopping it, believe me. I've watched love a long time, even helped out a time or two. When Dena's ready, love will come."

"When she's ready," Ellen repeated despondently.

"Yes." Louise nodded and winked as she gently squeezed Ellen's hand. "But in the meantime, this is what you do…"

Chapter 1

Breathe in, breathe out. Repeat, she reminded herself.

Dena Graham had walked by the window earlier, paused, glanced out then walked away. Ten minutes later she did the same thing. Now five minutes after that, curtains slightly drawn back this time, here she was again. "Oh, God, what is wrong with me?" she muttered with her eyes still glued to her secret treasure.

He, whoever he was, was her voyeuristic pleasure. He'd come a few times before and each time she'd watched from the safety of the house. But now, ever vigilant to his body's movements, she out-and-out stared. She just couldn't help herself.

A few weeks ago he'd stopped by and talked with her aunt at length. She still smiled her naughty obsession remembering his stance as they'd spoken. His hands firmly on narrow hips, rear end perfectly rounded, legs taut and firm; he was built and gorgeous. He'd turned at one point and glanced up at her bedroom window. She'd ducked back quickly then realized that there was no way he could possibly see her.

Then, to her lustful pleasure, a week ago he'd returned. He'd stopped by to move some oversize bags of soil into the greenhouse. Then he'd repaired the side fence, which her aunt had accidentally backed into with her small riding lawn mower.

Now here they were again, him outside and her inside looking out.

Unlike the previous times, this time her mouth hung open like a gapping black hole as the palpitations of her heartbeat shifted to a whole new rhythm. Her eyes riveted to every movement and her mouth salivating, she watched with anticipation each time his tool pulled back and slammed forward, hard and piercing. It was as if the force of his body was slamming into hers and she felt every sweet, savoring penetrating blow. Her cotton shirt did little to dissuade the sudden warmth of the stilled air around her that had suddenly heated up another ten degrees.

His body was perfection. Aptly muscled and strong, it was the kind that came with good genes and hard physical labor, not the kind that came from a monthly membership in a swanky urban gym and pseudo pick-up juice bar. Sweet, rich chocolate-brown, his shoulders sparkled with moisture as the hot sun washed over him and every muscle in his back responded to the pull of the hammer. He swung back, her head bobbed up. He swung forward, her breath halted. God help her, she was enjoying every second of her secret voyeuristic fantasy.

"Over four years of nothing and now out of the blue, you show up. Whoever you are, you've got a lot of nerve," she whispered through the glass pane, then shook her head and continued to stare. "Umph, umph, umh."

"What was that, dear?" Ellen asked.

"Nothing," she said, quickly turning away.

"Lord, it's so good to be home. I'll tell you those flower shows are wonderful, but all-in-all there's nothing like coming back home and being with family again," Ellen said as she sliced through the last lemon on the cutting board.

"It's good to have you back, Aunt Ellen," Dena said. "We missed you."

"I missed you and Dillon, too. But that flower show was breathtaking. I don't know when I've seen so many beautiful species of flower. And my friend, Louise Gates—you've heard me mention Louise, she lives in Virginia on Crescent Island—well, she had the most incredible peonies, big, colorful and full of life. They were truly a work of art. As a matter of fact she'll be stopping by in a few weeks to bring a few samples. I'm gonna try my hand at greenhouse peonies."

"Oh," Dena said matter-of-factly, finding her attention drawn back to the window again.

"I told her about the new soil mix I formulated for the layered flower bed in the greenhouse. After that fungus and infestation got ahold of my soil I didn't expect to get much, but using that new mix has really changed things." Ellen dropped the sliced lemons into the glass pitcher, added sugar and water then stirred. "Anyway, Louise and maybe a few other members of our ladies' flower club said that they'd stop by for a visit later in the month. I can't wait until she sees the new greenhouse producers."

"Oh," Dena responded absently.

"So how was your week?" Ellen asked as she added the last few lemon slices, mint zest and a peppermint sprig for garnish.

"Oh," Dena repeated.

Ellen looked up, seeing her niece distracted and looking out of the window again. "What on earth are you looking at? You've been at the window for the past twenty minutes."

Dena didn't answer, she couldn't. She'd heard the question, she just couldn't respond. The dryness in her throat wouldn't let her. All of her senses were trained on the single form and awesome power he exuded.

"Aha, yes." Ellen smiled knowingly. "Julian Hamilton. Now that's what you really need," Ellen said as she stood behind her niece and peered through the windowpane.

"This isn't gonna work," Dena suddenly said, dropping the curtain back in place but still staying at the window.

"What isn't going to work?" her aunt asked.

"Me, here, now. I can't do this. I thought I could but I can't. When you were away I started thinking, now that your wrist is better and you don't really need us anymore, there's no real reason for Dillon and I to still be here."

"Of course there is, don't be ridiculous. Dillon loves it here and this is where you belong."

"No, Aunt Ellen, not anymore. I think it's time I did something major, so we are going to move to California at the end of summer."

"California?"

"Yes, Dillon and I already talked about it and he's very excited. So right after his birthday party we're going to move."

"Dena, Dillon is three, he's excited about ants. This is your home. You're just restless. You need something to do besides think all day. I have my plants and flowers, and now Dillon has his morning and afternoon day school.

"What you need is a distraction or maybe a part-time job, something to busy your mind. You're in this house day in and day out. You need to get out and do something productive. And now for starters, do me a favor and take this outside. It's as hot as the devil out there. Go on, it's high time you got out there and met some new people."

Dena moved away quickly as if she hadn't been staring at the man for the past twenty minutes and two months. The instant she saw the pitcher of lemonade and glass on the table, she knew. "Aunt Ellen, I know what you're doing. Stop it. You can't just replace one man with another. They don't just pop up like tissues in a tissue box. It doesn't work like that."

"Of course it does. Child, in my experience, one is as good as another, and if anyone, I should know. Men come along every day, you just have to see the good in them and choose well."

Having been married four times, twice to the same man, Ellen Peyton, a slender, soft-spoken woman with a mane of salt-and-pepper hair, knew a thing or two about men or at least about falling in love.

Now twice a widow, she enjoyed life to the fullest with her plants. Years ago she'd opened and continued to run a small wholesale nursery that catered to a very select clientele. Interior designers, wedding consultants, upscale landscapers and a few high-end garden centers were privileged to carry her plants. With her botanist background she was an award-winning horticulturist who lovingly cultivated everything around her, including her family.

"I loved Forester," Dena said barely over a whisper, "even if he..."

Ellen reached over and draped her arm around Dena's waist and leaned her head on her shoulder. "Of course you did," she said, easily knowing also that the truth had blurred over the years as it's often wont to do. Death had a way of purging wrongs, creating martyrs and sweetening the bitter truth. She could see that the pain of loss, now just over four years, was still raw. So even now there was no way she could say what she really wanted to say.

"I know you loved him," Ellen added, leaning up to face Dena. "Forester came into your life at a time when you truly needed each other. He was there for you. That's all any woman can ask. But, child, he's been gone for over four years and you need to go on with your life."

"How can I?"

"You take one day at a time, you heal, you find peace and then you go on. But you never forget the good times."

"Do you ever miss having a man around?"

"I have men around here all the time," she said, glancing toward the window.

"You know what I mean," Dena added.

Ellen smiled and winked. "You're never too old to want a man around from time to time. Now, take this outside."

"I didn't come back here for this. Dillon and I just needed a refuge for a while, until I sell the house."

"Well, you were right in coming here. But you need to think of your future."

"I am. As soon as the house is sold, we're moving west."

"And then what?" Ellen asked plainly. "Dillon is going to need a father figure. You need to get back out there and enjoy life. It's been too long already."

"Dillon has me and the memory of Forester."

"Child, Dillon was only a few weeks' conceived when Forester was killed. He's gonna need someone in his life who's real."

Dena whipped around with anger but held her tongue. She didn't need a man in her life. Dillon didn't need a man in his life. They'd be fine just as they were, they had each other.

"And before you say it, yes, I'm the last one to go on about the role of a strong man in a young boy's life. Hell, I've raised your cousins alone most of the time. But having my husbands around wasn't just for my sons, it was for me. I needed companionship, I needed love, and so will you when the time is right."

"But that's just it, Aunt Ellen, I don't. I still have Forester, here, in my heart. He's all I need, at least for right now."

Ellen smiled and shook her head, knowing that a time would come when her niece would set aside her guilt and pain and come back into the world whole. But until then she knew that it was her job to take care of her.

She saw the hope in her great-niece's eyes. "You, child, have your grandmother's spirit, you've just been suppressing it for so long you've forgotten how it feels to set it free. My sister, bless her soul, was free and full of life, and she passed that zeal on to your mother. But when your mother got married, she forgot, just like you did. Marriage doesn't change a person's true nature, it only makes them better or worse."

"Aunt Ellen, this isn't about Mom, Dad or Grandma, it's about me and how I feel. I know what I'm doing for Dillon and me. We need a new life away from here."

"Child, just take this out to that man. He's been working for near about two hours straight in that hot sun without as much as a sip of water. I'm not asking you to marry the man, just take him a pitcher of lemonade."

Dena looked at her aunt then shook her head. Stubbornness obviously ran in their family. When her aunt put her mind to something, that was all there was. Usually soft-spoken and composed, there was no arguing the fact once she made up her mind.

She had a heart of gold and was a tender touch that'd been known to save a stray cat in the middle of a raging thunderstorm. She was always helping others and trying to fix things—sinks, stoves, cars, and now, apparently, her niece's life. Unfortunately most of her fixes were made worse. So as such, Dena took the pitcher and walked outside, knowing that this was just another disaster waiting to happen.

Damned if I didn't do it again. Julian Hamilton pulled back and with one fierce, penetrating swing slammed hard, using every ounce of strength he could muster. The fury and anger that had built up inside came out each time the sledgehammer met the solid cinder-block wall. He must have been crazy from the beginning.

He remembered his brother's warnings in a quote that would go down in his mental history. *Do you have wedding bells in your pants?*

But he'd done it anyway. He'd married then divorced less than a year later; the first of several romantic mistakes that nearly cost him everything, including his sanity.

The latest being the constant phone calls from his ex-wife. Although he hadn't actually hadn't spoken to her, she made a point of relaying her intentions. Unfortunately her intentions were getting back into his life.

He gritted his teeth harder. *Damn.* He just needed to stay as far away from women as possible. Every time he invited a woman into his life, he wound up neck-deep in drama.

Enter Stephanie Hall, his ex-wife, married just one year before she'd left him as soon as her child's father came back into the picture. A child he hadn't even known she'd had until after they'd returned from the honeymoon.

He'd been furious, then devastated. But since the adoption had not been finalized yet, he'd had no claim on the child he had grown to love. That was the beginning of a trend of disastrous relationships. *Slam.*

With both gloved hands securely fastened on the handle, he swung again. The heaviness of the metal head, the long swinging range of motion and the surging anger increased the momentum's impact. The more he thought about it, the higher the hammer arched, requiring added control on his part.

Next there was Jessie Bennett, his ex-fiancée of only seven months, whom he hadn't seen in a year until the day she'd stood before a judge and swore through a stream of crocodile tears that the child she carried in her arms was his. She'd wanted palimony and child support. Thank God for whoever invented the DNA paternity test. Last he heard, three tests later and she was still trying to figure out who the father was. *Slam.*

And finally his ex-girlfriend, Kellie Howard. Beautiful, bright and befuddled, she'd carried enough baggage to fill a super oil tanker. Her split and splintered personality issues had him completely confused. On any given day he had no idea who was going to walk through the door: a sweet, adoring woman or a satanic shrew. Either way, enough was enough.

He needed to listen to his older brother, Darius; he had the right idea. He always said that women were trouble and beautiful women were trouble times two. And beautiful women with children were completely off the radar. All they wanted was a father for another man's child and one was as good as any other.

Disciplined and self-controlled, Julian nodded to focus harder. Every muscle in his body screamed but he didn't care, he'd worry about that later. Right now all he needed to do was to release this pent-up energy. And knowing only two ways to do it, he chose the one least likely to land him before a family court judge. *Slam.*

The release of tension and anxiety was working. He stepped back, preparing for another swing just as his phone rang. He knew exactly who it was even without looking. She'd been calling him all morning and all morning he'd been ignoring her. *Slam.* "What is with these crazy women?"

With a stretched, swinging arch, he drew the hammer back once more. A split second later he heard a shriek and instantly stopped. The hammer, weighing just over ten pounds, suddenly lurched downward in midair, wrenching and twisting his arm as gravity took over. Plummeting to the ground, it seemed to weigh a ton. The last thing he'd expected was a scream in answer to his rhetorical rant. He turned, looked down. His jaw dropped open at seeing a woman lying at his boots.

Breathless, Julian dropped the hammer and hurriedly bent down over her. His long legs straddled her body, giving him full view to assess any injuries. "Don't move," he ordered, resting his hand on her shoulder as she began struggling to get up. "Are you okay?" he asked with ardent concern, fearful of a mass concussion or head trauma.

Dena lay on the ground covered from head to toe in ice cubes, lemons and sweet lemonade. Unable to speak, she just lay there completely drenched and completely humiliated.

"No, yes, I'm fine," she said, not only winded by the sudden jolt to the ground but also chilled by the frozen ice cubes in her shirt. She quickly unfastened the top buttons and removed several ice cubes from inside her shirt. In doing so she inadvertently revealed a very lacy, very lavender bra and the moistened swell of her bosom. "Are you crazy, swinging that thing around like that?"

"Me, crazy? Are you kidding? Any sane person would have enough sense not to sneak up behind a man swinging a sledgehammer." She attempted to get up. "No, lie still, you might have injured yourself in the fall." He took off his glove and tipped her chin up to see into her face and look into her eyes. "Look at me."

"What?" she asked, batting his hand and jerking away from him.

"Look at me," he repeated more persistently.

"What are you, a doctor or something?" she asked.

"Yes, in another life," he said as his years of medical experience clicked in and he looked deep into her big brown eyes. Clear and steady, he quickly concluded no sign of concussion. But signs of another kind took form.

"I'm fine, really. You didn't make contact."

"I know, but you fell back. Did you hit your head?"

"No, I fell on my…" She paused and looked away. "Uh, you don't need to tend to that."

"Are you sure?" Julian asked. She looked up at him, obviously questioning his bedside manner. "That's not what I meant. Are you sure you didn't bump your head?" he clarified, then swallowed hard just as a wave of desire hit him like a swing from the sledgehammer. This obviously wasn't going to be easy.

"Positive," she muttered.

"Good," he said, still looking down at her.

"Yeah," she muttered.

"Then are you insane or something?" he asked huskily, averting his eyes from her exposed cleavage.

"Excuse me?"

"Didn't you see me with the sledgehammer?"

"Of course I saw you." *All morning I saw you.* "And no, I'm not insane. You would have heard me coming over if you hadn't been talking to yourself."

"So what exactly were you doing behind me like that?"

She didn't reply. *Watching you.*

"Didn't you see me with the hammer?"

Are you kidding, I couldn't take my eyes off of you.

"Do you have a death wish?"

No, not anymore. To her surprise the answer came quick and clear and suddenly the thoughts she'd once considered seemed ludicrous.

"You could have been killed."

Dena smiled wide at the obvious realization.

"You're smiling?" His rant didn't faze her until she realized he was finished and was staring at her, waiting for an answer.

"I was, uh, distracted, by…" She paused, seeing the full beauty of his glorious brown chest hovering over her. "The sun." It was a lie, of course. She'd been distracted by his body. Each time he'd drawn the hammer back, the muscles in his back tensed and rolled, and she'd moved in closer.

It had been a long time since she'd seen a man's chest

over her. And even then, nothing remotely similar to his. Forester had been thin and wiry. Something she had grown to treasure.

"The sun?" He looked, seeing the now-overcast sky. "You must have hit your head harder than you thought," he said.

Still holding the lemon slices, he saw that her nipples had perked up through her open wet shirt. Still feeling the pull from his body, he closed his eyes and scrambled back, then stood and reached out his hand to help her up. She took his offered help and was pulled to her feet. In a split second she was slammed up against his body.

They stood there a few seconds until he stepped back and walked away. "You need to be more careful, I could have killed you."

Seeing that he was physically shaken by the incident, she softened. "You didn't, and I'm fine. I guess I should be delighted that you have so much control over your hammer."

He looked at her and tilted his head, feeling his body's urge. Everything she said and did seemed to send one message straight to his wanton body. The awkward moment lasted only a few seconds but seemed to go on forever.

He nodded then swallowed hard. "Sorry, I overreacted. I've been a little stressed lately."

"There's a lot of that going around." She muttered her affirmation. "I'm Dena, Ellen Peyton is my aunt."

"Julian." He removed his other work glove and held his hand out to shake. Hers sticky, his dusty, they shook, holding on slightly longer than necessary.

"Are you the handyman who reconnected her gas stove after my great-aunt moved it to the other side of the room a few months ago?"

"Yeah," he said, remembering the fire marshal's outrage when he'd found out what she'd done and ordered her never to attempt another remodeling job like that again.

"And I guess you helped her with the fireplace, too?"

"Yeah, that, too."

"Thank you."

"For what," he asked, "nearly taking your head off?"

"No, actually, that wasn't such a good idea. Thank you for looking out for my aunt, she means well."

"You're not from around here, are you?" he asked.

"No. I grew up in California but I lived here with my aunt for about a year and a half after my folks died."

"I'm sorry."

"Thanks, it was awhile ago, I was sixteen. Anyway I haven't been back to live here in years." She looked around, taking her eyes off him for the first time since she'd walked outside.

"Well, I'd better go change and get another pitcher of something for you to drink."

He cleared his suddenly dry throat, nodded and smiled. He bent down, picked up the glass pitcher and handed it to her. "Thanks. I'd appreciate that, thanks."

She nodded politely, half smiled in return, then turned and left. Without thinking she rubbed her thigh and rear, knowing she'd have a nice black-and-blue bruise in a few days. When she entered the back door of the Peyton house she turned, sensing that he'd been watching her.

Julian lowered and shook his head to steel his wayward body. He'd watched as her heart-shaped rear clad in perfectly taut shorts hurried away, but for him it was like slow motion. The sway of her hips accentuated the sweet taunt of her body. He'd watched as she'd reached down and rubbed her rear. That was his undoing. There was no way he could continue watching her. Of its own accord, his body went into overdrive as thoughts of her beneath him continued to test his resolve.

Still holding the lemon slices that he'd plucked from her neck and shirt, he popped them into his mouth and bit down hard, letting the sharp bitter-tart fruit pucker his mouth as a distraction. Then he replaced his work gloves, picked up the hammer and took another swing, nearly leveling the crumbling wall in a single blow.

"No," he said out loud, answering his body's needful yearn. He refused to go there. She was attractive, sure, but that was no reason to go back on his word. He'd vowed to focus on work and that's just what he intended to do. Like it or not, celibacy was his new calling.

Chapter 2

Ellen innocently looked up as soon as Dena walked through the door. "My goodness, was Julian that thirsty?" she asked, after seeing the empty pitcher in Dena's hand.

"No," Dena said as she looked down at her sticky, soggy shirt and shorts. "I spilled it." She placed the pitcher in the sink, rinsed and dried her hands then walked over to the refrigerator and began pulling out more lemons.

Ellen brought over the cutting board and, seeing Dena's shirt up close, shook her head. "What in the world? Looks like you spilled the whole pitcher down the front of you."

"I did," Dena said, pulling the sticky shirt away from her body.

"There are easier ways of getting a man's attention."

"I wasn't trying to get his attention," she insisted with a deep blush and hesitant stammer. "I walked up just as he was swinging that big thing…hammer thing of his. He didn't hear me until I screamed. He nearly took my head off with that thing." She looked at her smiling aunt, knowing exactly what she was thinking. "You're smiling and the grim reaper almost tapped me on the shoulder with his sickle." Ellen continued smiling. "What?"

"Nothing," Ellen said innocently.

"What?" Dena repeated as Ellen shook her head silently. "If you have something to say, Aunt Ellen, go ahead, say it."

"Me?" Ellen feigned innocence. "I didn't say a single word." Dena looked at her aunt, knowing better. Ellen had a way of looking that spoke loud and clear. A horrible poker player, she couldn't keep exactly what she was thinking from spreading all over her face. "Now go get yourself washed up and changed, and rinse those sticky things out before you get attacked by every ant in the county. I'll make another pitcher and take it out."

Dena saw the suggestion as her exit, so she took it. She hurried up the back stairs, stopped and peeked into the bedroom next to hers. Dillon was still asleep. He'd had a long, exciting day and passed out right after getting home.

She tiptoed over to his bed, smiled as she pulled the sheet up, removed his hard hat and tucked his teddy bear beside him. Then quietly she turned and continued to her own bedroom.

As soon as she entered she heard the sound of the sledgehammer slam against solid wall, and casually strolled to the window. Knowing that she'd have a perfect vantage point to the backyard from her large window seat, she carefully pulled the curtain back expecting to have an even better view.

Unfortunately she'd forgotten about the fullness of the

giant oak tree outside her window. Her view was completely obscured by branches and leaves. Squinting and peeking through and around didn't do any good. As the hammer slammed again, she closed the curtains and headed to the next window and then to the next one.

Not getting any better view, she tiptoed back into Dillon's bedroom and looked out his window. Unobstructed, she looked down as Julian hammered away at the solid wall. The guilty pleasure of watching him made her warm. The power of his motions excited her. Then the thought of making love to him drifted through her mind again. She closed her eyes and smiled, feeling the pounding against the wall as against her body.

The hammering stopped. She opened her eyes, seeing that he had taken a break and was now looking up at the house. She quickly closed the curtains and stepped away from the window, then went to her bathroom to wash and change.

Standing at the sink she sighed wearily as she looked at herself in the large mirror. She was a mess. Her ponytail and bangs had frayed and her face was shiny and sticky. Suddenly the thought of Julian seeing her like this mattered.

She peeled out her damp socks, slipped out of her sticky clothes and turned on the shower. Knowing what would come next, she stepped into the tiled stall and ducked beneath the stream of water. The cool refreshing blast poured over her. She tilted her head up, taking the full intensity of the flow with her eyes closed and her mouth slightly open.

This is when they usually came, the onslaught of tears, the sadness of being alone and the emptiness of possibility.

Ellen knew what had happened, of course, she'd been watching from the kitchen window. She'd gasped out loud, seeing the near miss, then smiled, encouraged as Dena lay on the ground and allowed Julian to crouch above her, straddling her body with his long legs.

Maybe this was what Louise meant when she'd said that love would come only when she was ready. Maybe, just maybe, Dena was finally ready to live again. At any rate, it was a good sign and she was more than encouraged.

She finished the second pitcher of lemonade and placed it on a tray to take outside. Just as she added a glass and her homemade cookies, the telephone rang. "Hello?"

"Hi, Mrs. Peyton, this is Willamina Parker at the Hamilton Development Corporation. Is Julian there, by any chance? He must have turned his cell phone off again."

"Yes. As a matter of fact, he's right out back."

"Great, I've been calling his cell phone for the last fifteen minutes. Would you please ask him to call me here at the office? I need him to stop by before he goes home this evening."

"Sure, anything wrong?"

"No, not at all, he just needs to pick up some employment applications and look them over before tomorrow morning. We're interviewing for an administrative assistant since I'll be on maternity leave for the next few months and Mattie Carmichael is still out with her broken ankle."

"Of course. I'm headed outside right now."

"Thanks. 'Bye, Mrs. Peyton."

"Wait a minute, Willamina," Ellen said quickly, "you said that you're looking for a replacement for a few months?"

"Yes, I have all intentions of returning to work and so does Mattie. It's just that the timing is crazy right now. We're so busy and with Mattie out another two months and me going out in a week and a half, we really need someone competent to fill in. The last few applicants just didn't work out. They were more interested in getting a Hamilton husband than working for the company."

"Interesting. My niece, Dena Graham, is looking for a job. Something temporary until she gets herself together and decides what she wants to do next. She's an attorney on personal hiatus."

"Does she have any administrative office experience?"

"Tons," Ellen answered, having no idea at all.

"Great. Why don't you have her stop by tomorrow around five-thirty? I'll make her my last appointment before the weekend. The position isn't anything glamorous but it's busy work and definitely challenging."

"Thanks, sweetie, I'll let her know, and I'll give Julian your message right now." Ellen hung the phone back on the wall, smiled and chuckled, then picked up the tray of lemonade and oatmeal-raisin cookies and headed outside, completely amazed by how quickly things turned around.

The front part of the barbecue pit, once a mass of hardened cement and cinder blocks, lay as rubble at his feet. Breathless, Julian looked down at the crumbled mess, feeling particularly pleased with his effort. His body ached and his muscles screamed for relief, but he had focused and gotten most of the job done.

As he leaned the hammer against the back wall of the grill he noticed a lemon slice on the ground and instantly thought about Dena. Remembering her lying there beneath him as he straddled her urged his body again. The memory of the sweet lemonade poured over her made him close his eyes and imagine what she might taste like. Tart and sweet, juicy and succulent; he unconsciously licked his lips. His body stirred so he quickly picked up the lemon slice and tossed it in the trash.

Then he rolled the wheelbarrow closer to the rubble and began picking up and tossing large chunks of cinder block and cement into the large metal container. Single-focused, he finished in no time and was using the broom, gathering the last remnants and the smaller chunks when Ellen called out to him.

He stopped and turned to her, quickly removing his gloves and going over to help her with the heavy tray. "Perfect timing," he said as he looked at the refreshing pitcher of lemonade. He placed the tray on the side picnic table and Ellen poured him a tall glass as he walked over to the outside faucet and doused his head under the water and washed his hands.

Drying his face, he walked back over and took the offered glass. Drinking it down in just a few gulps, he let the cold refreshing beverage chill down his throat. After the third glass he picked up a cookie and began munching.

Ellen walked over and looked down at his handiwork, shaking her head. "Well," she said, "it looked just fine to me. I don't see why I have to get anyone's permission to build a barbecue grill in my own backyard on land that I've lived on for over forty-five years."

"It's the law. You have to abide by the city codes, get permits and check zoning regulations, Ms. Ellen. You can't get around it."

She shook her head sadly. "Doesn't make any sense to me whatsoever."

Julian smiled as he took another bite of the oatmeal-raisin cookie.

"Oh, before I forget, Willamina called. She needs you to stop by the office before you go home this evening. You need to pick up some applications."

"Oh, right," he said, realizing that he'd forgotten to get them on his way out earlier.

"So how's Mattie doing?" Ellen asked casually.

"She's getting better, still has to take it easy and stay off her feet for a couple more months. I still can't believe she broke her ankle teaching her grandchildren how to jump rope. She's usually so careful."

"Accidents happen to the best of us. So she's out and now Willamina's going on maternity leave soon," she offered rather than asked. Julian nodded as he crunched into another cookie. "How long will she be away?"

"She said possibly a few months, although I can see her coming back sooner. She loves the job. I think it has something to do with the power of ordering us around that gives her a secret thrill."

Ellen laughed. "I can imagine," she said, knowing, of course, that the three Hamilton brothers were a handful when they were younger. Now the three, all grown up, were on testosterone overdrive, and every single and almost-single woman in a four-country radius wanted a chance to try to tame one.

Impossible of course, although Julian had been married and engaged, so the possibility of his ability to commit was there. But the other two, Darius, the oldest, and Jordan, the youngest, were adamant about staying single, and made sure everyone knew it. Ellen wondered what her friend Louise would say.

"Have you decided yet?" Julian asked, getting her attention again.

"About what?" Ellen asked, distracted and completely forgetting the now-open space where her homemade makeshift barbecue grill had been.

Julian pointed to the open area. "For this space, the back wall is too solid for the sledgehammer so I'll get a backhoe over Saturday morning and take it down. Have you decided what you'd like to do once it's down?" Julian asked.

"Oh, well, I need another one, obviously. I can't go the whole summer without a grill in the backyard. And besides, I have a huge birthday party to throw at the end of the summer. I'm gonna need it done quickly so I'll take care of it myself. I have a few ideas." She turned to the open space. "This time I think I'll build one with..."

"Maybe it would be a good idea to get a professional to come and build it this time. That way it would be up to code and Reggie Marshall won't have any complaints."

"Oh, that man is absolutely ridiculous. For a fire chief he's just too picky. He complains about everything I do. The stove, the fireplace, the supporting wall, the electrical system, he's always got something to say."

"What supporting wall and what electrical system?" Julian asked, almost afraid to hear the answer.

"I had a short in my living room lamp, so I fixed it."

"You fixed it?" Julian asked, knowing of course that when Mrs. Ellen said she fixed something, a disaster was in the making.

"It was easy. I saw them do it on television."

"Mrs. Ellen, some things are better left to professionals, in this case a qualified electrician. I know it looks easy on the half-hour do-it-yourself and fix-up shows, but every job is different. The solutions they show on television are often the simplest fixes and even then they're professionals. Having someone who knows what they're doing is a good idea, especially when it comes to something as dangerous as your electrical system."

"Nonsense, and I still say that the two-block blackout wasn't my fault."

"The two-block blackout, no. Of course not," Julian said, remembering the minor blackout a few weeks back. He should have figured that it was Mrs. Ellen and another one of her little fix-it projects. "Did you get someone in to fix it?"

"I told you, I fixed it," she insisted.

"Right, but I'll be happy to check it only to make sure that Reggie won't have anything to complain about."

"Your brother already came by. Reggie suggested that he stop by. I insisted that it wasn't necessary but he called him anyway."

Julian nodded, delighted that the electrical system had been checked out. Either Jordan or Darius would have been thorough. "And the supporting wall?"

Ellen shook her head. "Don't even get me started. I saw this perfect little patio sitting area on television a few weeks ago. So I thought I'd just build it onto the side of the house over there, with a walkway connecting to the grill area I built." She pointed to the general area. "Anyway, I went down to the hardware store and lumberyard to put an order in and told Pete that I was thinking of knocking a hole in the side of the house. I also wanted to rent a backhoe and a large Dumpster. The next thing I know Reggie is at my door again. I declare if I didn't know any better I'd say that man has a serious crush on me."

Julian smiled, trying not to chuckle. The possibility of Reggie having a crush on Ms. Ellen was completely plausible. Not surprising, most days his whole conversation centered on Ms. Ellen and her latest do-it-yourself projects. He even once stated that he might just marry her and save the state the cost of rebuilding the county once she got a project in her head. It wasn't long after that he and Pete got their heads together and decided that whenever Ellen placed an order, Reggie knew about it.

"Wouldn't you know it, the first thing he said was that I needed a professional. Can you believe that?"

"It might be a good idea, knocking down a supporting wall can be tricky even for a professional."

"It didn't look that difficult when I saw it on television. They knocked a hole in the wall during the first commercial break. I figure three minutes, five tops."

"I tell you what, I'll ask Darius to work up some ideas. Maybe together you can get the patio working to Reggie's satisfaction."

She nodded, smiling. "Jordan said the same thing when he stopped by to look at my electrical system. Speaking of which, I need you to turn up my hot water pressure. I think your brother lowered it again."

"Sure," Julian said, and he finished the last of the lemonade and cookies.

"Go ahead in, you know where everything is," she said, and she began walking toward the terrace garden he'd helped her put in for her prizewinning flowers.

Julian shook his head then rolled the wheelbarrow to the ramp attached to his truck. He secured the heavy load then went around to the back of the house. The grill area, aside from the solid back wall, was now spotless and, seeing Ellen heading toward the greenhouse with her small wheelbarrow, he headed inside to check out the water pressure setting.

It was just as he suspected. Jordan had turned it down to the standard pressure level and Mrs. Ellen had turned it up. He readjusted it again. A few minutes later he heard the second scream that afternoon.

Without thinking he ran upstairs just as Dena was running downstairs. They met midway, stopped, mouths dropped open and wordlessly both turned and headed in the opposite direction.

Chapter 3

Late Friday afternoon Dena ran through her to do list a third time in her head. This was her first job interview in almost six years and everything needed to be perfect. Even starting out as temporary administrative assistant was something.

She still couldn't believe her aunt was able to get her the interview so quickly. The position wasn't even advertised in the newspapers. It had been listed privately because the company, Hamilton Development Corporation, was so well-known and highly selective.

Having clerked for Judge Hughes years ago, she knew most of the who's who in the area. The company was one of the largest black-owned construction companies in the state. They handled multimillion-dollar projects and were well-known for their sizable charitable donations.

Nervously she checked her list a fourth time.

Clear nail polish, unchipped, check. No runs in stockings, check. Soft-hued lipstick on and unsmudged, check. Breath mint dissolved, check. The list, one of many, composed mainly of superficial formalities, continued with another ten items. They were the things she could care less about but the new reality of her life had suddenly made her appearance a necessity.

She looked down at her left hand, devoid of jewelry; she focused on her ring finger. The band of gold had been missing for years yet she still felt the weight of its meaning pulling at her. She had failed at something else. But this wasn't the time to reminisce about her wayward life, this was a new beginning and she needed to make a good impression.

Her aunt was right; she needed a distraction and a job. This job would do fine. More than likely it would be mindless office work and that was easily something she could handle even in her scattered state of mind.

So, with her list all checking out satisfactory, she glanced at her watch and noted the time. She needed to get a move on if she wanted to be on time.

With the executive offices on the upper level she looked up as the escalator stairs continued upward. It was now or never. Okay, everything was set, she was ready. She stepped on, ready to begin a new chapter in her new life.

Smile and for heaven's sake be nice.

The words popped into her head like a jack-in-the-box. *Yes, yes of course,* she'd promised her aunt. She smiled. Then Dillon's tiny voice echoed, *For heaven's sake, be nice and smile.* Her smile broadened, instantly lighting her face like sunrise at midnight. The tickle of his voice always made her smile. She looked over at the down escalator then up at the three men just stepping on above.

She'd know him anywhere dressed in anything.

Julian Hamilton stood at the top of the escalator along with two other men. They joked and talked easily until his eyes shifted in her direction. Her heart lurched. No longer was he the shirtless handyman in the too tight jeans, instead he wore a professionally-tailored-to-fit-his-body business suit and carried a leather briefcase.

What a difference a day makes.

He nodded, keeping his eyes focused on her face. She returned his slight gesture as they met and passed each other side by side. Willing herself not to turn around, she stood firm and grasped the escalator railing tighter. There was no way she was going to turn around. No way. No, way. Way.

She turned around to see that he had turned around. He nodded silently again as the two men he was with caught sight of her with inquiring expressions. She quickly turned to face forward.

A nervous chill at seeing him again gripped her and had her misstep and nearly trip while coming off the escalator. She quickly gathered herself and calmed her nerves. She needed this job.

Following the signs, she walked down the short hallway and stood outside the offices. She took a deep breath and entered.

"Whoa, what was that vow," Darius began then paused briefly. "I've had it with women. I'm through with love, never ever again." He glanced at Julian and chuckled. "Now where did I hear that?" he added as he witnessed his younger brother turn around to nod at the woman on the escalator. "Oh, that's right, you were tired of all the games and all the drama. I remember now."

"He can't even get out of the building without suffering whiplash," Jordan added. "Have you ever seen anyone so determined to fall in love again?"

"Unbelievable," Darius concluded. "And remember that word he used, now what was it again?" he asked of his brother Jordan as Julian's face began to burn.

"Celibacy," Jordan answered, slowly and deliberately.

"That's right. How long ago was that?" Darius asked.

"I believe that it was just two weeks ago," Jordan said.

"It was seven months ago, two weeks, three days and sixteen hours," Julian said briskly.

"It can't be genetic. The rest of us are fine. Must be something he contracted in med school," Darius added.

"My thoughts exactly," Jordan confirmed. "But he's always had the tendency to fall in love at the drop of a hat. Remember his kindergarten crush on Kylie Grimes."

"Yeah, he gave her his milk money for three months." In unison they shook their heads, seemingly saddened by the comments.

"If the two of you are finished with the jokes and levity, I'd like to get back to our previous conversation, if you don't mind."

"Oh, but we do mind," Darius insisted. "I want to know what all this head-nodding is all about."

"True that. You're not getting off that easily. Who is she, the hopeful Ms. Lucky number three?"

Julian looked at his brothers threateningly. "She's Ellen Peyton's niece. I was there yesterday tearing down the grill she put up, remember."

"Yeah, I also remember that you asked for that particular

assignment to relieve some of your pent-up anger. I guess the sledgehammer didn't do the trick." Darius and Jordan looked at each other and smiled knowingly. Julian's playboy reputation had rivaled theirs and had even exceeded them at times.

"I know where you're going with this, and you're wrong. I almost hit her with the sledgehammer. I turned around and she was there out of the blue. She spilled lemonade down the front of her shirt."

"Wet T-shirt?" Jordan asked.

"Interesting approach," Darius said as he and Jordan nodded their approval, knowing that Julian was getting more and more annoyed with them as they enjoyed every minute.

"No," Julian answered too quickly, "it wasn't like that. She had a regular cotton shirt on and, not seeing her, I swung the hammer back and nearly clipped her. She spilled the lemonade when she fell back on her… I'm sure you get the idea. Now can we please get back to business?"

Instead, Darius and Jordan continued. They laughed and joked but Julian had totally tuned them out by then. The wet T-shirt had reminded him of the scant towel wrapped around her body and the quick way she'd run back up the steps after seeing him. She was soaking wet, the towel was wrapped haphazardly, so when she'd turned and ran he had a perfect view of her two impeccably formed brown cheeks.

Instinctively his body reacted.

"See, he's not even paying attention now."

"You know who he's thinking about, of course."

"Of course. But who could blame him. She is fine."

"It's not that I'm not paying attention." Julian finally spoke up. "I simply choose to ignore you. Now, can we get back to business, please."

"All in all, not exactly the best first meeting."

"I'd have to agree there. I've found that basic introductions are usually best. The dramatic approach can sometimes backfire."

Julian's piercing stare made them laugh harder.

"Relax, little brother," Darius said as he continued jokingly, then laughed again seeing Julian's reaction to his "little brother" remark.

"I was relaxed. I mean, I am relaxed," Julian said angrily, "until you two stopped by the office. Now can we please get back to business," Julian affirmed more forcefully.

"Fine with me. Speaking of getting back to business, what about Mrs. Peyton's barbecue grill. Did you finish the job?"

"No, not even close."

"Distracted?" Darius and Jordan asked simultaneously then tapped their closed fists together approvingly.

"No," he insisted firmly, "although she cemented the front and side cinder blocks in place, she secured the back row by pouring a ton of cement into each one. Tearing that back wall down by hand is close to impossible. I'll have to use one of the machines."

"So you're going back?"

"Yeah, you know how Mrs. Peyton is, if we don't take care of her she'll do it herself and you know what that means."

The brothers nodded. "Disaster," they said in unison.

"I'm sure you remember the gas stove incident, she nearly blew up three square blocks of the neighborhood with her handyman self-installation."

"Not to mention the two-block blackout a few weeks ago."

"All right, do you need anyone with you?"

"I've already taken care of it," Julian said. "I have a small crew going over there Saturday to take the rest of the wall down. She needs you to come up with ideas for the new grill and better make it sooner than later. I think I saw that there was a special on this weekend about installing swimming pools."

Darius nodded. "I'm already on top of it."

"All right, we'll cover the rest of the jobs pending. But we need you in the office Monday. We need to jump on this county contract as soon as possible. Are you going back up to your office?"

"Yes, for an hour or so. I need to check on a few things before the start of the weekend." Darius and Jordan eyed each other and smiled. Julian ignored them.

By the time Darius and Jordan reached the garage and their respective cars, the conversation had completely turned to business. Except Julian's thoughts still lingered on Dena and their meeting the day before. The ponytailed temptress with the Godsent body had changed into a woman, and once he saw her it was all he could do not to trip while getting off the escalator.

It wasn't so much the wet shirt or the embarrassed expression as she came barreling downstairs soaking wet in the towel, it was the sadness in her eyes behind the forced smile. Even just now on the escalator, her strained smile never seemed to reach her eyes, at least not until the last second. Whatever touched her and made her smile so genuinely had to be some kind of wonderful.

"All right, if that's it—" they all nodded in agreement "—we're out."

"Have a good weekend," Julian told his brothers, knowing that they were headed to the family beach house.

"You, too," they responded in unison.

Darius got into his SUV and Jordan got into his sports car.

They waved as they pulled out and drove away. Julian watched them go. Although it was his turn to stay in the city for the weekend, he was relieved and more than happy not to drive to the beach house. Staying at the family house had gotten to be too much of an effort for him. He turned to go back to the office. Then, looking down, he noticed a narrow stream of dark greenish liquid coming from beneath one of the cars.

Knowing what it meant, he made a mental note to talk to the attendant then went back into the office building wondering what Dena was really doing here.

Dena sat in the interview chair and answered the questions with ease, surprising even herself considering she'd just seen the man she'd dreamed about last night. Her voice was even-toned yet interested and her responses were concise. All things considered, everything went as well as could be expected.

The interviewer, Willamina Parker, seemed to be eleven months pregnant and ready to give birth any second. Happy and upbeat, she was excited that with this being her third child, she'd have some time to be with her other two small children in the coming months. After they discussed the basic duties of the job, her background and the company they began talking about motherhood and the strain on personal time.

Each had a different perspective, as Willamina was married to one of the company's project managers and they worked at the same job. So their relationship included seeing each other constantly. Dena said that she'd been widowed for over four years and that her late husband had never even known she was pregnant.

Having nearly forgotten that they were here for an interview, they talked about infants and toddlers and the fact that they each had an almost-four-year-old little boy and the trials of their adventures and, of course, misadventures. Laughing at similar stories and comparing notes, they got along perfectly. And since Dena hadn't bothered to make any friends since she'd come back to town, talking with another adult other than her great-aunt was a joy.

"Okay, I just have one more question, or rather, one last remark," Willamina said. "Your résumé reads like a legal who's who. You clerked and interned with a number of law firms and judges, then worked at legal aid. Why aren't you practicing law?"

"I need a change and being a lawyer just isn't what I want anymore, at least not right now. I guess you could say that seeing what the law and lawyers can do up close and personal, I don't want to be a part of that world anymore."

Willamina nodded. She knew that there was something else behind the words and she was curious as to what had led to the stark change but didn't pursue it. "All that is to say that you are completely overqualified for this position," Willamina added.

Dena smiled without responding.

"Well, as far as I can see you're the best applicant by far, so I'd like to offer you the position pending a background check, I'll have to run it by the owners of the company. They gave me complete control, but I still want them to meet with you."

Dena smiled; all she really heard was that she'd gotten the job.

Willamina went on to describe more of the job's details.

The position title was actually executive office administrator to operations. She, as the administrative assistant, would be directly answerable to the company's three owners. She would also be responsible to make sure that everything ran smoothly since the office would be under her total control, and that all projects ran on time and on budget.

They ended the interview with a hug as Willamina wished her the best, and Dena returned the gesture.

As she exited the building Dena realized that the smile she'd faked for so long actually outlasted the promise. She was happy and giddy and pleased with herself. She'd done it. She'd actually found herself a job.

The feeling seeped into her brain like morning sunshine after a miserable midnight storm. On her own she'd gotten a job, albeit less than what her degree might have offered, but nonetheless she was once again employed. Giving up her old life was one of the hardest things she had to do but there was no way she could even consider continuing in law after what she'd been through.

Aunt Ellen was right, getting back out into the world had definitely lifted her spirits. It had been a long time since she'd felt like herself. Well, maybe not so long ago. She suddenly remembered the day before and the construction worker, Julian, and the way her body reacted as he'd hovered above her, looking down.

Hot and sweaty from thinking about the encounter, Dena had taken a cool shower, until the water temperature spiked and she'd gone running downstairs in a towel only to run into him on his way up. The look on his face had no doubt mirrored her own. But she was sure that the inner burn she felt was hers alone.

There's no way that a man that gorgeous and built that perfectly could be single and unattached, yet she didn't recall seeing a wedding band. But of course that didn't mean anything. Forester hadn't worn a wedding band; he'd complained that his was too tight and cut off his circulation, and at the time confrontation avoidance was all she'd known. Now, of course, she knew better.

"Well, that's more like it."

The man's voice, taking her by surprise, interrupted her private jubilation. Looking up, she turned to see her hunky construction worker leaning against a car, apparently waiting. "Hi," she said joyfully, as if they'd known each other for years. But the fact that she was just thinking about him and here he was, was both startling and welcoming.

Julian's insides melted as the smile he'd so longed to see was amply rewarded. Bright and sexy, as he'd assumed, it nearly melted his shoes. She had a very definite twinkle in her soft brown eyes that tilted his stomach like a roller coaster on crack.

"Hi. We kind of got off on the wrong foot yesterday."

"Nearly killing me can kind of do that," she quipped, then watched as his expression darkened. "I'm joking," she said quickly, then waited a second for his expression to lighten again. "So, were you waiting for me?" she asked still half-jokingly and still in an unusually good mood after her interview.

"Actually, I was, in a roundabout way," he said shyly. "I saw you earlier and I recognized your car from the driveway yesterday. I thought I'd hang around to say hi and, of course, I wanted to apologize again for the sledgehammer and running up stairs like that. I heard a scream and just reacted."

"That's really sweet in a scary stalker kind of way."

He laughed, making her smile widen. The sound was warm and inviting. Forester had seldom laughed at her humor.

"Truthfully, I had to take care of some last-minute business in the office and I noticed..."

"So you work here?" she asked, interrupting.

"Yes."

She nodded. "Really, I just interviewed."

"As?"

"A temporary administrative assisstant."

He nodded. "It's a great place to work."

"You do construction here?" she asked.

He nodded. "And other things."

"Like coming to my aunt's rescue?"

"Yeah."

They stared at each other wordlessly, each half smiling for no real reason. The silence seemed comfortable then curious then odd then awkward. "Well maybe we'll see each other again, if the job comes through that is," she said.

"Good luck, I hope you get it," he offered, making a mental note to check with Willamina later that evening.

"Thanks. Well, I gotta get going. See you later." She got into the car and closed the door.

He waited for her to start the car. She did, but as he suspected, the engine moaned and grunted like a dying beast then sputtered and choked. She tried the ignition a second and third time with the same results. She opened the car door and stepped outside.

"Sounds like a problem," he said, having already expected the engine to fail. He stepped back and pointed to the greenish-black slick trail of shiny goop coming from underneath the car.

She wrinkled her nose. "What is that?"

"My guess would be oil."

Dena followed and looked where he pointed. "My aunt Ellen volunteered to change the oil for me yesterday. I guess she worked on a few other things, as well." She turned to him hopefully. "You wouldn't happen to know anything about fixing cars, would you?"

"Sorry, I'm afraid not, that's not exactly my strong suit. I can, however, call a tow truck then give you a lift home if you like."

"That would be great, I'd really appreciate it." She looked at her watch, noting the time, then grabbed her purse from the car and followed him. She looked around for the truck she'd spotted the day before or at least one that he might be driving. There was no truck in sight.

He walked over to the car he'd been leaning against and opened the door for her. She slipped inside easily, relaxing back against the smooth leather interior.

As Julian got into the car and started the engine she inhaled the aromatic spice of his cologne. It was nice. She smiled and chuckled to herself. "What?" he asked of her humored expression.

"Nothing. I guess I just assumed you had one of those big flatbed trucks you see on television commercials. You know the ones, a macho man's truck that can pull half the city and three tons of dirt."

"Sorry to disappoint. I'll bring the truck next time."

"I'm not disappointed," she said as she glanced at her watch again.

"That's the second time you checked your watch. You gotta a hot date?" he asked, half joking, half hoping not.

"As a matter of fact I do, with a three-year-old and a batch of chocolate-chip cookies."

He came to a traffic light and braked harder than he intended. "A three-year-old." He asked, "Yours?"

"Yes. His name's Dillon, he's a cookie fiend and it's our little ritual every Friday night."

"Ah," Julian said, trying not to sound as surprised and disappointed as he felt. "I didn't realize you were married." He glanced down at the left hand, still not seeing a ring or even an empty ring indent.

"I'm widowed," she said, her voice strained and tense.

"I'm sorry."

"It's been over four years ago," she added.

"How long were you married?" he asked.

"Almost two years."

"You were just married?"

"Yes," she said, then paused. "He was killed in a car accident."

"I'm sorry," he repeated, not sure what to say.

She stared out the front windshield in a trancelike state remembering the night with crystal clarity. "It happened so fast. I barely knew what was going on. We skidded on a patch of ice and spun out. I was thrown from the car and wound up with just a few scratches. He was still inside. I watched the car roll over and over again. It was so loud and so fast. When it stopped, I ran to the car. I held his hand and watched him die."

The mood went silent. Julian reached over and took her hand. She looked down at the tender embrace. It felt good, better than she expected. "Sorry I went on like that. It's the first time I've actually talked about it outside my—" she paused and took a deep breath "—family."

"Hey, I'm glad you feel comfortable enough to tell me. Did you want to stop and grab a cup of coffee or something?"

"No, thanks, I better get home."

"Chocolate-chip cookie night," he said.

"Yep, that's right. Chocolate-chip cookie night."

"Want to hear a secret?" he asked.

"Sure," she said.

"Your aunt makes the best oatmeal-raisin cookies on the planet, but I haven't had a homemade chocolate-chip cookie since I was about ten years old. My mom used to make them." What he didn't say was that she'd made them just for him and ever since she'd died, he'd refused to have another one.

"Really. Well, I'm going to have to do something about that." He pulled up in front of Ellen Peyton's house and an awkward silence stilled them as he switched off the ignition. They sat silent for a few seconds, neither wanting the time to end. He got out and walked her to the front door. "Thanks again," Dena said.

"Anytime."

She turned to go in then stopped and turned back around. "Would you like to come in for coffee or something, maybe a chocolate-chip cookie?"

Julian looked at the half-open door and at the beautiful woman, but declined. "I'll take a rain check."

She nodded. "Okay, good night."

He nodded and waited the few seconds it took for her to enter and close the door behind her. Julian moaned as soon as he got back into the car. An attractive woman with a child. Would he never learn? It was his ex-wife all over again.

He drove down the street shaking his head. What was he thinking? He was about to fall into the same trap all over again. Correcting himself, he made a mental note to ask Willamina not to consider Dena for the job. Having her around would definitely work against his pledge of celibacy.

It was her vulnerability that moved him. When she'd told him about her husband, there was something in her voice that touched him. He could very easily see himself consoling her. And he couldn't go there. But he didn't want her hurt, either. So the least he could do was find her other employment, hopefully as far away from him as possible.

If she needed a job so badly he'd ask one of his friends in the city to hire her, anything as long as she wasn't working near him. In the past two days he bumped into her three times and each time his body reacted.

He nodded, the decision had been made. First thing Monday morning he'd set his life back on course again. But for right now, thanks to Dena, he needed an ice-cold shower again.

Chapter 4

"You hired her?" Julian asked.

"Of course we hired her. She came highly recommended."

"A glowing recommendation from Mrs. Peyton about her niece isn't exactly impartial," Julian said.

"Willamina liked her, that's all I needed," Jordan said. The three of them knew firsthand of Willamina's unparalleled judgment. She was demanding, a perfectionist and nearly impossible to please, particularly when she was pregnant. And having unceremoniously dismissed three previous candidates for the job, it was a miracle that anyone else would even apply. "She actually called me Friday evening at the beach house and raved about Dena. She even faxed me her résumé."

Darius nodded. "I got the same phone call on the boat. Have you seen her credentials? She has a law degree and a master's degree in criminal and child psychology. She clerked with superior court Judge Hughes after graduation then worked in family court, then legal aid and has an impeccable record. I spoke to his assistant this morning. She said that Dena was brilliant and that the judge adored her. She even sent over a copy of the judge's personal recommendation."

"She's a lawyer?" Julian asked, having had no idea.

"Looks like," Jordan answered.

"So why isn't she practicing law somewhere?" he asked.

"She did," Jordan said as he picked up the résumé lying on the desk. "She's even connected to some extremely prestigious law firm in the city." He scanned the résumé, "Here it is, Graham, Whitman & Morris. I wonder if the Graham is a relative."

"She told Willamina that she wanted to go in another direction," Darius said. "That works for me. Having someone with legal experience on the books is a bonus as far as I'm concerned. She's definitely an asset."

"But what does that mean, she wants to go in another direction? Was she disbarred or something?" Julian asked offhandedly. Jordan and Darius looked at each other, not knowing the answer. The question hadn't even occurred to them. "Well?" he prompted. "Would she be legally obligated to list disbarment on her résumé?"

"I don't care. She's perfect for this position and she has the job as far as I'm concerned," Jordan said.

"I agree," Darius added. "The administrative assistant position doesn't have a legal prerequisite. What she brings to the table is a bonus. And somehow I doubt she was disbarred, she doesn't seem the duplicitous type."

"What makes you so sure?" Julian asked.

Darius and Jordan looked at each other again, knowing of course Julian's drama with women. "Because your eyes nearly popped out of their sockets when you saw her on the escalator Friday evening. It was only right that we ease your pain and hire her."

"Not funny," Julian said flatly.

"What do you want us to do?"

"Tell her that it was a mistake."

"You mean, fire her before she even starts? Isn't that a bit of an overreaction, not to mention probably cause for litigation? And perfect that she's a lawyer, she can handle her own case against us."

The three brothers went silent for a moment until Jordan spoke up. "Maybe I'll put on the old charm and…"

"Don't even think about it," Julian warned firmly.

"Is she married?" Darius asked.

"No," Jordan said.

"Already seeing someone?" Darius asked. Julian looked up with interest.

"She's not," Jordan said. "I already checked."

"She's widowed with a three-year-old son," Julian said.

"Oh, that's perfect." Darius began, "You suggest we fire a widowed attorney with a three-year-old son. I can just see it now."

Jordan smiled suspiciously at Julian. "I want to know what the big deal is. I mean, we have women around here constantly. Why this one woman? Is there something we don't know?" Darius looked on with added interest as Jordan continued. "You obviously don't want me to pursue her, why so protective, Julian?"

"Good question," Darius said as he and Jordan looked at Julian for a response.

"Okay, fine, don't fire her. Just keep her away from me.

And you—" Julian specifically pointed to his younger brother "—don't you even think about it." Jordan raised his hands as if to surrender at gunpoint.

"All agreed?" Darius asked. Jordan nodded, Julian looked away. "Two to one, she's hired."

Julian looked at his two brothers murderously. Apparently they had all intentions of winning this wager by any means necessary and that meant putting as much temptation in his path as possible. "Fine, whatever, she's your call, you hired her, but I don't have to deal with her." He stood and headed to the door as they began laughing. He turned looking at each brother as they began laughing harder.

"What?" he said tightly.

"Actually you do."

Fortunately for Dena the weekend sped by in a flash. After a miserably sleepless night spent, to her surprise, on not-so-innocent thoughts of Julian, she was awakened early Saturday morning by a crew of three men who stopped by with a small backhoe to tear down the remainder of her aunt's cinder-block barbecue grill.

Her bedroom window was open and she heard her aunt talking to the workmen below, knowing of course that her aunt was probably giving them further instructions. She got up and peered out the window curiously wondering if Julian was back. He wasn't. She was disappointed.

She watched as two of the three men spoke with her aunt for a few minutes then they unrolled and showed her plans, presumably a new grill. The three of them conferred briefly then the men went right to work with as little disturbance to the household as possible.

Moments later a small machine driven by the third man rambled through the yard and she knew that it was only a matter of time before Dillon came to tell her all about it. She needed to get dressed.

As if on cue, just as she finished dressing, Dillon charged into her bedroom fully dressed in jeans, T-shirt, snow boots and his mini-construction-worker tool belt and hard hat. He excitedly went on and on, relaying everything he saw and heard, including the fact the men had waved at him. Then he announced that he was going outside to help them. Dena insisted that he have breakfast first and, after much debate, he finally relented.

Thankfully within the span of twenty minutes and before the end of breakfast, the five-foot, double-thick cement walls were reduced to a pile of rubble, then removed as if never having been there.

Dillon, who had gone outside, was devastated that he didn't get to help out. Dena, on the other hand, was delighted. At times his single-minded fascination with large machinery was completely beyond her. Whenever they'd pass a construction site he wanted to stop and watch. She didn't mind once in a while but lately it had become his determined obsession. Once or twice she'd actually had to tempt him away with a special treat and even then he was disheartened.

Maybe it was because there was no man in his life or maybe it was his way of connecting on some level to something she couldn't give him and didn't understand. Whatever the reason, she was determined to keep him as happy as possible by being both mother and father.

They read and sang and learned new words, but mostly he enjoyed anything related to building and construction, so of course the last thing she wanted to do was disappoint him. He was the joy in her world and she couldn't imagine her life without him.

Without knowing it, he had literally saved her. And in return she had poured her spirit and her soul into his well-being and everything she did revolved around his happiness, even at the expense of her own happiness, much to her aunt's chagrin.

"They're gone," Dillon said disappointedly as he walked into the kitchen and climbed up onto the first rung of the stool at the center island counter. His tool belt got caught and his hard hat slipped toward the front.

Dena glanced up from filling the dishwasher as soon as he entered. She looked at her aunt Ellen, who returned her smile as she followed him into the kitchen. "I'm sure they'll be back," Dena said.

"Of course they will," Ellen said, holding the rolled plans the men gave her. "These are plans for a wonderful new brick barbecue grill and patio we're going to build just in time for your big birthday party bash."

"Really?" Dillon asked with renewed excitement.

"Really," Ellen assured him while picking him up to sit comfortably on the stool. "This is going to be the grandest four-year-old birthday party this side of the Mason-Dixon Line."

"What's the messy-dissy lime?" Dillon asked.

Dena closed the dishwasher. "Never mind about that right now, young man, I need you to run upstairs and wash your hands and face. We have some shopping to do today."

"In town?" he asked hopefully, tilting his hard hat back from the front of his face.

"Yes," Dena said as she removed the hard hat completely and unbuckled his tool belt.

"By the big building."

"Yes," she repeated, knowing exactly where this conversation was leading.

"Can I bring my hard hat and tool belt to help 'em?"

"May I," she corrected.

"May I bring my hard hat and help?" he repeated.

Dena smiled and placed the construction gear on the counter. "Not this time, sweetie."

"Aw, Mom," Dillon moaned, and poked out his bottom lip to show his disapproval.

"Don't 'aw, Mom,' me." She lifted him to the floor and turned him to face the back staircase to the second floor. "Off you go, and use soap. One, two, three, four…" By the time she got to five Dillon was tearing around the corner of the island counter and hurrying upstairs. She heard his giggling when he reached the top step knowing that he'd gotten upstairs before she counted to ten.

Ellen shook her head, smiling. "He is such a darling."

Dena nodded. "I don't know what I'd do without him."

"God willing, you'll never have to find out." She unrolled the plans and placed them on the countertop then sat down on the stool. Dena placed a trivet on each of three corners and a cookbook on the last then looked at the plans, as well. They studied the plans a moment in silence until Dena spoke.

"Wow, can they really do all this?"

"It's not exactly what I had in mind…" Ellen said as she frowned while running her finger over the details of the plans. "I really expected something entirely different."

"Aunt Ellen, look at these plans, these are incredible. Look at this. They're planning to build a roaster, a grill, a smoker and an outdoor cookery. You've got to be impressed with all this."

"Oh, I am," she said, then sighed openly. "It's just not vhat I expected. It's so detailed. On television they had all his on the other side and a bit more counter space."

"Maybe you can talk to Julian about making a few changes."

Ellen nodded. "Well, it's not just that," she said, sighing ieavily. "I really had my heart set on doing it myself."

Dena cringed inwardly as would half of Gilford County vhenever Ellen Peyton had her heart set on doing something ierself. "But, Aunt Ellen, I was hoping that you'd help me."

Ellen looked up quickly. "With what?"

"If I get this job with the Hamilton Development Corpo-ation I'll be working long hours and Dillon will need omeone he…"

"Say no more, of course I'll be here for Dillon."

"Thank you. Aunt Ellen, maybe instead of building the vhole thing yourself, maybe you can supervise. I'm sure vith your background you'll be more suited in that position."

"Perhaps you're right."

Dena nodded and smiled; the last thing she wanted was for ier aunt to start mixing cement again. They were still chipping iardened cement globs off the washer and dryer and she still iad no idea how her aunt got cement on the front porch ceiling an. "Can I get you something in town?" she asked.

"No, thanks," Ellen said. "My show, 'You Can Do It, Be Iandy Around the House,' comes on in about ten minutes. I ust might get a few new ideas."

"Is that really such a good idea?" Dena asked.

"Of course it is. Why wouldn't it be?"

"Well, maybe because you already have these great plans nd besides, you don't want to worry about doing all that hard vork, do you? Let the guys take care of all that."

"Oh, I don't mind a bit of hard work."

"Still, maybe you should let them handle it."

"What do you mean?"

Dena sighed, summoning all the tact she could muster. "I mean, maybe it's a good idea to let the professionals handle this job. I mean, this one time." Ellen considered her suggestion a second and was about to speak when Dena continued. "I have an idea, Aunt Ellen. Why don't you spend the day with us? Dillon would love to show you around the new toy store in town and I need to get some new office clothes. I know how much you love shopping."

"Maybe next time. You two go have a good time. I'll be just fine right here. Today on 'You Can Do It, Be Handy Around the House,' they're installing a new kitchen sink and I've been considering making a change." She glanced around the kitchen, smiling.

Dena instantly remembered the gas stove fiasco. "Aunt Ellen, promise not to do anything until we get back," Dena nearly begged.

Ellen laughed. "Of course not. I can't get the materials that quickly anyway."

Moments later Dena gathered Dillon and left feeling victorious but still slightly concerned. Leaving her aunt in an empty house with her favorite television show on was dangerous but she decided to have a little faith. After the little arrangement she made with Reggie the fire chief and Pete the owner of the hardware store, she was sure that between the three of them her aunt would be safe and so would the county.

The rest of Saturday afternoon was spent with Dillon at the local library, the playground and park, then in the local mall picking out new summer clothes for him and work clothes for her. An exceptional day as usual, Dena was delighted, and forgot all her troubles as the two sat in the food court eating a special treat, chocolate ice cream.

"When is my party?" Dillon asked, swinging his feet.

"In about a month and a half."

"Why-come I can't have it now?" he asked.

Dena smiled. "How come," she corrected. "Since it's a birthday party you'll have to wait until your actual birthday and your birthday isn't until another month and a half."

"Why-come?"

"How come?" she corrected again.

"How come," he repeated. "How come my birff-day is a month and a half and not now?"

"Because that's when you were born and you can't change it, like ice cream, one per customer."

"How come?"

"A birthday happens only once, one time only." She held her finger up to show him.

"Nah-uh," he immediately rebuffed. "I have a birff-day three times, see." He held up three fingers to show her.

"Very good," she said, proud that their numbers and counting games were going so well. "But actually, you only have one birthday, the others celebrate the special day each year after that."

"Can I invite everybody?" he asked.

"Well, maybe not everybody, but yes, some people. Your very closest friends in the whole world." She reached over and kissed his forehead. He instantly ducked away and wiped his head.

"Mom," he complained, "you can't do that here. I'm a big boy and big boys don't get kissed." He looked around as if to make sure that no one saw them and witnessed the kiss.

"Oh, that's right, I'm sorry. I'll try to remember next time." Dena smiled and chuckled at the newfound sensitivity of her son. He was growing up so fast. She knew that in the blink of an eye he'd be on his way to college and she'd be left alone. She pushed her dish of ice cream aside. Suddenly she didn't feel like a treat anymore. She looked away as Dillon continued spooning chocolate into his open mouth.

Across the room she saw a man walk by dressed in tight jeans and a white T-shirt. He was built strong and he instantly reminded her of the first time she'd seen Julian. Then as if on cue random thoughts of Julian with the sledgehammer appeared. She smiled. He looked so good. Each muscle in his back tightened and pulled, his triceps and biceps contracted and released. The awesome forceful power of his body in perpetual motion warmed her body all over again.

Then her dream resurfaced and his body hovered over her like before but this time it was more sensual. He leaned down and gently touched his mouth to hers. Their tongues touched and a sweet surrender welcomed them.

They were locked in a heated embrace.

"Can I invite my dad to the party?"

Like a record needle on a vinyl album, the screeching sound was Dena's mind racing to return. "Huh? What?"

"You said not to say huh," Dillon said. "I'm finished. Can I have some more ice cream, please?"

"No, sweetie," she said, almost breathless as she looked around guiltily as if she'd gotten caught in her sexy dream and everyone knew about it. "Come on, get your stuff together, we need to go now."

"Okay," he said excitedly, knowing that they'd walk past the construction site to get to the parked car. He slid then hopped down off the plastic chair, grabbed his empty dish and his mother's half-full dish and marched them over to the trash can just as she'd taught him.

Dena watched as he went. The pride on her face was undeniable even as the thought of being alone gripped her again. She gathered the shopping bags, took his hand and left.

The phone call came while she was out. Sooner than she anticipated, it was definite, as of Saturday afternoon, then officially Monday morning, she was gainfully employed at least temporarily by Hamilton Development Corporation as the new administrative assistant.

Thrilled by the possibility of getting back to work and earning her keep, on Monday morning Dena arrived an hour early. Seeing Julian's car parked in the same spot as it was Friday evening sent her thoughts focusing on him again. She smiled, remembering their last conversation, then blushed remembering her wayward dream.

Talking with him was easy and relaxed, and made her feel good, something she seldom felt even with her late husband. Forester had been so focused on himself, work and his career, then on his family, particularly his mother. She'd always felt that she came in a distant third, fourth or fifth on his list, although it hadn't started out that way.

Their grad school romance had been whirlwind and ended in a Las Vegas chapel officiated by Elvis Presley and witnessed by two Martian aliens. His mother, Adel Graham, had lain in the bed for a month when she found out that her youngest son, her angel, her baby, had been tempted into marriage. Everything from then on went slowly downhill. Forester, once kind and gentle, had become cold and distant.

His mother had convinced him that the marriage was a mistake. He'd believed her as twenty-eight-plus years of momma's boy pull and influence far outweighed their budding love. Forester had succumbed and the marriage was all but over.

Julian seemed to be nothing like that. There was something innately exciting about being with him that piqued her interest. Although they'd only had a few conversations and granted their first meeting would be considered more of an altercation than introduction, they had started something and made a connection.

Being with Julian was like being the only woman in the world. He gave his total attention. He listened completely as she'd talked even when she confided in him the pain of her loss, surprising herself. She'd never spoken of the accident outside of her doctor's office. Even with her aunt Ellen, as close as they were, she never opened up completely. Julian seemed patient and kind, and she'd decided while making cookies with her son that he was different. She didn't know him well, obviously, but she got the sense that he was a good man. And she needed to know a good man.

So early Monday morning she packed up a small basket of chocolate-chip cookies and took them into the office. It wasn't until she asked around that she found out that Julian was actually one of the company owners. Then she realized that he must have been instrumental in her securing the position in the company. Deciding to thank him personally she found his office and left a short note along with the small basket of cookies.

Shortly afterward Willamina gave her an abridged tour of the facility then introduced her around to coworkers, including to the other two owners, Jordan and Darius, Julian's two brothers. They were near carbon copies of Julian, the same strong build, the same smooth-chocolate complexion, the same gorgeous eyes and the same jovial smile. Dena couldn't believe it when she heard her first bit of office gossip, that all three brothers were currently unmarried. She was sure that the women in the county must be mad or at the very least crazy.

After the tour and a brief conversation with Darius and Jordan, Willamina took Dena to her new office and gave her detailed records of the company's newest client, the county government. A multimillion-dollar account, they had been awarded a bid to build a new office complex. It was a major undertaking and everyone in the office was excited about it.

So for the next few hours Dena immersed herself in the exact details of the project, including records and files both computer-generated and hard copy. She spent a good bit of time sorting, purging and reorganizing to get a basic handle on what was going on.

The start of the project's files, several months ago, was accurate, concise and detailed, but as of a month ago they'd turned scattered and confusing. And going through the process was like putting together a puzzle without actually knowing what the finished picture looked like. As she dug deeper into the files, she discovered a number of questionable accounting practices. It wasn't until she heard the slight knock on her open door that she realized how late it had gotten.

She looked up from the computer monitor and the mass of papers and files already cluttering her desk and smiled. Her heart jumped as soon as she saw him. "Hi," she said, removing her reading glasses and pushing back her hair. Dressed casually in slacks and a polo shirt, he looked like a breath of fresh air standing there. His eyes, light in color, focused on her and she nearly fell out of her chair.

"Good afternoon. Welcome aboard," Julian said as he stood in the doorway. His expression was firm and stoic, which made him that much more sexy. Her stomach quivered as she remembered the last time she'd seen that expression, when he was leaning over her. "May I?" he asked.

"Yes, please come in," Dena said, standing to greet him.

Julian walked into the office and stood across from her desk. "I see you're already getting acclimated."

She nodded, looking down at the numerous files in front of her. "Trying. I'm getting there slowly. It's an exciting opportunity. I'm looking forward to being involved."

"I see." He nodded while still looking around, avoiding eye contact. "Well, how do you like us so far?"

"I didn't realize that you were one of the owners. Somehow I think you had something to do with me getting this job."

"Not at all," he said truthfully. "We needed an experienced administrative assistant with ample knowledge in tax law and tax codes on board, especially for this contract. You applied, Wilamina did the hiring. Believe me, I had nothing to do with it."

She smiled, not really believing him. "Well, thanks anyway, and thanks again for the ride home last Friday."

"Don't mention it. How's it going so far?"

The businesslike demeanor put her off at first; she hadn't anticipated the drastic change. "There's a lot of information and the previous records are pretty scattered and some of the computer files are incomplete."

"Unfortunately just before Mattie broke her ankle, Willamina went out on bed rest for a few weeks. With both of them out, we hired a few temps to fill in."

"No offense, but they didn't do a very good job."

"Which is why they're no longer employed here. Needless to say Willamina was furious with us when she came back. That's when she suggested we hire someone more suited for the position."

"Well, I'm no CPA but I'm catching on quickly. I do have a few questions about the contract and several of the subcontractors you hired. My predecessor left quite a few things open. Maybe in the next couple of days, if you have the time, you could sit down with me for a little bit and brief me on some of the particulars. Your brothers told me that you were the point man on this job."

"Sure, of course," he said, and took a seat.

"Now?" she said, surprised by his prompt attention and immediate response.

"Yes, I'm all yours. What can I do for you?"

Oh, Lord, don't ask that. Dena's thoughts veered quickly away from the stack of files on her desk and traveled along a straight line into her bedroom. She literally had to snap her wandering mind back to reality.

"Great," she muttered, nearly breathless as she opened her notebook and checked the questions she'd written down earlier. She handed him a file and asked him for an update, then prayed she could get through the next few minutes without making a complete and total fool of herself.

She did, barely. For the next half hour they discussed the particulars of the contract, the bid and the job. There were several points of contention that they both agreed could be worked out later. At one point she referred to some figures on the monitor. Julian stood and walked over to stand over her.

He leaned one hand on the desk and the other on the back of her chair. The close proximity was maddening. At one point she turned to say something not realizing just how close they were. Their faces were just inches apart. Suddenly she remembered him hovering over her when she was drenched with lemonade and then again in her dream. She lost her concentration three times and actually needed him to repeat himself. It was embarrassing, yes. Mortifying, definitely. But having him that close was also heaven.

As a distraction she shuffled the papers on her desk in the guise of looking for a particular invoice. She found it and handed it to him. Much to her relief he leaned up and walked back to the seat across from her, sat and studied the paper.

Then midway through another one of their discussions his cell phone rang. He excused himself and answered. Dena glanced away, recognizing a personal conversation when she heard one. There was obviously a woman on the other end and as per his end of the conversation, he wasn't too happy to hear from her.

When he hung up, he apologized and prepared to get back to work when his phone rang again. A shadow of frustration darkened his face as he answered, obviously expecting a repeat of the previous conversation. But apparently it was someone different. He agreed several times, apologized then promised to be wherever as soon as possible.

He stood as he hung up. "I've got to go. We'll have to work on this later. But feel free to talk to Darius or Jordan, either will be happy to answer any questions you might have."

"Sure," she said.

He walked to the door then turned. "By the way, I got the cookies. Thanks, they were delicious."

"You're very welcome."

As he left Dena closed her notebook then turned back to the monitor screen she'd been scanning before he arrived. She sighed, realizing that her focus had been shot. Frowning she cupped her head in her palm and leaned on the desk. What was wrong with her? It seemed that every time she saw Julian her hormones raged like a high-school student on prom night. She needed to do something about it. One way or another she needed Julian Hamilton out of her system.

Chapter 5

It was the perfect interruption.

Ten minutes more in the office with Dena, and Julian was sure he'd need crutches to walk out. He shook his head miserably. His brothers had known exactly what they were doing when they'd hired her. He'd forgotten that it was the start of a calendar quarter and since they each took turns in the office each quarter and it was his turn, he wasn't sure how long he was going to last.

And the brilliant idea he had of going into her office stone-faced and aloof disappeared as soon as she'd looked up and smiled. This had to end. There was no way he was going to survive much longer.

"You're late," Ellen said as she met Julian in her driveway with her hand on one hip and the rolled up plans slapping against her leg. "Your crew dropped off some supplies and is long gone."

"Evening, Mrs. Peyton," Julian said.

"Don't 'Evening, Mrs. Peyton' me. I called you over two hours ago. You're losing daylight and you know that I need this grill up and running by next month."

"Yes, ma'am," he said, smiling and shaking his head. He got out of his truck and walked around to the backyard. She followed. He looked around the open space seeing the more than adequate job his crew had done the Saturday before. Gone were the remains of the horrendous cinder-block wall and the hunks of dried cement. The patio, which he had put in a year earlier after another Ellen Peyton disaster, was back to its original state.

He walked over and bent down, checking the cracks and dents unavoidably left by the heavy machinery. Rubbing his hand over the surface he eyed the level plane. It was as he suspected, he needed to do some prep work before beginning work on the built-in grill station. "Did you see the plans Jordan worked up for you?"

"Yes, they'll do just fine with a few alterations."

"Changes?" he said, knowing that there would be.

"A few. I had one or two new ideas, but all in all, it was a good start."

Julian nodded. "I'll have him call you or stop by tomorrow if his schedule isn't too tight."

"Not necessary, we've already discussed my alterations. He sent over revised plans this afternoon." She unrolled and gave Julian the altered plans. "Mind you, I'll be happy to do it myself if you're too busy."

"No, not at all, Mrs. Peyton. I've already put you on my schedule, but if I get tied up at work either Jordan or Darius will be over to continue the job. We know that you'd prefer working with one of us."

She nodded, slightly disappointed that she wouldn't be more hands-on involved. "Have you eaten yet?"

"Thanks, but I grabbed a bite earlier," he said evasively but with good reason. Many an evening, he or one of his brothers sat in Ellen Peyton's kitchen enjoying a tasty home-cooked meal after working on something in her home. He headed back to his truck to get his supplies.

"Are you sure? I was just about to start dinner. I believe it's one of your favorites, smothered pork chops, mashed potatoes and gravy, collard greens, homemade apple pie and sweetened iced tea."

Julian's mouth watered instantly but there was no way he could stay knowing that Dena would be home soon. He needed to stick to the plan. He'd come to level the cracked and gouged patio surface and prep for the next phase of work. "Maybe next time," he said, hoping she didn't hear his stomach growl as he lowered the back flap of his truck.

"Suit yourself, but I'll make a platter for you just in case you get hungry later."

Julian smiled. "Thanks, Mrs. Peyton, that would be great."

"So how do you like my niece so far?" she said, changing the subject drastically. "I knew you'd want her as soon as you met her."

Taken off guard, Julian, without a firm grip on the load, turned and wrenched his back as he tried to lift a bag of cement. He dropped it. "I beg your pardon?" he said, wincing from his strained back muscles.

"And of course I just knew she'd be perfect for you," Ellen continued.

"Huh?" Julian added, presuming now that he must have been sucked into an alternate reality.

"Dena, my niece. I knew she'd be perfect and that you'd want her in the office as soon as you met her. Her credentials are impeccable. She knows all the office computer programs, she's a hard worker, organized and detail-oriented, and did I tell you she also has her law degree? She's not practicing right now, of course, but still, I knew she'd be an asset to Hamilton Development Corporation. I knew you'd want her."

"Yes," he said, then muttered, "I certainly do," just before closing his eyes and taking a deep breath. "She is a definite asset."

Ellen smiled, seeing Julian's reaction. "My sister's only grandchild, she's had some recent heartache, poor dear. Mind you, don't let those construction workers of yours give her a hard time or you'll have to answer to me. And don't let that tough-as-nails demeanor of hers fool you, she's as sweet as my homemade apple pie. Oh, Lord, speaking of apple pie, I'd better check on my pie. It's still in the oven. Do you need me for anything?" she asked.

"No, ma'am. I'll call you if I need you," he said, giving the standard reply. Ellen nodded and hurried back into the house. Julian sighed with relief. The conversation had taken him off guard. He knew of course that Dena was Ellen's great-niece, it was just the way she'd put it that had taken him off guard. *She's perfect for you.* She didn't know how right she was.

His thoughts started down that path and he could feel his body harden. Dena was plaguing him again and she wasn't even here. There was no way he was going to keep his vow if she was around. He had to do something.

Now focused on work, he unloaded a few bags of dried cement and carried them around to the back of the house. He stopped when he was nearly run over by a young child on a training-wheel bicycle.

The young child stopped suddenly, making a loud screeching sound of bad brakes with his mouth, then looking up at Julian with a helmet ill-fitted to his tiny head. "Hi, who are you?"

"Hello," Julian said with laughter in his voice. "I'm Julian Hamilton."

"Hi, Mr. Toolyian Hamydon. I'm Dillon, I'm three." He held up four tiny sausage fingers, rechecked and held one finger down. I'm almost four, see." He let go, allowing the fourth finger to pop up.

"Well it's nice to meet you, Dillon." He shifted the heavy bags of cement in his arms and continued to the work site. He dropped the bags and looked around again. A load of red bricks, a wheelbarrow and several other supplies had been left by his crew. He visually checked everything and made a mental picture of what needed to be done to get the job started.

As he stood with his hands on his hips he realized that Dillon had come up beside him and was mimicking his stance with the huge bicycle helmet still on his head. He chuckled. "Okay," he said, looking down at the top of the helmet.

"Okay," Dillon repeated in a squeaky deep voice, trying to imitate Julian. "I guess we better get started, right?" he asked, looking up at Julian as his helmet slipped forward to cover his eyes.

"Yep, I guess we'd better." Julian, realizing that Dillon was by his side for good, didn't even bother dissuading him. Julian reached into his tool belt and pulled out his work gloves.

Dillon looked at his tiny hands and frowned. He reached up and tugged on Julian's jean leg. "I don't got no globes."

Julian smiled wide. "You don't have any gloves." Dillon shook his head sadly. Julian walked back to the truck and dug in the glove compartment and pulled out a pair of men's soft suede leather gloves, a gift from an old friend. Dillon, right by his side, looked at the gloves and frowned.

"They're too big," he complained.

"We'll make them work," Julian promised as he pulled out a strip of Velcro and wrapped it around the suede gloves. When he finished the fit was perfect, albeit visually outrageous.

Now gloved and ready, together they gathered more tools. Julian carried a mixing shovel and trowel, and Dillon carried several rags. When they went back to the job site Julian strapped on his tool belt and Dillon took off. Moments later he returned with his play-school plastic tool belt and his brand-new yellow hard hat. "Ready," he said proudly.

Julian burst with laughter.

Dena left the office far later than she intended but she was so engrossed with the work set before her that she hadn't realized that dusk had begun to settle. She hurriedly left but drove home with thoughts mingled with tomorrow's chores. It felt good to get back to work and to just for a few hours not think about her troubles.

That's why she loved law so much. She enjoyed being totally engrossed, of straightening and figuring out problems and finding workable solutions while staying within the parameters of the law. As she drove down her aunt's street she noticed an unfamiliar truck in the driveway. She pulled up beside the truck and got out.

Dena climbed the stairs and opened the front door instantly feeling the cool of the air conditioner. "Hello?" she called, then listened for the typical response. Nothing. She called out again.

She walked into the empty kitchen and looked around, spotting the mess. Never a spoon out of place, there was definitely something wrong with this picture. Three soiled plates were in the sink, one of them being Dillon's favorite construction plate. Pots and pans were still on the stove and a plastic-wrap-covered, half-eaten apple pie was on the island counter. Odd. She heard a man's laughter and hurried over to the window and looked out.

Julian was holding his hand up and being splashed by Dillon as he tried to hold the water hose up to his mouth to get a sip. As water splashed everywhere Julian reached out and took the hose, bent down and held it while pinching it so that only a small stream would flow out. Dillon leaned in and sipped the water then giggled as it ran down the front of his already wet shirt.

Then Dillon reached out and, following Julian's exact instructions, grabbed the hose and pinched it then reveled as a small stream flowed. He held it up to Julian who leaned in and took a sip. Then Dillon's little hand slipped and again water splashed everywhere. Both laughed and fell back onto the wet grass.

Dena laughed with them as she closed the curtain and went to the back door. She opened it and walked outside, finding a new scene. Julian was holding a big fluffy white towel as Dillon dried off. He spun around and wrapped himself up, giggling as he went. He looked up, seeing his mother, and shrieked with joy.

"Mo-omm," he hollered, "looked what I did. I made it all

by myself, but Mr. Toolyian Hamydon helped, too. I held the water and mixed the teement and put it on the brick and stamped it down with the big rubber thing." Finally out of breath, he stopped as his little body slammed into her and she picked him up still wrapped into the towel.

She kissed his cheek and he moved back, avoiding her. "Mom, don't do that in front of my assistant, you promised," he whispered, then glanced over at Julian and wiggled until she let him down. He removed the towel and marched back to Julian's side.

"Hello," she said, looking down at Julian as he continued securing the water hose back in its container.

"Hi," Julian said.

"You're late, Mom," Dillon said as he knelt down and picked up his hard hat, gloves and tool belt.

"I know. Sorry. I was distracted at work. What are you doing here?" she asked Julian.

He reached down and helped Dillon strap the tool belt back on. "I'm helping Dillon start the new barbecue pit."

"Oh, I see, and how's that going?" Dena asked, then looked behind them, seeing a small, natural-stone block circular retaining wall half-complete. "It looks great." She walked over to get a better look. The detail work was perfect, but the size seemed a bit off. "Kind of small for a barbecue grill, don't you think?"

Dillon laughed and shook his head. "That's not a barbecue grill, Mom, that's the fire pit. We needed to build that first. The barbecue grill is next after we're done."

"Oh, I see," Dena said. "Why exactly are you building a fire pit?"

"That you need to take up with your aunt, she had changes and specified the exact requirements," Julian said.

"Speaking of which, where is she?"

"In the greenhouse."

Dillon hopped on his bicycle and drove it around the yard, ending up in front of the greenhouse. He got off then ran inside to apparently tell her that his mother was home.

"So I see you met Dillon."

"Yeah." Julian immediately smiled and chuckled.

"I hope he didn't get in your way too much or distract you from doing what you needed to do. He loves anything having to do with construction at the moment. You being here was probably a dream come true for him."

"Not at all, I enjoyed having him help me. He's quite the charmer, a great kid, full of life. His exuberance is refreshing."

"Yeah, he's exhausting sometimes, but I can't imagine being without him."

"Just like you were at that age?" he asked.

"What has my aunt been telling you?"

"Not a thing."

"Uh-huh." She blushed. "Well, actually yeah, by all accounts I was a bit of a handful. But Dillon is special. Today was the first day we've actually been apart for a full day. It was hard, really hard. Thank goodness work was so consuming."

"Glad we could help, ma'am."

They smiled and their eyes, hers having avoided his the entire time, met, and a quiet thought passed between them. She opened her mouth to speak but stopped suddenly, her breath caught trapped in her throat. The loneliness she'd felt for so long poured out to him.

She could see that he knew what she wanted without her

even speaking. His eyes gazed at her as she reached out and touched his face. The connection was something more than casual. At that moment they both knew that more had passed between them. "Dena, I'm sorry, I can't let this happen."

She gasped quietly then slowly backed up. "Um, I'd better clean this up," she said, turning away to the picnic table covered with a bowl of Cheerios and carrots. Her heart beat a mile a minute and the butterflies in her stomach began flying around with jet-propelled engines. How could she so freely expose herself again?

"Dena, let me explain…" he began as he came up behind her. He reached out and touched her arm.

"No, really, there's nothing to explain."

She grabbed the bowl of Cheerios and carrots and hurried to the back door. Her thoughts whirled dizzyingly. She made it to the kitchen and dropped the bowls in the sink. Leaning over with her eyes closed, she'd been mortified. It was one thing to be sexually turned down by her husband, now she'd been turned down by a near stranger. So Forester was right, she was inadequate. Breathing hard and fast, she was just seconds away from hyperventilating.

"Dena, are you okay?" he asked.

She opened her eyes at hearing his deep voice too close behind her. Still standing at the sink, she didn't move. Julian came up behind her and placed a half-full juice box and a half-full diet soda in the sink beside the bowls. He leaned in closer and loosely wrapped his hand around her waist. "It's me, not you. Dena," he began, but stopped when she suddenly turned and wrapped her arms around his neck. She kissed him with all the feeling and emotion she'd held back for what seemed like a lifetime.

It had been too long for both of them.

He returned her embrace and kissed her with equal fervor and commitment. The seven-month buildup of want and hunger nearly exploded inside him. Blinded by desire, taking her, making love to her, having her, right here, right now, at the sink in the kitchen was all he could see.

Their mouths engulfed the swirl of desire around them. Hot searing kisses continued to her neck, her cheek, her chin, then back to her mouth. Hard and passionate, their mouths met in an explosive relief. He moved forward, pressing his hard body against hers, trapping her against the sink. His hands held, touched and caressed everywhere. She was the spark that had ignited a raging fire.

"Dena," he whispered before he suckled then kissed the sweet sensitive underside of her earlobe.

"Julian," she moaned, light-headed by the tender tickling sensation while breathlessly feeling the hardness and evidence of his excitement pressed into her. She molded her body to his, taking everything he offered and feeling filled, desired and wanted for the first time in a long time.

Then he stopped, their bodies held perfectly motionless but still pressed together. Breathing hard, she rested her head against his chest, welcoming the thunderous beat of his heart. "I can't. We need to stop," he whispered softly, nuzzling his chin to her loose curls.

Rejected and dejected, Dena closed her eyes in pain. Her body slackened in response.

"I want you so much right now," he muttered then inhaled sharply. "You have no idea." His body twitched as he sighed. "Right now, this instant, I want you, but we can't. I can't," he added.

Dena smiled her relief. Of course, what was she thinking? Her son and her aunt were right outside and here she was attacking a man in the kitchen. And not just any man. Julian was her boss, someone she had to see and work with every day. Thank goodness, at least he was thinking.

"Are you okay?" he finally asked.

She nodded. "I know, I want you, too," she muttered as the fog of desire continued to cover her. "But I…" She stopped, hearing the slam of the back door and small footsteps running toward the basement steps.

"Mo-omm," Dillon called.

Julian took her hand and backed away slightly. She smiled even as her heart continued to beat wildly and her mouth still tasted of him. She licked her swollen lips. It felt good to have a man desire you again even if it was just a physical attraction. It was still something she'd seldom got with her husband.

Julian turned and walked over to the kitchen window. He looked down at the start of the fire pit below. But his focus was gone. His body still yearned for Dena and she was still too close.

Dillon climbed the back stairs and dumped the open box of Cheerios on the table. It tipped over then fell, sending three or so whole grain snacks scattering across the table. He smiled, happy that he'd joined in with the cleanup. "Thank you, sweetie. I'm gonna walk Mr. Hamilton out. Would you go upstairs and get ready to take your bath? I'll be right up."

"'Kay," he said, then turned to tear away but stopped and smiled at Julian. "'Bye," he said. "We finish later, right?"

Julian turned, his eyes instantly pulled to Dena then to Dillon. "Right," he confirmed.

With that Dillon disappeared up the back stairs singing the

theme song from a construction cartoon show he loved. Dena turned to Julian. "Is this going to be impossible?"

"No."

"I mean, us working together and..."

"No," he repeated.

"I have a child..."

"Guess what, I know."

"I mean, my life is scattered enough already. I know we can't do this. It would be impossible. Working together and..."

Julian moved back to her side and kissed her lips tenderly. "Why don't we see what happens? In the meantime, I need to leave now."

"Sure." She nodded and followed as he led the way through the dining room to the living room. "So it was your truck out front."

"I didn't want to disappoint you so I drove my truck."

"Thanks," she said as he held her hand, walking to the front door. "See you later."

"Tomorrow," he said, smiling warmly.

"Tomorrow?" she said, momentarily distracted.

"At work," he added.

"Oh, right, at work, yeah, see you tomorrow."

He leaned down and kissed her again. Long, loving, insistent and demanding, and filled with passion. Her arms wrapped loosely around his waist and held him close. She could feel the effect their kiss had on his body. He wanted her and, God help her, she wanted him, too. "Goodbye, Dena."

He stepped outside and walked to his truck. She waited in the doorway until his truck pulled off. As she turned, she was startled to see her aunt standing in the living room right behind her. "Nice," she offered with a huge, exaggerated smile. "And it's about time."

"Aunt Ellen, it's not what you think," Dena protested before her aunt spoke again.

"Somehow, I doubt that." Ellen smiled again.

"Mo-omm," Dillon screeched from the upstairs landing in a long exaggerated singsong tone. "I'm ready for my bath now."

Dena looked to the stairs then to her aunt. "It's not what you think," she repeated as she hurriedly left the room to help Dillon with his bath.

Ellen smiled. "Thanks, Louise."

Chapter 6

"Only when she's ready," Louise repeated. "Maybe we were wrong, maybe neither one is ready."

"Believe me she's ready. He's ready. Hell, at this point I'm even ready, but still nothing. It's been seven days since I saw them kiss and I haven't heard a single thing since. Nothing's changed."

"Are you sure they're right for each other?"

"Positive. I know they'd be good together but for some reason they just won't allow it to happen. They're their own worst enemies. I've never seen anything like it."

"And you saw them kiss?" Louise asked.

"Passionately. Louise, let me tell you, that kiss nearly rocked my world and I just walked in on the end of it. And I'd bet you good money that certainly wasn't the first time.

Not the way he was holding her and she was holding him. They have intimate knowledge."

"Well, the way you describe, it sounds like they're perfect together. But you're right, something is defiantly standing in the way."

"I have no idea what it could be. Dena is so lonely. My heart just breaks when I see her just sitting around reading or listening to music or watching television. She should be out there enjoying life."

"Well, maybe we can come up with something when I visit in a few weeks. Is that barbecue picnic still on?"

"Yes, my new patio should be finished by then."

"Don't worry, Ellen. I've helped dozens of couples find their way through a muddled mess. I don't intend to lose one now."

"Thanks, Louise. I'll see you in a few weeks."

Her door was closed and her head was lowered but she knew that she couldn't avoid him much longer. For seven days now she arrived extra early and left extra late. But she knew that she'd have to eventually run into Julian. She was just surprised that it hadn't happened already.

Thankfully he'd been out of the office for the past week and the one time he was in the office she made it a point to personally introduce herself to several of the company's major suppliers. It was the coward's way out, sure, but she was willing to go that route. Of course she knew hiding would only last but for so long.

A knock on her door startled her and she looked up. "Come in," she said hesitantly.

"Hi, how's it going?"

Recognizing the voice, Dena smiled her relief. "Hi, Jordan. Everything's good so far, thanks again for this opportunity."

"Don't mention it. You're actually doing us a favor. With Mattie still out and Willamina leaving for maternity leave there was no way we could survive without someone here. I'm just sorry that I haven't been around the past few days to help you out."

"I pretty much have a handle on the job so far. Are you back in the office now?"

"No, my brothers and I usually have a quick meeting at least once a week to check schedules and review details," he said, moving farther into the room.

"Sounds like a good idea," she said.

"And everyone's treating you well?"

"Yes, this is a dream job for me right now, just what I needed."

"Good," he said, then glanced at the one picture she had on her desk. "And who's this young man?"

Dena smiled. "That's Dillon, my son."

Jordan chuckled. "Let me guess, he wants to be a construction worker when he grows up."

"How'd you know?" she joked.

He chuckled again, eyeing the phone closer. "The hard hat, tool belt, overalls, hammer in his hand and huge smile on his face were a dead giveaway."

"He'd just turned three when this picture was taken. I purchased a suit and shoes, but he adamantly refused to wear them for the photo. When I insisted, his smile told me it wasn't in his heart. So I relented."

Jordan laughed openly. "It sounds like he's got your number."

"He certainly does. But I guess you'd understand and relate since I'm sure you did the same thing."

"Me, nah, when I was a child I wanted to be an artist. I painted, sculpted and sketched everything in sight."

"Really, that's interesting," she said, surprised.

"Oh, yeah. I went to school for architecture and even worked in a top L.A. firm for a few years."

"Then you just stopped and came here?"

"Yep, we all did. I was an architect, Darius was a New York stock broker and Julian was a doctor in Boston."

"What? How? Why?"

"Our dad owned a small construction company when we were growing up. He and our mom divorced and he bent over backward to give us everything within his power including our own lives. He got sick suddenly and died. We didn't want to see his dream disappear so we changed careers and took over."

"Wow, that's so incredibly touching."

"We never regretted a moment," Jordan said as he placed the photo back down on the desk. "So how old is Dillon?"

"He's three going on four in a few weeks going on sixteen."

"Now with that, I can relate." They chuckled. "How's Mrs. Peyton?"

"Fine, and as long as her favorite television show only comes on Saturday afternoons, I think we're all safe."

He laughed. "I love her spirit."

"Me, too. I sometimes wish that I had her steadfast courage. She takes whatever she has and moves on to build something new. That's the spirit."

"But you have that quality, don't you?"

"Me, no, I wish."

"You're a widow with a small child and you're moving on with your life. That has to take a tremendous amount of courage and bravery."

She smiled at his kindness. "Thanks."

"Don't thank me. You're the amazing one." They smiled happily. "Okay, enough of this pep talk, time to crack the whip. Get back to work."

Dena laughed and saluted. "Yes, sir, boss."

Jordan turned to leave then turned again. "Oh, one more thing. I have some revised plans for your aunt's patio. Would you pick them up and drop them off before you leave tonight?"

"Sure," she said. "I'll be leaving in a few minutes. I'll stop by and pick them up."

"Thanks."

Jordan left Dena smiling. The story he'd told her about their lives was truly touching. She knew that he was the youngest of the three brothers and Darius was the oldest, leaving Julian as the middle child. But that's pretty much all she knew about him. Now she wondered about Julian's past career. He was a doctor in Boston. Did he have a wife there, children of his own? She actually knew little about him.

"Knock, knock."

Dena looked up, slightly startled, then relaxed when she saw that it was Willamina standing in the open doorway, her protruding stomach taking up most of the open-framed space. "Hi, what's up?" Dena said.

"Oh, nothing. I'm on my way home and just stopped by to check on you. But actually I do have a favor to ask."

"Sure, what can I do?"

"I wanted to invite Dillon over for dinner this evening then maybe go out for some ice cream. My boys would love to meet a new playmate."

Dena smiled and brightened instantly. Dillon had both

older and younger friends in the neighborhood, of course, but she knew that he would just love meeting children his own age. "That sounds wonderful. Dillon is dying to meet some new friends. Thank you so much."

"Great. Is it okay if I stop by on my way home?"

"Sure. I'll call my aunt and let her know you're picking him up for the evening. He's going to be so excited."

"Good, glad to do it. Also I stopped by for another reason. I wanted to make sure everything was all right."

"Are you kidding, everything's great."

"Are you sure?"

"Positive," Dena said. "Why do you ask?"

"You seem to be…" Willamina paused and shrugged. "Oh, I don't know any other way to put this, so here goes. You seem to be hiding out the past few days, maybe even a bit jumpy."

"No, I'm fine, really. Maybe a bit too much caffeine, but I'm certainly enjoying working here, particularly the adult conversation. After being home with Dillon the last three years, I almost forgot what it was like. But really, I'm fine."

"Good, just one more thing, go home."

"Huh?"

"Go home, relax, take a break, get some rest. Whatever works for you, do it. You've been working like a madwoman for the past seven days. You get in early, leave late and take lunch here in your office. You need to let go, fourteen hours of this is too much, and I don't want you burning out on me. I need you at least until I get back from maternity leave or Mattie returns in the next month or so. So I'm kicking you out this evening. Go home and spend some time doing something you want to do. I'll take good care of Dillon and have him back a little after eight."

Dena sighed, knowing that Willamina was right. She was overdoing it. "Actually that's a good idea. I think I'll do just that."

"Good, I'll see you later when I drop Dillon off."

"Thanks again, Willamina."

She nodded and smiled then mouthed the words, *Go home.*

Dena immediately picked up the phone and called her aunt to tell her about Dillon's play date. Afterward she sat a moment longer, thinking. Willamina was right; she was hiding and she was being silly. Hiding from Julian was childish. They had a connection and the attraction was certainly real enough. They were both consenting adults and whether or not anything happened or would happen between them was no one's business but theirs.

She grabbed her purse from the lower drawer, stood and walked out. She was headed to the elevator when she remembered that Jordan wanted her to take plans home with her. She turned and headed toward the executive offices then paused, realizing that Julian might be around this late.

But then she remembered that Jordan mentioned that he and his brother would be in a meeting this evening so running into Julian was remote. Finding her way through maze of offices, she heard voices and immediately recognized Julian. Picking up the new plans on the desk, Dena stopped, stunned by what she'd just overheard.

As often as possible, the three Hamilton brothers met after work at least once a week to discuss business-related issues. It was a practice they started shortly after their father died as a way of coming together and consoling each other, now it was a way of life.

Tonight Julian sat in Darius' office waiting for Jordan to

get off the phone. They'd already discussed the more immediate issues and now the conversation continued to a more personal nature.

"I can't do this," Julian insisted.

"You're gonna have to," Darius said firmly.

"Fine, then you take this quarter and I'll take your next two quarters."

"No."

"Darius, seriously, I can't do this."

Darius looked at his brother, recognizing his angst. "Julian, this ridiculous kick you're on is absurd. No grown man in his right mind would even consider something so insane. Just give it up."

"You don't get it. For the first time in a long time, I feel calm and in control. No drama, no worries and no women. Now I'm right back where I started. Yeah, I get the occasional phone call from Stephanie or Jessie, but I can ignore them. I can't ignore Dena."

"Yeah and don't you think that should tell you something? All your angst is over one woman. Why? You come in contact with attractive, interesting women all the time, we have dozens of women walking through here every day and you've never said a word about dismissal. Now this one woman shows up and is affecting you to this extreme, that says something."

"It says nothing, only that I need her gone."

"She's affecting you, you said it. Did you ever stop to think why? Stephanie is your ex-wife, she didn't do this to you, neither did Jessie or even Kellie. There's obviously something about Dena that touches you."

"No," Julian said, still resisting.

Julian turned his back. Darius was right, but he wasn't going to give him the satisfaction of admitting it. For more than seven months he had successfully avoided any physical interaction with women and he'd had plenty of opportunity, yet he was never even tempted. Now, in the span of about a week, Dena Graham came into his life and had him so worked up that he was seriously reconsidering his vow of celibacy.

They'd kissed a week ago and he'd been avoiding her ever since. She set a fire in him and his was still burning for her. But last night was the final straw. The dream he'd had was too vivid, waking him up in a heated sweat. He wanted her and he was agonizing over it. She was a woman with a child and all the drama of his ex-wife surfaced. He couldn't go through with that again and keeping his distance was getting more and more difficult.

He successfully avoided her at her aunt's house easily enough by making sure not to go when she was there. Unfortunately there was no way to continue avoiding her in the office. So the best thing to do was to get rid of her.

"Sorry I'm late, what'd I miss?" Jordan said as he entered Darius' office, seeing Julian at the window and Darius behind his desk with his back turned. The tension in the room was telling. "What's going on?"

"Julian wants us to get rid of Dena," Darius said.

"Are we doing this again? I thought this was settled," Jordan said as he entered the discussion.

"It's not," Julian said, turning.

"It is," Darius corrected.

"I don't see how you have a problem with Dena," Jordan said, taking a seat across from Darius' desk.

"Well, I do. She needs to go, now," Julian insisted.

"We can't do that even if we wanted to," Darius said. "Legally we don't have a leg to stand on and besides that, the suggestion is absurd."

"Well, then, I'm going on vacation for the next three months or until either Mattie returns or Willamina comes back from maternity leave."

"Don't be ridiculous," Darius said.

"I'm serious. I've already got a position lined up for her."

"I bet you do," Darius muttered under his breath, seeing firsthand the distress Dena was putting his brother through. Julian turned to him.

"No, way," Jordan insisted. "I asked around, everyone thinks she's great and so do I. As a matter of fact, I was just in her office, we talked a bit. She's nice and I really like her. Actually I was thinking I might ask her to the beach house this weekend."

Julian turned to him. "What?"

"Yeah, Mrs. Peyton can babysit her son and she and I can spend some quality time together, get to know each other better." He smiled, looking directly at Julian.

"Over your dead body." Julian glared with an empty threat but still the anger in his eyes sparked piercingly.

Jordan laughed and pointed to Darius. "I told you, interesting response for a celibate man wallowing in self-pity."

"You're not asking her anywhere," Julian said.

"Why not? You don't even want her here in the office let alone in your life, so why shouldn't I ask her out?" Jordan chuckled and Darius joined in.

Julian realized that Jordan was just teasing to irritate him and that he had no intention of actually asking Dena out. "If this meeting is adjourned, I have things to do."

"Anyone I know?" Jordan asked, still chuckling.

Julian glared at him one last time before walking out the door, hearing Darius join in the laughter.

She was hurt and angry and just plain pissed off. Another man's rejection should have been nothing to her but this one hurt even more than the others. Her father rejected her and then her husband rejected her, but at least on some level they knew her or at least thought they did. No, Julian's off-hand dismissal hurt worse than the others. He didn't even give her a chance.

She got in the car and drove on automatic like a zombie on Prozac. Windows down, the once gentle breeze whipped recklessly through her loose curls as she drove detached, emotionless, stilled by what she'd just heard. Anguished images stirred her mind to wonder.

Her lowest point was just after Forester died. She remembered the feeling well. He was pronounced dead right there in front of her at the scene of the accident. She expected the world to stop, but it didn't. Nothing changed. She looked around and curiosity-seekers looked on and cars continued to drive by as if nothing had happened.

In that instant her world had collapsed and the ripple she expected to follow didn't even tremble. She was in a bad place at that point. Her heart was broken and the guilt of surviving a deadly crash that took three people plagued her. She was ripe to be taken advantage of.

But what did follow, the arguments, the rebuffs and the rejection from her mother-in-law drove her to near insanity. That's when she learned to fight back and to stand up for herself and be strong. Her great-aunt always told her that no one can beat you down if you don't let them. She had let them, but no more, never again.

Then fighting back had become her mantra. She fought Adel, Forester's mother, and she fought the law. And now she intended to stand strong and fight again. Pointing her car, she arrived at her aunt's house before she even realized it. She pulled up in the driveway, got out and walked inside.

"Hi, sweetie, you're home early," Ellen said.

"Hi, Aunt Ellen," Dena said, dropping her purse on the kitchen counter then looking around. "Where's Dillon?"

Ellen looked at her strangely. "You called me, remember? Willamina picked up her twins then stopped by to pick up Dillon for dinner. He was so excited. She said that they'd probably be back late, around eight o'clock."

"Oh, that's right," Dena said, obviously distracted.

"Are you all right? What's wrong?"

"Nothing." She faked a half smile. "I'm just tired."

Ellen stood, walked into the living room then returned with a letter. "This came for you. It's from your attorney."

Dena looked at the letter as if it would bite her. She took it gingerly and opened it. Sitting down, she read silently then reread its partial contents out loud. "It's from Adel's attorney to my attorney then copied to me."

"Anything good?" Ellen asked.

"It deals with Adel, you know better than that," Dena said, then cleared her throat and began reading the interesting part of the letter.

> "'Defendant, Adel Graham, has supplied verifiable proof that the child, Dillon Graham, is not biologically related to her son deceased, Forester Graham. Further-

more said wife/widow/plaintiff, Dena Graham, entered into an adulterous affair after the death of Forester Graham resulting in said child. As a direct result all inheritance life insurance policies, property and personal assets on Forester Graham's behalf will remain in the custody of Adel Graham.

A tentative appointment has been scheduled to review information stated in this letter, please contact me at…'"

"'Verifiable proof,'" Dena repeated wearily as she looked up from the letter. "That woman still won't let go of those apron strings."

Ellen chuckled. "She damn near choked you with her vindictive lies. I'm so glad that part of your life is over."

"Not quite over."

"I don't know how you do it. This lawsuit has dragged on for over three years. Adel is just plain spiteful. She knows good and darn well that Dillon is Forester's son. And tell me please, how the heck is she privy to what did or didn't happen in your marital bed?"

"I told her that Forester and I hadn't had intimate relations in months before the accident."

"You did what?"

"I told her. It was the truth as far as she needed to know. But a month before he died Forester came home drunk one night and we were together." Her voice trailed off and a pained expression clouded her face.

"He raped you, didn't he? That son of a…"

"Dillon was conceived that night, how and why doesn't matter."

"So tell her."

Dena half smiled. "Tell Adel that her perfect angelic son forced himself on me. Yeah, she'll believe that," she said facetiously. "The only reason I'm even doing all this is that Dillon deserves it. He shouldn't be penalized because of his father."

"It'll all come out in the wash. Are you going to the appointment they've set up?"

"I'll have to contact Lynn and see what she suggests. I'd like to go. At this point I just want to get this over with."

"I'm sorry this has been so difficult for you."

"You know, the funny thing is that Forester's ex-girlfriend was also pregnant at the same time I was. She told Adel that it was Forester's child and Adel has taken the child into her home."

"Is it his child?" Ellen asked.

"I have no idea. I just want Dillon to have what he deserves."

"He will," Ellen said, patting Dena's hand gently. "Now, how about something to eat? I made fried chicken, macaroni and cheese, green beans and homemade corn bread."

"Nah, thanks, I'm not really hungry."

"You have to eat something, Dena. I'll fix you a plate." Dena nodded. "Oh, by the way, Julian stopped by earlier."

"Did he?" Dena said coolly.

"Yes, he let Dillon play with his cell phone and forgot to take it back when he left. He asked if he could stop by and pick it up this evening. But I need to go out, so would you make sure he gets this? Oh, and I fixed him a food platter, too."

Dena looked at the phone her aunt handed her. Her day was going downhill on jet-propulsion skis. A few minutes later Ellen left and Dena was alone. She walked through the house, her thoughts clouded with images of Forester then Julian then Dillon, the men in and around her life.

To find some relief she walked out back and stood at the

edge of the patio. Disheveled in its renovation stage, the framework for a breathtaking sanctuary was visually emerging. Quiet but still restless, she continued her walk along the well-worn garden path toward the greenhouse that had been constructed years earlier and had since been renovated and modernized to suit her aunt's needs.

Her aunt's house stood on ten pristine acres of land, giving her plenty of room to roam freely. She passed the large greenhouse, finally reaching the narrow path beyond it to the small brook traversing the property. She stood listening and watching the water. There she found her contentment. Moments later she turned and headed back to the house.

Walking back she enjoyed the dancing lightning bugs' glow while listening to the ardent crickets rub their legs together in hopes of finding a mate. She returned just as dusk had begun to settle and a full moon climbed high in the clear night sky. A warm breeze blew by as she sat relaxing, resolving to herself that being alone was good.

She closed her eyes and dreamed.

Then hearing a noise, she awoke and looked around. "Who's there?"

"Dena, it's me, Julian. I came to…"

"Yeah, right, I know. Your cell phone. It's in the kitchen on the counter, go and get it," she said, her voice cold and detached as she relaxed back in the chair again.

He didn't. Instead he moved to where she was sitting and sat down on the lounge beside her. "How are you?"

"You tell me. Or better yet, don't. Let's not play this, okay. Just get your phone and go."

"Excuse me?" he said as she sighed heavily, stood and walked away from him. "What's wrong? Have I offended you?"

She laughed.

"What's so funny?" he asked, still following.

"You, you're a trip."

Julian continued to follow. "I don't get it."

"If you have a problem with me, tell me, I won't sue and you certainly don't need an extended vacation just to get away from me."

"What?"

"Sorry I don't fit into your pretty little package."

"You have me at a disadvantage," he confessed.

"You, disadvantaged?" She whipped around quickly. "You, made uncomfortable by a mere woman like me? Somehow I doubt that." She marched across the greenhouse and slammed open the door.

"What are you talking about?" Julian asked as he followed her into the greenhouse.

She turned on a dime to face him. "Don't act like you don't know. I heard you tonight in your brother's office. I'll have a letter of resignation on Willamina's desk first thing in the morning and you don't have to farm me off to someone else, I can find another position."

"Dena," he began, "it's not what you think."

"As I said, let's not play this game. Your precious honor is safe. I'm not looking for some kind of consort. I know what happened between us was inappropriate. I just didn't realize you were so disgusted. I'm truly sorry if I offended your sensibilities."

"Dena—" he began but was cut off quickly.

"I don't want to hear it." She turned and walked away, and began closing the windows and vents and shutting down the sprinkler system for the evening.

He followed. "Are you finished? Can I please say something now?"

She turned again. He stopped short. "No. But you may inform your brothers that litigation takes too long and I don't sue over trivial matters."

"Are you finished now?" he asked humbly, following her outside and back to the house.

"No." She turned again. "How dare you presume you can change my life to suit your needs. I dealt with that crap for too long to have to put up with it again. I don't need you or this job."

"Are you finished now?" he asked again.

She hesitated then started in again and really let him have it. "This is exactly what's wrong with men today. What makes you happy, what pleases you, what you want—you never think about anyone else but yourself. Men may rule the world but you don't rule all the women in it," she said, then stomped up the stairs to the kitchen.

"Are you—" he attempted to ask again.

"No. I just want to know one thing. Why are you so threatened by me? What are you afraid of? If you aren't interested, just say so," she said then stopped and, breathing hard, went silent.

"—finished now?" he continued his question, half smiling by her less than focused tirade.

"Yeah, I'm more than finished." She picked up the cell phone and slammed it into his hand, then turned to the back staircase and headed upstairs. "Goodbye, Julian. Close the door on your way out."

"I've chosen to be celibate," he confessed.

She stopped on the third step, stunned by his statement.

Chapter 7

"Celibate."

She turned.

He nodded. "And you, woman, are driving me crazy." He lowered his head, leaned forward against the counter, his arms wide and his hands grasping the edge firmly.

"Celibate," she repeated, unbelievably stunned.

"I'm no monk. I've been tempted, yes. But for the last seven and a half months, I avoided any and all physical contact with women. But you..." He took a deep ragged breath and shook his head. "You come along and everything goes right out the window."

"Celibate," she whispered.

He looked up at her and cocked his head impatiently. "You want to stop saying that now," he requested calmly.

"Sorry." She smiled and silently chuckled. "Why? Or is

it a spiritual thing?" she asked as she came back into the kitchen area.

"It's not a spiritual vow and the particulars of the why don't really matter. The point is, having you around is killing me."

"Oh, no, you don't. You're not going to blame this on me. There are half a million women in this county—"

"That haven't affected me as you have," he continued.

"No," she said plainly. "Flattering, yes, but I refuse to believe that," she stated firmly as she moved closer.

"Believe it." He looked at her deeply, his eyes glazed with undeniable truth. "I can't do this with you in my life," he near whispered as she came closer.

"I'm not in your life," she said.

"You know what I mean."

"And how is this fair to me?" she said.

"It's not," he agreed, "but I don't know what else to do. You stir urges in my body, strong urges, and every time I see or am near you, I want you. I want you so bad," he said, gritting his teeth.

She smiled, feeling a certain power. "Is that right?"

He nodded.

She nodded.

They stood face-to-face, staring into each other's eyes feeling what lovers feel when passion calls. Then without moving, in his mind's eye he took her in his arms and kissed her. Her lips melded to his as he wrapped his arms around her body, holding her tight to his own. His thoughts devoured her with an embrace so intense the world stopped spinning as their assent to pleasure and their surrendering to passion gave way.

It was his fantasy and his mouth dried even with the thought of the long lustful sensation. His overwhelming unrestrained craving yielded to nothing but reality. But in his thoughts, she was his and he was hers. His eyes, sad and wanting at the same time, stayed steadily focused on hers as a vacuum of air continued to still around them.

Dena sighed inwardly. Unfulfilled desire; she knew what it was like. The wanting, the arousal, the hunger, the longing all culminated in one fierce intensified need. She had lived her life wanting more, first from her parents then from her husband and now from herself. And in this moment her want was Julian. But there was no way she would deliberately defy his promise of celibacy, yet the idea was tempting.

She herself had been celibate or at least abstinent for the past four and a half years, not by choice but by circumstance. Now the slow, steady attrition had built up inside of her. She had finally found someone, but he, of his own volition, was beyond her reach. But oh, the possibility. Wild and wicked, they were many, varied and then some.

Rapturous thoughts clouded her mind and he never even touched her. Breathless and patient, she felt his eyes touch her and she nearly trembled, transfixed by the unquenched passion. They drowned in desire having never even dipped into the pool. The dream, a fantasy, in reality was set aside. Relenting would be effortless, but they didn't.

Each held controlled strength, knowing in this moment gratification would not come, imagining was one thing, but actually making love was not to be.

"What were you just thinking?" Dena asked.

"You know exactly what I was just thinking," he said.

She smiled. He was right, she did know what he was

thinking because she was thinking the same thing. How easy it would be to surrender to the moment, when wanting each other was all there was and all that mattered.

"Condoms?" she joked.

He shook his head and smiled.

"You?" he queried, adding to the joke.

She shook her head and smiled.

A relaxed expression touched their eyes. The connection they'd made quickly dissipated.

"Mo-omm, I'm home," Dillon called.

They laughed just as Dillon and two other little boys rounded the corner. They were all three dressed like super-heroes with bright red, white and blue capes.

"Hi, Dena. Sorry we're so late, we were having too much fun. We really need to—" Willamina, following to boys to the kitchen, stopped and smiled, seeing Julian standing at the counter. "Julian," she said, smiling broader. "I didn't realize you were here."

"Hello, Willamina," he said. "Hi, guys."

"Hi," the three boys said in unison.

"Willamina, thank you so much," Dena said.

"Don't mention it, it was fun. I actually got to sit and relax. These three superheroes rescued me from an evil villain six times. All I had to do was sit with my feet up and eat ice cream."

"Really," Dena said, laughing, "that's fantastic."

Dena turned her attention to the three superheroes. "You three deserve something very special."

"We had chocolate ice cream, Mom," Dillon began excit-edly. "This is Caleb and Justin, they're my new friends. They have a big construction in their house. We played with trucks and dug holes in the sand. It was fun. Can I go back and play later, cause we're gonna build a castle and then—" he yawned "—we're gonna build a spaceship and then a house and a castle again. Can I show Caleb and Justin my room?" He finally finished then took a breath. Caleb and Justin moved back to lean against Willamina's legs. They also yawned.

"Why don't we discuss that tomorrow? Right now, Dillon, you need to thank Mrs. Parker for inviting you over tonight." He did.

"You're very welcome, Dillon, anytime. Well, I'm gonna say good night and get these guys home and right to bed."

Caleb and Justin sang a collective, "Aw, Mom."

"It's late, buddies, and we have to go now."

"Can we come back again?" the twins asked hopefully.

Willamina looked at Dena. She smiled at the boys. "Caleb and Justin, you have an open invitation to visit Dillon anytime your mom says you can."

"Yea," Dillon yelled as Caleb and Justin joined in.

"But for right now, its bedtime, young man, so say goodbye and good night."

"Aw, Mom," Dillon said, then, seconds later complied.

"Good night, Julian," Willamina said as she walked away.

"Good night, Willamina. Check you later, Caleb, Justin."

"'Bye," the boys called in unison.

"Thanks again, Willamina," Dena said.

The three boys ran back to the living room then out onto the front porch. Willamina and Dena followed. "Julian, huh?"

"It's not what you're thinking," Dena said, stepping out onto the porch.

"Uh-huh, it never is, is it? See you tomorrow."

"Good night." Dena watched as Dillon said 'bye to his new friends then walked back into the house. She stayed outside and watched as Willamina secured the boys in their seats then got in, buckled up and drove off.

As she went back inside she heard Dillon telling Julian everything he did that evening in machine-gun rapid secession. "Okay, mister-man, its way past your bedtime."

"Aw, Mom," he said, apparently his new catch phrase. "Can't I stay up longer?"

"Nope. Say good night and head upstairs. I'm right behind you." She removed his cape and placed it on the back of the chair then kissed his forehead. He didn't pull away as he usually did when they weren't alone.

"Night," he said to Julian while yawning.

"Good night, buddy," Julian said as they slapped each other a high five then Dillon slowly walked up the back kitchen stairs to his bedroom.

"He's such a great kid," Julian said, surprising himself by the open admission. He was obviously beginning to feel attached.

"He's my hero," Dena said. "He saved my life."

Julian looked at her. Her focus was on the back stairs but he knew that she was miles away in her thoughts. She turned and their eyes held. "So," they said at the same time then smiled. "You first." Again in unison.

"Look, Julian, I don't know what led you to make your decision and I'm sure it took a lot of thought and consideration. I may not fully understand, but I can certainly respect it. I won't make this any more difficult for you. I'll stay on my side of the desk but if you still find my presence difficult, I'll get another job, simple. So, colleagues?" she offered as she held her hand out to shake.

Julian's heart lurched. He didn't expect her to say what she said. He was actually ready to give up celibacy but her offer touched him. "Friends." He finally conceded, shaking her hand.

"Mo-omm, I'm ready," Dillon called from upstairs.

"I'd better go," Julian said, and he began walking to the front door. "Good night."

"Good night," she said, watching him walk down the front steps then to his car parked across the road.

"Mo-omm, I'm ready again," Dillon repeated.

"Coming," Dena said, closing the door.

Julian looked in the rearview mirror, seeing Dena go back into the house. He smiled. The evening hadn't started as he expected, but it had ended favorably enough. As he and Dena came to an understanding he wondered just how long he could hold out knowing that the temptation was too strong to ignore.

Chapter 8

She'd gotten a new look.

She was going to meet with her attorney and Adel's legion of suits, and that in itself required change. The last time Adel saw her she was a pathetic pitiful wreck sniveling and crying about the sale of her house. Although it was only a few months ago, she felt as if it were a lifetime ago.

Thankfully, Willamina granted her a full day off to handle personal business.

It was exactly as she remembered, Graham, Whitman & Morris, only there was no Whitman or Morris. Graham had long since bought them out but they still carried the letterhead for purely professional purposes. Dena walked to the reception area, her attorney was already there.

Lynn Brice turned and smiled, surprised. "Dena."

"Hi, Lynn," Dena said as the two women hugged warmly.

Old college friends, they had started in Judge Hughes's office years ago. They were both on the fast track to partnership success but then Lynn assisted in a case for her firm. Their client was accused of kidnapping and assault. Her firm got the man off then in return he kidnapped Lynn and held her hostage for three days. The ordeal was horrendous. Once resolved and the man imprisoned, Lynn eventually quit her job and took time off, then came back stronger then ever.

"Look at you," Lynn remarked. "You look fantastic."

"Thanks," Dena said, proud of her new look. "I feel fantastic."

"Whatever your aunt's doing, she's a miracle worker. I might stop by and check her out myself."

"Are you kidding, you look fantastic." They hugged again then chatted briefly to catch up.

"So are you ready for this?" Dena asked, looking up at the grandfather clock in the main lobby.

"One question," Lynn offered. "Why me? You know my history, I haven't practiced law in over five years. My practice is small, very small, you know that. There are so many other attorneys and firms who would love to take Graham, Whitman & Morris on. Why me?"

"Because you're my friend and because you know what it's like to go to hell and come back stronger. So I figure another trip won't be so bad." The two chuckled, remembering the times they consoled each other through the lowest points in both their lives.

"Ain't that the truth," Lynn said.

"This isn't going to be easy. They're gonna play their games, try to intimidate us, even scare us, that's just how they roll. Adel always gets her way, period. There is no compromise as far as she's concerned."

"I've been in the lion's den before," Lynn said. "I've grown quite comfortable there."

"This isn't the lion's den," Dena said. "This is the lion's mouth and I'm the main course. You can turn back if you'd like, I'll understand."

"Nah, I've turned back too many times in my life already. Let's do this for Dillon."

Dena nodded. She was proud of her friend. They grasped hands, squeezed for moral support then headed to the elevator.

"Warning," Dena said as they walked, "their main strategy is the positioning in the conference room. They'll have us face the bright sun streaming in from the windows. We'll be off balance and blinded most of the meeting."

"Do you have sunglasses?" Lynn asked.

"Yes," Dena answered.

"Good, then follow my lead, everything else we need is in this bag." She patted the large purse-style bag on her shoulder. "Let's do this," she said ruthlessly, like a general going into battle. "And by the way, lunch is on you."

Dena smiled. This was new. The tone in Lynn's voice was harsh and fearless. She seemed almost ferociously angry as a single, focused glare covered her eyes. She was on a mission. And for some reason, at that moment, Dena pitied Adel.

The executive offices of the prestigious law firm were exactly what might be expected. Large, impressive, masterfully and meticulously designed for maximum effect. "Appearances make statements," Adel was always fond of saying. The show of power and money was the perception of power and money. And Adel, thanks to the death of her husband and two sons inherited an amassed fortune worth in the millions.

Having grown up poor and on the wrong side of town, Adel Cooper Graham worked her way to the top of the food chain through grit and determination. She kept to her goal, focused and remained true. A formidable foe, she was a dangerous woman but only to those who challenged or threatened her.

Dena threatened her.

They walked into the main office then were escorted to the nearby conference room. Stately and majestic, again for appearances' sake, it was covered and filled with tedious worker bees all humming around for a single entity, Adel Graham.

The exalted queen, presumably absent, wasn't a lawyer but she knew more about the law than most of the men in the room.

Gaylord Till walked over and needlessly introduced himself having known Dena and Forester for years. He was Adel's eyes and ears at the law firm. A senior partner, she handled him and he took care of her and her interests. "Ladies, please come in, have a seat," he said with the scant Southern accent he often used to the extreme to throw his opponents off guard with an exaggerated Southern mild-mannered gentry.

Dena knew his tricks well; after all, she had been part of the family for two years. They were corporate law and she was family law, not even in the same league as far as they were concerned. So, mostly ignored and overlooked at family and business occasions she tucked herself away and just listened closely.

Never mindful of her, they spoke openly of battle scars, weaknesses and leverage. So Dena learned all the office gossip, the deadly secrets and the bits and pieces of interesting hearsay, that only an insider would be privy to. Yes, she remembered Gaylord Till very well.

"Coffee?" he offered, nodding across the room. Two blank-faced assistants stood instantly to retrieve coffee as the two associates leaned in to talk between themselves.

"No thank you," Lynn said calmly. "We'd just like to get started."

"As you wish," Gaylord said, nodding to an associate. He walked across the room and opened a side door. Two more associates entered followed by Adel Graham. She glanced at Dena, half smiled maliciously, then nodded confidently. It had begun again.

They ushered her to a seat against the far wall below the row of uncovered windows as each of them took a prominent place at the conference table in front of her. The men remained standing until Adel sat, then as Dena and Lynn positioned themselves opposite and sat. They sat in unison then opened their folders as if cued.

Lynn side-glanced Dena. The absurdity of the placement was beyond humorous. Resembling a football front line protecting a quarterback, the positioning was supposed to be intimidating; she'd remembered the strategy well and was glad that she'd briefed Lynn as to what they might expect.

Gaylord cleared his throat. "Shall we begin," he prompted. "The law firm of..." He paused as Lynn reached into her large purse and pulled out a standard tape recorder then placed it on the table and pressed the record button.

"Ms. Brice, we have a stenographer available if you

haven't noticed." He motioned to a older woman sitting in the corner with a small device in front of her. "We usually take full dictation and send out transcripts upon request."

"That's very generous, but no thanks, I got this."

Gaylord turned to his associates, cleared his throat again then continued. "The law firm of Graham, Whitman & Morris would like to again offer our sincere condolences to Mrs. Adel Graham and to Dena Graham…"

"Mrs. Forester Graham," Lynn corrected immediately.

"Yes, of course, Mrs. Forester Graham. As such, Mrs. Adel Graham has been extremely generous in offering a sum equal to the due tenure of the union of…"

"Legally sanctioned marriage," Lynn corrected again.

"Yes—" Gaylord cleared his throat "—legally sanctioned marriage, in as much…" He paused.

Lynn leaned over to Dena and they both reached into their purses and pulled out dark sunglasses, covering their eyes against the brightness of the morning sun glaring at them. "Continue," Lynn prompted humorously.

Dena smiled, barely able to contain herself. The absurdity of them sitting at a conference table in the middle of a meeting with dark sunglasses on was hysterical. Yet here they were.

The assistants turned to each other curiously questioning protocol.

"Is the glare of the sun too intense?" one of the associates asked, smirking.

"Not at all. We're fine, please continue."

Gaylord asked an assistant on the end to lower and dim the blinds. He did but Lynn and Dena kept their sunglasses on. "We'll continue now," Gaylord said, then nodded to an assistant on the opposite end of the table. He stood and handed out a sheet of paper to Adel, Gaylord, the associates, the assistants and finally to Lynn and Dena.

"Mrs. Adel Graham has been extremely generous in offering a sum equal to the due tenure of the legally sanctioned marriage of her son, Forester Graham to Dena Graham. That offer has since been adjusted. Please feel free to discuss this, but mind you the terms are nonnegotiable. Signing today will end this, finally. A continuance is unacceptable."

He reached into his pocket, pulled out his favorite fountain pen that had to cost him at least six hundred dollars and placed it in the center of the table. "I'd like to offer you my pen," he said graciously.

Lynn smiled and reached for the pen. "Thank you, Gaylord, that's very generous of you," Lynn offered. Gaylord smiled and turned to Adel who was also smiling.

When he turned back to the table he saw Lynn place the pen in her big bag, then she picked up the paper placed in front of her and tore it up in eight equal pieces without even looking at it.

She stood.

Dena stood.

Without saying a word they walked out.

Everyone's mouth in the room dropped wide open. Seconds later the room went into an uproar as everyone began talking at once. "Wait a minute, wait a minute, get out," Adel said to the stenographer who, stunned by the turn of events, had since stopped dictating. When the door closed behind her, Adel turned to Gaylord. "What the hell just happened here?" she asked.

"She took my pen," Gaylord said.

"Screw the pen, what just happened?" she repeated.

"They obviously turned down your offer," an associate said, slightly impressed with the countered theatrics.

Adel gritted her teeth. "That much is painfully obvious, thank you. What are we going to do about it?" Gaylord didn't answer. Adel turned to him and repeated her question. "I want ideas and suggestions now."

Instantly a new strategy was planned and several particulars for consideration were proposed. From the absurd to the ridiculous and there in between comments ranged and were vocalized.

Adel, completely silent throughout the proceedings, took point, detailing exactly what she intended to do and have done to several of them not exactly legal or legitimate.

A knock sounded and the door opened. Everyone stopped, hushed and looked. Lynn poked her head in and smiled, then chuckled. "Sorry, I'd been practicing that exit forever and wouldn't you know I'd blow it." She giggled like a schoolgirl as she walked over to the conference table, turned off the tape recorder and placed it in her bag. "Thanks, for everything." She left. The exact repeat of the earlier openmouthed surround room returned this time a bit more fearful.

"What was that?" Adel asked.

"That was our asses in a sling," an associate said.

"File a motion to suppress the tape," Gaylord ordered one of the associates.

"On what grounds?" someone asked.

"Interfering with due process, violating client attorney privilege, eavesdropping on private conversations, Peeping Tom, I don't care, damn it, just file something, now. Now," Gaylord said, raising his voice. Two associates immediately rushed out of the conference room.

"Why do we need to file a suppression?" Adel asked.

"Do you have any idea what damaging information is on that tape recorder?" Gaylord said, rushed. "The other partners will be livid when this is made public. A conference room at Graham, Whitman & Morris filled with its attorneys conspiring to commit fraud, conspiracy, malicious intent and even murder would ruin us."

"I wouldn't worry about all that now," Adel said.

Everyone turned and looked at her as if she were insane.

"Mrs. Graham, if anyone ever heard it, this firm would be a laughingstock. We'd all be up on charges," an associate added.

"Not everybody, some of those suggestions are downright illegal. In particular the one to have Dena Graham permanently quieted. I believe we even mentioned a name, a previous acquitted client, as someone we could use to perform the act," another spoke. Several curse words pitted the room. "Neither the police nor the law review board would find that too humorous if indeed something were to happen to Ms. Graham."

"We wouldn't even have to be involved to garner reasonable suspicion," another associate added, "our reputation…"

Another round of curses sounded.

"Let me get this straight. Seven lawyers in this room and no one saw that the tape recorder was still sitting there turned on and recording every word we said?" Gaylord asked. Blank stares looked around the room then back at him. "This is completely unacceptable, gentlemen."

"Forget about the damn tape recorder, what are we going to do about Dena?"

"Pay her," an associate said. Everyone turned to look in his direction. "Why not?"

Adel walked over slowly. "What is your name?"

"My name is Hollander. Craig Hollander, ma'am."

"Mr. Hollander—Craig, get this straight. That is not an option, understand?" she said pointedly. He nodded.

"It might have to be," Gaylord said. "We can't drag this on for much longer. If her attorney files with another arbitration..."

"We'll fight it, the same way we fought it the time before, and before that. Buy the arbitrators again. This goes all the way to the Supreme Court if necessary."

"Exactly how much money are we talking about here?" an associate asked.

"Seven point three million dollars not including interest accrued for over four years."

"I will not pay her," Adel lashed out.

"That's not all, it's not all about the money," Gaylord said. Adel whipped around fiercely and her eyes blazed hot. She made a statement without saying a word. "Adel, this firm has hundreds of unbillable man-hours invested in this, we need to cut our losses. Maybe it's time to walk away," Gaylord offered humbly.

"No, something, some leverage, some deep dark secret, I don't care what it is, find it, create it, again I don't care or I'll close this place down and turn it into a parking lot." She opened the side door and slammed out. Gaylord followed.

"Do you think she meant it?" an assistant whispered.

"What do you think?" the other assistant answered.

Adel eyed Forester's picture on her desk in her late husband's office, now unused. Nelson Graham had been a formidable attorney and he would never put up with this mess. "It seems that I misjudged her."

Gaylord nodded. "Her commitment and passion in this matter is astounding."

"I agree," Adel said curiously.

"A mother's wrath protecting her young," Gaylord added.

"Interesting, perhaps there's more to her claim than I anticipated."

"What do you mean?" he asked.

"Get me a current photo of her child. I'd like to see this Dillon for myself."

Gaylord nodded. "Good, it's time. We can end this as soon as possible."

"This ends, everything does," she pointed out.

"It won't come to that," Gaylord said. "Thus far Dena only knows about the trust and the corporate insurance policies. As stated, that's merely seven million and change. She has no idea about the rest."

"And she won't. I owe it to Nelson, Kirkland and Forester. She'll never get her hands on the trust fund, the Graham estate, the insurance policies, the seat on the board of Graham, Whitman & Morris or the company shares."

"Worth conservatively over fifteen million dollars." Gaylord shook his head and smiled. "You really have a set of brass ones."

Adel returned his smile. "Funny, that's what Nelson always said."

"That was a thing of beauty," Dena said, raising her iced tea glass to toast. "To you."

Lynn raised her glass. "To us. Round one scored. Hell zero, us one." Lynn licked her finger and drew an imaginary one in the air. "I hope you grabbed that paper they handed out," she said.

"I did," Dena answered.

"Good," she said. "Now, I need you to give me a dollar."

Dena looked at her strangely. "A dollar, for what?" she asked as she reached into her wallet and pulled out a dollar bill.

Lynn took it. "Thanks. You just purchased a tape recorder with a very valuable cassette." She reached into her big bag and pulled out the tape recorder and gave it to Dena. "Keep it safe. We might need it one day. Adel is not just gonna roll over and play dead and neither will her law firm."

"That's a given," Dena agreed, looking at the cassette. "What's on it exactly?"

"I have no idea. But we're delving into criminal law and in this state I'm not allowed to know or possess certain things. A tape recording from an opponent's private conference is one of them. I suggest that you sell the recorder to someone else, but keep the cassette close."

"Sure," Dena said, nodding, then she smiled and chuckled, shaking her head in amazement.

"What?" Lynn asked.

"You. You were awesome in there. You always had a flair for the dramatic, but you outdid yourself today. It looks like the old Lynn Brice is back and better than ever."

"Took me long enough. I was just so scared. Scared to look forward, scared to look back, just plain scared," she admitted.

"All things in time, right," Dena said. They nodded in common understanding. "You know, I found that when my reality warped, getting back to the person I was, was damn near impossible, so I had to build a new me from where I was."

"I learned that the hard way. I was too arrogant to change until I was forced to. But it's not where you start, it's where you end that matters, right?"

"To endings." Dena toasted again.

"To beginnings." Lynn clinked glasses.

"Looks like a celebration."

Dena looked up, seeing Darius Hamilton standing by their table. His eyes locked on Lynn then back to her. "Darius, hi. What nice surprise," Dena said.

"Hi, Dena, how are you?" he asked.

"Fine," she said.

"Willamina mentioned this morning that you'd be out all day. I had no idea you'd be here in town. I hope everything is well."

"It's getting there," she said, smiling and nodding to Lynn.

"If there anything I can do to offer assistance?" he asked, shifting his gaze back to Lynn.

"No thanks, we have it under control. Darius, this is a friend of mine, Lynn Brice. Lynn this is my boss, Darius Hamilton."

"Hello, Darius," Lynn said, extending her hand. "A pleasure to meet you."

"Indeed, likewise, a pleasure. May I offer you ladies a ride back?"

"No thanks," Dena said. "I need to make a few stops before heading back."

Lynn looked at her.

Darius turned his hopeful attention to Lynn. "And you, Ms. Brice?"

She returned his attention. "I live here in the city," she said, "but thanks for the offer.

"You're quite welcome," Darius said. "I come into the city quite often."

"Really? Perhaps we'll meet again." Lynn was flirting.

"That would be my pleasure," he said with obvious delight. "I look forward to that."

Lynn blushed and nodded. "As will I."

"Well, you ladies have a good lunch. I'll see you back at the office tomorrow, Dena."

She nodded as Darius smiled at Lynn again then left.

"Wow." Lynn sizzled watching Darius walk away. "Is he yours?"

"No, he's my boss—one of them. There are three brothers. I work at Hamilton Development Corporation."

"I've heard of them, nice, very, nice. I'm obviously doing something wrong opening my own office. I should have gone into corporate law."

"No law, I'm the temporary administrative assistant."

"You're an AA with a law degree?"

"My official title is executive office administrator to operations. It's easy and comfortable work. I like it so far."

Lynn started laughing. "So that's why you've got this guilty pleasure smile on your face."

"I'm sure I have no idea what you're talking about."

"Please, girl, who do you think you're talking to? We didn't just fall off the turnip truck together yesterday. You and I have been dishing this for about ten years plus."

"Please don't tell me it's been that long."

"Yep, there about and then some, through thick and thin and a hell of a lot in between, so give," she insisted.

"Okay. His name is Julian Hamilton, Darius' brother, and he's…" Dena paused, not finishing.

"Um, yummy. That fine, huh?"

"Oh, yeah, that, too. He's gorgeous, built, handsome, sexy, but that's not what I was going to say."

"Hell, girl, what's left?" Lynn said.

Dena moved in closer. "Lynn, this is serious, you have got to promise never to repeat this, ever, to anyone, not even back to me."

"Dena, I'm your legal representative. That means I get to rot in jail for life before I reveal attorney-client privilege, you know that, not to mention I'm your girl from way back when."

Dena leaned in closer still. "Celibate."

Lynn frowned and leaned in, nearly bumping heads with Dena. "Say again? I think I missed that."

"I'm not saying it again, you heard me the first time," Dena whispered. Lynn shook her head as Dena continued. "Go ahead, say it."

"I'm sorry," Lynn said, still shaking her head.

"Go ahead. I know you have serious jokes."

"Honey, that's nothing to joke about. When I say I'm sorry, I mean it." She reached across and squeezed Dena's hand. "Poor baby, just your luck to find a man who's cut his own flow."

"Well, it happens."

"But you still work with him, right? You still see him regularly." Dena nodded. "So, seduce him. March your butt right over to his house and seduce that man. Dress in a frilly low-cut, wrap dress with ankle-strap stiletto heels then let nature takes its course."

Dena's mouth flew open in shock. "No, never. I respect his decision. I would never do something like that."

"Are you sure?" Lynn asked.

"Positive, kind of."

They laughed.

"Uh, uh, uh, two others like him," Lynn said, looking toward the exit. "I still think I should have broadened my options."

"I'd say that you already have—if you ask my opinion, he was seriously into you."

"I wish." Lynn sighed dreamingly. "Um, um, yummy."

Dena chuckled at her friend's vernacular. "Let's order."

Chapter 9

Restoring a 1968 Ford Shelby Mustang GT500 convertibl
to vintage condition seemed easier than it actually was
Powered by a 428 cubic-inch, eight-cylinder engine, the ca
was classic perfection if indeed he could get it to work. Th
body, once rusted and corroded in key places, had bee
replaced with vintage parts from all around the country
Finders, bumpers, cushioned seats, tires, and period rim
were all either in place or ready to be.

Julian had been working on the project for the past six an
a half months. He'd purchased a shell from a nearby deale
and via the Internet located everything he needed to refurbis
the classic piece by piece. Painstaking patience was not hi
forte yet he trod along diligently.

He never professed to be a mechanic but the detailed focu
of completing each step was well worth the time spent. It gav

him time to think and time to assess his life. With the car as with his life he'd made mistakes, yes, but persistently rectified each in turn with planning and focus.

This week he continued focusing on the carburetor, a Holley 600 CFM capable of reaching over 250 horsepower. It wasn't that he actually wanted that much power under the hood but just in case he needed to go from 0 to 60 in seven seconds then drive 130 mph, he'd be ready.

Seeming easier at first, but to his surprise, the carburetor, a small gadget, was trickier than he'd expected and it had taken him three weeks of patient shredding labor to put it together and recalibrate per its specs. Six times he had put it together and all six times he had failed to pass the metered test. After his frustration finally ebbed he decided to choose a new direction.

Darius stopped by earlier with beer and a large pizza. They ate, sat and talked then went out into the garage. "Aren't you finished playing with that tinker toy yet? You know Freud would have said that it's just a two-ton pacifier."

"Actually a bit less, it's a 3780-pound pacifier," Julian said, looking at the complete chart of specs.

"Either way, it's a poor surrogate for the real thing."

"And what might the real thing be?" Julian asked.

"Having a life," Darius said.

"I have a life, a very fulfilling life."

"You go to work and then come home and play with this thing. You don't have a social life."

"I don't need a social life."

"And women, you don't need women?"

"Exactly," Julian stated proudly.

Darius shook his head, knowing better. He knew his brother would come around in time. Julian, the hopeful of the three, had experienced three consecutive disappointments, leaving him classically lovelorn. But it was only a matter of time before he snapped out of it.

"So where was Dena, I hadn't seen her all day," Julian said casually when Darius refocused the flashlight for him.

"Oh, make up your mind," Darius said with annoyance.

"What do you mean?"

"You wanted to get rid of her," Darius said.

"You fired her?" Julian said, quickly stopping and turning to him in horror.

"I thought that's what you wanted. As a matter of fact you even had another job lined up for her. Make up your mind."

"No, no, no, tell me you didn't."

"You sat in my office not twenty-four hours ago and damn near demanded that Jordan and I get rid of her, now you've changed your mind. What happened between last night and this morning? Or don't I even need to ask."

"We came to an understanding."

"What kind of understanding?"

"I told her about my celibacy."

"And she was all right with it?" Darius questioned.

"Yes, we decided that we can keep our emotional and physical attraction at bay. But I guess it doesn't matter now since she's gone."

"So, do you want her or not?"

"Yes, I want her." Julian finally relented.

Darius nodded and smiled victoriously. "Now was that so difficult to say?"

"What are you talking about?"

"Willamina told me that Dena needed a personal day to clear up some legal business."

Julian glared at his brother. He wasn't amused.

"Funny you should mention Dena, though. I ran into her this afternoon in town. She was having lunch with a friend of hers."

"Male friend? Julian looked up, interested.

"Female friend," Darius corrected, deciding not to torture his brother further.

"Lunch, huh?" Julian said, turning his attention back to his carburetor. Darius nodded. "Interesting."

"Very interesting. Her name is Lynn Brice."

Julian looked up, seeing his brother smile that smile that always meant trouble. Ever since they were younger they each fit into very distinct categories. Darius was the brains, he thought of the schemes. Jordan, the youngest, was the lookout and he, Julian, executed the plan.

Julian hunkered down over the carburetor plans. He reviewed each detail slowly. Nodding at each step, he was sure that he'd gotten it this time. He picked up the metered instrument and attached it to the carburetor, connecting several wires. He unraveled a cord and prepared to plug a metal rod into a cylinder.

"Maybe I'd better stand back," Darius said.

Julian looked him. "Funny. Very funny."

"I know I've asked this a million times," Darius said, picking up several sheets of paper with specifications on them, "but do you have any idea what you're doing?"

"Not a clue, that's what makes it so much fun." He plugged the rod into the hole. Darius came closer and peered over his shoulder. They both watched the thin red arrow slowly turn to point into a green zone.

"Is that it?" Darius asked.

Julian smiled. "Yep, that's it."

"You did it?" Darius asked.

"I did it."

Slow, easy chuckles broke to joyous laughter as Darius congratulated Julian on his accomplishment. Jordan drove up mid-excitement. He got out and walked over to where his brothers were laughing. "What's so funny?" he asked.

"I did it," Julian said happily while wiping his hands on a cloth.

"Well it's about time," Jordan said approvingly. "I knew that little rant of yours wouldn't last. Dena's a nice lady. Good for you both." Then to Darius he held his hand out. "Pay up."

"That's not what he's talking about," Darius said.

Jordan looked at Julian questioningly. He held up the carburetor and the meter. Jordan shook his head, obviously disappointed. "This affectation of yours is getting a bit tiring, isn't it?"

"On the contrary, I'm enjoying myself," Julian said, then walked over to the car's open hood and placed the carburetor into the chamber. He maneuvered several other mechanical pieces to attain a precise fit. Nodding his approval, he stepped back.

Both Darius and Jordan walked over and glanced down at his achievement. The spit shine of the engine cavity was no doubt very impressive. "Admit it, not a bad evening's distraction, is it?" Julian said as he looked at Jordan and Darius smugly.

"Compared let's say with spending a romantic evening with Dena. Are you sure?" Jordan asked. "In my opinion, not even close."

Darius chuckled, seeing Julian's reaction. "Point and counterpoint," he said, refereeing.

"Will we be discussing Dena Graham all evening?" Julian asked. "I'm just asking."

"Probably," Jordan said, then continued, "I figure she's still mourning to some extent."

"No, I don't think so. She's been hurt, but not still in mourning," Darius added.

"Her husband died, of course she's hurt," Jordan said.

"No, I think there's more to it than that. It's like she's living half a life, like she's hiding half herself away for some reason. She's built a safety wall around herself," Darius said.

"Curious," Jordan pointed out. "I wonder what he was like, her husband, I mean."

They both looked at Julian as he faked disinterest. He continued beneath the hood tinkering and adjusting nothing in particular having long since lost interest in the car. He listened and formed his own conclusions.

The evening pretty much continued to run along the same lines. Julian worked on his car and his brothers pitched in joking about his love life or lack thereof. Thankfully for Julian they left fairly early, leaving him in peace with his thoughts, which were troubling enough without his brothers' assistance.

It was late when Julian decided to call it a night. After a quick cleanup in the mudroom, he passed through the kitchen, grabbed a bottle of water and continued through. His house, a large, farm-styled, split-level rambler was the perfect home for him. Large and roomy. With housekeeper assistance, he kept it immaculate and comfortable.

He grabbed a quick shower and chilled out, expecting nothing more than to watch the late news then fall asleep. In complete serenity he went to his bedroom and stepped out onto the overhung deck. The stilled night whispered gently as he sat in his lounger and relaxed for the first time that day. Hours later the news came and went and Julian was still awake, sitting on the deck. Jordan's joking comments stayed with him.

Dena had been on his mind and he knew for a fact that easing his thoughts and his body was going to take a while. Their last conversation and her willing acceptance of his celibacy was unexpected, yet appealing. He smiled in the darkness. She amazed him. He chuckled, and Dillon was a joy. His jewel-like effervescence for life was addictive. He laughed openly. His cell phone rang. Without thinking or checking the number he grabbed it and answered. He immediately regretted it.

"Julian," the ultrafeminine voice cooed. He didn't answer. "Julian, I know you're there. Talk to me."

"I have nothing to say to you," he responded.

"Fine, then I'll talk. I miss you."

"Stephanie, this is moot, you made you choice years ago, calling me is senseless."

"Actually it's not. Jamie left us. We broke up. I found out that he was using me and our son."

"I'm sorry to hear that," he said, increasingly coolly.

"Aren't you going to ask about him?"

Julian paused. He was in the wrong state of mind to deal with this. "How is your son?"

Her voice was quiet. "He's fine, he asks about you all the time. He wants to see you."

"He doesn't remember me. He was only two when you walked out."

"But he does, he really remembers you, I swear," she vowed earnestly. "May we come see you sometime?"

"No, that's not possible."

"Julian, don't penalize our child for my mistake. I left

because I wanted the best life for our son and his father promised me that he would be there for us. He lied."

"That's not my problem now, Stephanie."

"You can't just ignore us. We're in your life."

"No, you're not. You left, remember? Five years ago you walked away with a friend without looking back. You're not in my life, I question if you ever were."

"How can you say that? We loved each other fiercely."

He didn't respond, realizing for the first time that his relationship with her was all a farce. She played a waiting game until a better offer came along. He, Dr. Jamison Gray, did and she walked. Now that they were over, she wanted back in. "Did we? I'm not so sure."

"Julian, I was wrong, okay, I said it, I admit it. Please, I just want to see you, our son wants to see you." He didn't respond. "Julian." Her voice was gruffer.

"We talked. Goodbye, Stephanie." He hung up.

Sleep never did come after that.

Dena arrived back to her aunt's house later than she expected. It had been a long day and she was exhausted. After her lunch with Lynn she'd stopped at the bank to change an account then she'd gone home for the first time in weeks.

Walking into her house was strange. Musty, hot and stale, the closed house was unwelcoming and unfamiliar. She felt like a stranger in a place she once belonged.

The house was a five-bedroom, four-bath modernized Tudor with high ceilings and large stained-glass windows. It was the quintessential family home. Surrounded by an acre of manicured landscaping it was going to be their home forever.

Although it was Forester's choice, and she often suspected with his mother's strong influence, she'd grown to love the house as much as he had. Purchased in full before it was even completed, each and every detail was lovingly chosen by her since Forester yielded to her taste and decisions. She'd made it a welcoming home and a place to grow old.

Now she walked through like a stranger, devoid of emotion, feeling no loss and no passion.

The melancholy of the memories here often drained her, but not today. Today she felt strong and in control. She immediately busied herself, gathering, boxing and finally discarding.

It was time to clear away the pain and sorrow. Forester's clothes had long since been carted off to local charities. Now she needed to dig deeper and purge the rest to start a new beginning. It was time. Three hours later she returned to her car.

Looking up through the front windshield she smiled feeling a surge of emotional progress in her life. A new job and a new life awaited her. It was time to let go and move on. Since the house sat vacant, the idea of selling it seemed more real than ever. There was interest but nothing substantial, but she was hopeful. The sooner it sold the sooner she'd move on to a new life with her son.

Paid in full by the one mortgage policy Adel didn't control, the house was all hers. The upkeep was minimal and she used what money she had in the saving accounts for maintenance, water, electricity and landscaping.

She glanced up, taking one last look. Her beautiful dream was gone and it was time for something new. She shifted gears and drove away. The house she loved was silent again. A while later she was back at her aunt's house.

"Hi," she said, walking into the kitchen, seeing her aunt reading through some recipe books piled high on the kitchen table.

"Hey, sweetie, when'd you get back?"

"Just now. How's Dillon?"

"He's fine. He had a great day out back and passed out early. I told him you'd wake him up to say good night when you got in." Ellen looked at her watch and frowned. "I thought your appointment was earlier."

"It was. I ran a few errands afterward then stopped by the house to get a few things."

Ellen sighed wearily, knowing the turmoil that usually came after her niece went home. The house often drained her, which is why she was so insistent that Dena stay with her for a while. "Are you okay?" Ellen asked, knowing she wouldn't be.

Dena half smiled. "Actually, yeah, I think so." She half chuckled. "I'm good."

Ellen looked at her oddly. "Are you sure, after dealing with Adel and her lawyers and then going to the house?"

"I'm sure. Lynn was phenomenal this morning. Every trick they pulled she countered brilliantly. Thanks to her, I actually got the upper hand for once, at least for now."

"Wonderful, that's great news."

"And then going to the house was different this time. It was strange. I was there but I felt nothing—no pain, no love, nothing. It's like I got lost somewhere along the way but now I'm back."

"I'm glad to hear that," Ellen said happily.

"So Dillon played in the backyard. I thought he had a play date next door."

"Julian came over so he decided to stay and help him finish the fire pit."

"Julian, huh," Dena said.

Ellen nodded. "He's really attached."

"That may not be such a good idea," Dena said.

"Why not?" Ellen asked.

"Well, first of all, Julian is a busy man and I'm sure he doesn't want a three-year-old hanging around while he's trying to get work done. Also, I don't want Dillon getting too attached to any man, we'll be moving on soon."

"Did someone make an offer on the house?"

"No, not yet, although several people have walked through and seemed interested," Dena said, seeing her aunt's despondency. "I know we never really talked about this but we both know that we can't stay here forever."

"That's just plain ridiculous, of course you can. This isn't some bed-and-breakfast or flophouse, this is your home and you're family. You're welcome to stay as long as you please and yes, forever is just fine with me."

"Thanks, Aunt Ellen."

"Don't thank me. Now get up stairs and say good-night to Dillon while I heat something up." Ellen opened the refrigerator.

"That would be a great idea. I'm starved. What was for dinner?"

"Your son's favorite, meat loaf, mashed potatoes and green beans," Ellen said.

"Um-yum, sounds perfect," Dena said as Ellen began pulling covered dishes out and placing them on the counter. She stood by her great-aunt and laid her head on her shoulder, holding her warmly. "You've been a godsend, Aunt Ellen. I don't know what I would have done without you." Dena kissed her cheek, turned and headed up the back stairs to Dillon's bedroom.

She opened the door, finding him fast asleep with his teddy bear, hard hat, tool belt and crime-fighter cape beside him on the bed. Dena smiled warmly and removed the items. She tucked the covers up to his chin then reached down and touched his cheek. The gentleness of her touch and the sweet softness of his face warmed her. She leaned in and kissed his forehead. He never stirred. "Good night sweetheart," she whispered.

Chapter 10

The next few weeks sped by in a blur of dreamlike busyness. Dena kept her distance while at work with Julian, but the evenings and weekends were tricky. As he still came over to work on her aunt's yard, she made sure to busy herself elsewhere while the backyard work continued uninterrupted. Always noticeably absent, she decided that avoidance was best since the last thing she wanted was another awkward moment.

"Why don't we take a break?" Willamina sighed.

Dena looked up, seeing that Willamina looked completely drained. "Great idea. This is your last day and you must be exhausted."

"Actually I just need to go to the bathroom again. I know it's to be expected, but it's really a pain in the butt. I spend most of my waking hours either going to or coming from the bathroom. And right now this kid is sitting right on my kidneys, kicking my ribs," she added as she stood.

"Oh, I remember Dillon, he was a kicker and puncher. I thought I was going to give birth to the next prizefighter."

Willamina laughed, shaking her head, commiserating completely. "I'll be back in a few minutes," she said, then opened the door to leave.

Dena welcomed a break and a brief distraction. She and Willamina had been going through last-minute details for the official transition. It was Willamina's last day and Dena wanted to be completely up to speed with all assignments. They'd been at it all morning and afternoon.

Dena stretched her neck and relaxed back in the comfortable chair. Although they'd been swamped all morning, it was the fact that she'd gotten very little sleep that had worn her down the most. She picked up a few papers and reviewed some files then decided to close her eyes and lay her head down on the conference room table for a few minutes.

"Dena, are you all right?" Julian asked from the doorway. Her head popped up like a jack-in-the-box.

"Yeah, fine."

"Are you sure you're okay?"

"Yeah, of course, I was just resting my eyes."

Julian, standing in the doorway, walked into the room and stood beside her. "I haven't seen you around in a while."

"I've been really busy."

"I guess we've been working you kind of hard. It's just that with Mattie out and Willamina leaving we just want to make sure we're covered."

"Don't worry, I'm on top of it."

"Good," he said. "Just want to make sure you're not overdoing it. We don't want you burned out."

"No, not at all. Actually, I've enjoyed the challenge. It's a huge change from my previous position."

"You were a lawyer, right?" he asked.

"Yes, I worked as a Legal Aid lawyer for the city's Fair Housing Commission."

"Really, sounds fascinating," he said with interest as he leaned back to half sit on the side of the table.

"It was very rewarding although my husband and in-laws wanted me to join the family firm. I decided against it."

"More money at the commission?" he joked.

"Hardly," she said, smiling, "but the satisfaction of seeing a landlord forced to clean up his building was priceless."

"Well, I don't think we can offer you anything quite so exciting."

"On the contrary, this is very interesting work, very detail-oriented. I'm learning a lot. I had no idea all of this went into building and construction. Interestingly enough, I came across a few instances that your attorney might want to look into."

"Great," he said, pleased at her knowledge. "I guess having you is truly an asset," he said warmly.

"I hope so," she replied, looking up into his eyes. They stared at each other a few seconds as a warm feeling built inside. A sense of admiration and genuine respect passed between them. Unspoken, the attraction was always there just below the surface. And of that attraction they were always just seconds from yielding.

"Dena, about our last conversation, what we talked about—"

"No worries," she interrupted him. "I get it, nothing personal, just coworkers and friends. We—"

"Actually, that's not what I was going to—"

"Julian, you don't have to do this. I understand. Yes there is this thing between us, this attraction. But as adults and as colleagues we can resolve it and I hope become friends."

He nodded. "I'd like that."

"Me, too," she said, looking into his intense eyes again. The pull was there, she felt it. The desire still burned strong but she needed to resist. She lowered her head to look away. They paused, letting a few minutes pass before saying anything again.

"Are you almost finished here?" he eventually asked.

"Yes, just about."

"Good." He paused another moment.

"Is that all?" she asked.

"No, yes, Willamina's shower," he began.

"Today, yeah, I heard about it, sounds like fun."

"I just wanted to make sure you heard about it and planned to attend."

She nodded. "I did, and yes, I do. Is there anything else?" she asked again, nervously shuffling the papers on the table again.

"Yes, tell Willamina that I'm ready to get started whenever she is."

"Sure," she agreed. "Is that it?"

"That's it," he said, standing. "I'll talk to you in a few."

As soon as he left Dena breathed a heavy sigh of relief. This was getting ridiculous. Being in a room with Julian was torture. The whole don't-touch thing, wanting but not being able to have was more difficult than she thought.

He had seeped into her subconscious and she'd been dreaming and fantasizing about him for the last few weeks. She needed to quell her attraction once and for all.

"I'm back," Willamina said as she sat down in her chair. "Sorry about the delay, I got to talking and one thing led to another."

"Don't worry about it. Julian stopped by, looking for you. He said that he's ready whenever you are."

"Oh, good, we're about done here, so why don't you finish with him."

"What?" Dena asked.

"Julian's going to show you the rest of the process."

"Can't you show me? I mean, I know he's busy and I don't want to disturb him."

"He volunteered."

"Did he?"

"Yep. I just ran into him on the way to the bathroom. I was going to just use either Jordan's or Darius' office computer but since he volunteered to show you on his, this is even better," Willamina said as she began handing her files, piling one on top of the other. "The program is on only three computers. They usually take care of that part of the job, but since they're so busy we thought it might be worth it to show you. Then you can teach Mattie and me when I come back after maternity leave."

"But I'm temporary. I won't be here that long."

"But in the meantime someone needs to know it and that's you.

"Maybe it would be a good idea if we learned together, you know, help each other out. Two heads are better then one," Dena said, beginning to babble. Willamina looked at her strangely. "I mean, having both of us know this program can only be a benefit to the company."

"We will, just not right now. Besides I thought you and

Julian might want to…oh, rats. I need to go to the bathroom again. I'll see you later." Seconds later she was headed back to the bathroom.

Dena was speechless. She hadn't expected to spend the rest of the afternoon in Julian's office side by side learning a computer program. She reshuffled the files in her arms and headed to his office.

Keep your distance, be detached.

The mantra repeated in her mind over and over again. She needed to stay focused. No, she needed to have her head examined. There was no way she could spend the afternoon in Julian's office and not want to rip his clothes off. Was she really that horny? she asked herself. The answer came quickly. No. She didn't want any man. She wanted Julian.

Seconds after that affirmation, she arrived at Julian's open door. He was inside, on the phone. His back was to her but she couldn't hear the conversation and he hadn't realized that she was there.

Dressed in a relaxed fitted pair of blue jeans and a polo shirt, her eyes immediately went to the firm tightness of his butt. This was going to be impossible. Granted, he looked good in anything he wore, but in casual clothes he was spectacular. All she could do was stand and stare and shake her head. She was never one to have a heightened sexual appetite but the fact remained: she couldn't stop thinking about him.

Julian had gone back to his office then stepped outside on the balcony that ran the length of the building's upper level connecting his office to his brothers'. He stood looking up at the midafternoon sky wondering what in the world possessed him to offer to teach Dena the project software program.

A stroke of genius at the moment, now, not so much. How was he going to focus on teaching Dena when all he wanted was to make love to her? The logic of his brilliance made him chuckle. It was plain to see that his vow of celibacy had completely dissipated. He heard his office phone ring and went inside to answer. "Julian Hamilton."

"Julian, it's me."

"What do you want now, Stephanie?" he asked coolly.

"I need to talk to you."

"We already talked."

"In person, I mean, today, please," she nearly pleaded.

"I'm busy, Stephanie."

"I know, but it's important. I can stop by the house tonight. I'll even bring dinner, if you'd like?" she asked hopefully.

"I'm busy," he said.

"I can make your favorite, I'll cook it myself. I actually learned how to cook, you'd be proud of me."

"Good for you. I'm still busy."

"Julian…" she began, cooing softly in that way that always got her whatever she wanted, "please."

"I'm busy Stephanie," he said flatly.

"I can stop by the house afterward."

"No," he said emphatically.

She paused, hesitant by his sharp answer. "Okay, then anywhere, anytime you say."

Julian sighed heavily. Stephanie's drama was about to invade his life again. Although he'd moved on long ago he needed to sever ties completely. "I'll meet you outside the building in an hour."

"This is a private discussion, Julian."

"Outside the building in one hour," he repeated.

"Fine, but I'm not in the area, I'll take a while to get there. My flight is just boarding now."

Julian looked at his watch. He hoped to get this over with as soon as possible, hopefully while everyone was at the baby shower for Willamina. "All right, call my cell when you're on the way. I'll meet you outside."

"Outside? Why, I'm coming all this way to see you…?"

"If you'd rather not, that's fine with me."

"No, outside will be fine," she said with added gratitude, "thank you, Julian, I'll see you in a few."

Julian hung up.

This thing with Stephanie was beginning to wear on him. He had no idea what she wanted other than the obvious and he was tired of putting her off and delaying the inevitable. Stephanie was determined to see him and from past knowledge, whatever Stephanie wanted she got, and that included him.

They'd dated, they'd married and they'd divorced all in the span of ten months. Tumultuous and combative, their union was fraught with lies and deceit. From the very beginning she never mentioned that she had a child. Then she'd lied, telling him that her first husband, her child's father, was dead and that she was destitute. He found out later that she'd never been married and the father of her child was a friend of his and a fellow doctor.

After spending time overseas he'd returned to Boston. Stephanie found out a month later and within a week was trying to get back with him. Embarrassed but not particularly upset, Julian dealt with her deception with ease thanks to the help of his brothers. They of course warned him against the impetuous relationship, but all he saw was a way to help someone in need.

That was the last time he'd seen her.

He'd filed for divorce. She'd initially insisted on a huge monetary settlement but after his lawyers got through with her she wound up paying his court costs. Now she was back for more. He picked up his phone and called his friend. After explaining the situation, his friend, attorney Kenneth Fields, insisted on being present and assured him that everything would be handled.

Julian rounded his desk and sat down, pondering the situation. He looked up and saw Dena standing there.

"Hi," she said simply, almost breathless as she stood in the doorway avoiding his focus.

"Hey, you ready for me?" he asked.

The statement carried all kinds of innuendo and, given her recent lapses into the realm of lustful fantasy voyeurism, she decided that it would be best not to answer. Instead she smiled, looked out his window and nodded.

"Let's get started."

Louise Gates arrived for her visit with Ellen in usual grand style; Colonel Wheeler drove. Loving partners for years, they'd just returned from visiting her grandson and his wife, Tony and Madison, and her new great-grandchildren. The miracle of birth had a way of renewing her spirit, which prompted her to visit.

After a nine-course Southern-style lunch with all the homemade trimmings, Ellen and Louise bid farewell to Colonel Wheeler as he set off on a fishing trip for a few days with some military buddies. The women, having waved dutifully from the front porch, never made it much past that spot. They sat out relaxing on the hanging swing and gliding rocking chair. The tranquil comfort to the tranquil day eased around them like a pair of old slippers. The only stirred movement beside them was the energetic dashing of three-year-old Dillon on his bike and the gentle breeze blowing, adding to the genteel conversation.

"Julian Hamilton, I like that name," Louise said.

"He's a nice man. Charming and kind like his father, he's just what the doctor ordered, and as a matter of fact, he was a doctor a few years back. After his father passed on, he and his brothers returned to close the family business but found that they were more connected than they thought. That's when they each moved back home. Good men, all three of them," Ellen said.

"Three?" Louise asked. Ellen nodded. "All single?" Ellen nodded again. Louise nodded with added interest. "And he's been married before?" she asked.

"Yes, but it didn't count, she wasn't his type. As a matter of fact, she wasn't much anyone's type. Wild and headstrong, she nearly tore that family apart when he moved here."

"How's that?"

"Apparently they met in Boston when he was a doctor and apparently she didn't like the idea of not being a doctor's wife, at least that's what was said. I think there was more to it."

"I imagine there was, there always is," Louise said.

"Anyway, she took that darling little boy of hers and marched right back to Boston."

"So Julian has a son?"

"No, not biological. He was planning to adopt when the marriage broke up. Julian adored that child. Broke his heart when she took him away and never looked back. Right after that he got himself engaged to a nutcase."

"How long ago was that?"

"A year and a bit," Ellen said. "I haven't heard anything since. Guess he just tired of being disappointed."

"Indeed, I can see why," she said, sympathizing. "So what's going on with Dena?"

"She's keeping pretty quiet, getting stronger. She stopped by the house and came back in one piece. Usually a trip there tears her apart."

"That's a good sign."

"Aunt Ell-lllen," Dillon called as he came barreling around the side of the house on his bicycle. Ellen stood and looked over the open rail. Dillon parked his bike, got off and ran up the front stairs.

He smiled and handed each woman a crumpled yellow dandelion and a perfectly mud-free rock he'd found in the yard. "I got this for you," he said, proud of his accomplishment.

"Thank you, Dillon," Louise said, smiling from ear to ear at the thoughtful gift.

"Thanks, toots," Ellen said, and she kissed his forehead then looked at his dirty hands. "Have you been in my flower garden?"

"No-oo, not me," he said, shaking his head.

"Good. Tell you what, why don't you go wash up and change your shirt? Mamma Lou Gates and I will drive down to the ice-cream parlor and pick some vanilla ice cream to go with the apple pie for tonight's dinner."

"'Kay," he said, and hurried into the house, then stopped and came back to the screen door just as it softly closed. "But I want chocolate ice cream, 'kay?"

"All right, chocolate ice cream it is."

"Yea," he yelled, and he hurried upstairs.

Ellen and Louise laughed heartily.

"He is such a darling," Louise said.

"I don't know what I'm going to do when they leave."

"Dena's still moving, uh?"

"Yes, unfortunately. We talked about it last night. She insists that she needs to move on."

"That means we better see what we can do."

Chapter 11

It was self-sabotage, she knew it, but she didn't care. Ten minutes into the lesson and she was already feeling the familiar sexual attraction. She inhaled softly, smelling the spiced scent of his cologne. Pure masculinity exuded from every pore of his body as they sat side by side on the sofa at the small coffee table.

The program itself was more difficult than she expected. Uniquely developed, it was designed especially for Hamilton Development Corporation needs. More statistical than mathematical, in essence it shadowed every job from concept through to completion, showing and evaluating progress, anticipating shortages in material and manpower and even projecting losses.

A few keystrokes brought the entire company into view. Updated regularly by job foremen from satellite offices, the three owners had their finger on every job no matter when or where.

Dena did a test rundown, having received numbers from one of the foremen in the field. She entered his data and requested an update. The program ran through the algorithms and output the next few days' assignments. She approved them against a previous project and forwarded the information to the foremen's laptop.

"Perfect." Julian said after she completed the run-through. "It'll make more sense to you once you start working with the program on a regular basis." She nodded, keeping her eyes glued to the screen. He focused on her profile for too long. "Maybe we should take a break. We've been at it for almost two hours."

"Good idea," she said, trying to sound relaxed. He stood and walked over to his desk. She pulled up one of the projects she'd worked on earlier. "So you're renovating the Kellerman Building."

"Yes," he said without turning, "we're sixteen weeks into the project, looking to close out in twenty-three."

"That's a quick turnaround. That building is pretty messed up."

"You're familiar with the Kellerman Building?" he asked, turning to see her looking at him.

"Yes, actually it was one of my last assignments before I quit working a few years ago. I remember it well. It was so avant-garde for a 1970s bank building. Unfortunately it was used as everything except what it was intended. If I remember correctly, it was a storefront church, a halfway house, a rave club, a trash dump and then squatters moved in and it really went downhill. The housing commission came in to legally evict the squatters. Still the architecture is phenomenal and I always thought that the potential was limitless."

"I agree. Jordan drew up some really incredible plans and

we added some very interesting and innovative ideas, but still in keeping with the basic architectural structure and integrity. Our client is very happy with what we've done so far. I'm excited to see the finish."

"Me, too," she agreed.

"I think it's going to be one of our top jobs."

"That's really exciting. The place was such a mess and now to see the progress reports and the digital photos, I'm just amazed by the transformation."

"It just needed a little TLC."

"Tender loving care, don't we all," she added. "Taking a disastrous shell and bringing life back into it is a tremendous undertaking."

Julian knew she wasn't only talking about the Kellerman Building. He walked back over to the sofa and sat beside her. "So tell me more about the housing commission."

"There's not a lot to tell. I dealt with slum lords, wrongful evictions, housing discrimination, that kind of thing."

"Sounds interesting."

"It was. I never knew what each day would bring."

"Such as?" he prompted.

Dena began relaying interesting situations she'd dealt with while working at the commission. She told funny anecdotes and soulful, heartwarming stories of success and triumph. Julian listened intently, asking questions and just enjoying being with her. After a particularly touching story she stopped suddenly. "Oh, boy. I'm sorry, I must be boring you to death."

"No, not at all. I'm fascinated and I'm glad you didn't compromise your values and work for the law firm."

"Me, too."

"Ever think of going back into law?"

"Sometimes. I guess I will someday, just not right now. It would be too frustrating for me with everything that's happening. So, looks like you're stuck with me as a temp."

"Good, I'm glad to hear that."

"Are you?" she asked.

"Yeah."

"Why?"

"Because I like having you around and I'd like to get to know you better."

"As friends?"

"That, too," he said, his eyes burning into hers. "You know where this is leading, don't you?"

She reached up and softly stroked his cheek then quickly moved her hand away. "I'm sorry," she apologized.

"For what?"

"That was inappropriate."

"Then I guess this is way over the line." He leaned in, slowly kissed her softly on the cheek.

Dena closed her eyes, feeling the warm sensation of his lips on her face spread throughout her body. She held her breath as her stomach fluttered and her mind hazed dizzily in all directions. "Julian," she moaned. Seconds later he kissed her again, an inch away from the previous spot. "This will compromise everything for you."

"So be it," he said softly, then moved to kiss her lips tenderly. The smooth sensation of his lips gently pressed to hers sent tremors through her body. They'd kissed before, hungry, grasping and wanting. This was different. She was feeling everything—nervousness, excitement, happiness, exhilaration, anticipation—everything at once.

His tongue touched her lips and she opened to him. The

kiss, once sweet and easy, turned needful and devouring as she wrapped her arms around him, pulling him close. He held her tight with no intention of letting go. She savored his touch with her own longing. The hunger they'd both suppressed for so long intensified beyond measure.

How do you stop raging fire when all you want is to feel the burn inside? The question swirled inside her brain as their unrestrained yearning swelled.

He reached down and touched her breast through her suit jacket, once stylish business wear, now a hindrance to their desire. She opened the jacket to expose a silk lace bra. His hand covered her breast, tweaking the taut nipple to pebble beneath the lace. Her head rolled back as his kisses plunged downward, her neck, her shoulder, her arm, and finally to her breasts.

Reclining against the thick-cushioned couch she raised her leg as he adjusted his body to cover her. His full weight lay on top of her and his body felt so good. Both breathless, he kissed her neck then slowly rose to her lips. He moaned, she sighed, both knowing that this was neither the time nor the place.

He sat back, taking her hand to sit straight. He looked down the length of her body, seeing the lace bra still exposed. Shaking his head, he smiled. She mirrored his actions as he reached over and slowly buttoned her jacket. After a few deep, cleansing breaths, he took her hand and kissed it.

"I know," she said, agreeing to his silent frustration. "Our timing is lousy."

"Yes, it is." He stood and walked to his desk.

Dena watched him as she quickly restyled her mussed hair. The chances they were taking only added to the intensity of their desire. The door was unlocked and dozens of coworkers were gathered just down the hall celebrating a baby shower.

"I can't do this," he finally said.

"Do what?" Dena asked hesitantly.

"This, you and me, sitting here like nothing's up, like my body's not on fire, like I'm about to explode."

She stood and walked over to him. "I know, I'm sorry."

He turned to her. "No, never be sorry for passion. I want you and you want me. No regrets."

"What about…"

"Celibacy is my way of avoidance. It's easier to deny than o open your heart. For the last seven months I walked away, only to find you waiting for me in the end."

"Wrong place, wrong time."

"Well, I guess that is a problem," he said. They smiled nd half chuckled at their ill-timed destiny. "Have dinner with me tonight."

"I can't. Dillon."

"Bring him. I'll pick you up at eight."

She shook her head sadly. "It's too soon…Dillon…" she began, but before she finished he kissed her.

"I understand, but if you change your mind, call me."

The tempting offer hovered in the air between them.

The knock on the door startled them apart. Dena turned ack to the computer screen as Julian walked over to the oor. Kenneth stood on the other side, smiling. They shook ands as he entered. Seeing Dena sitting on the sofa looking t the computer screen, his smile faded. "Hope I'm not disurbing anything," Kenneth said, dropping his briefcase on the hair opposite the desk.

"Not at all," Julian said. "Kenneth, this a new employee,

Dena Graham. Dena, this a friend, Kenneth Fields. Dena is also an attorney. Dena is taking Mattie and Willamina's place while they're on medical and maternity leave."

Dena stood, meeting Kenneth midway. "Nice to meet you, Kenneth."

"Same here," Kenneth said. "So, you're also an attorney. Where have you practiced?" They shook hands and talked briefly about law school and people they knew in common.

"I'd better get going," Dena said, gathering up the folders and files she'd brought with her. Seconds later she made a quick, discreet exit.

"I thought you were doing the celibate thing," Kenneth said as he sat down and opened his briefcase.

Julian looked at him, surprised by his obvious perception. "I am."

Kenneth smiled. "Right," he said skeptically.

"Sounds like you don't believe me."

"Julian, I'm your attorney. I get paid to believe every word you say. Now, tell me about Stephanie." Julian began, telling him about her recent phone calls and e-mails. Kenneth strategized responses, offering several alternatives. Julian only half listened; Dena was still on his mind.

Within the span of two and a half hours the conference room had been completely transformed. Large pink and blue balloons floated on the ceiling and yellow and green crepe paper twisted and streamed around the room. Huge baby booties, pacifiers, bottles and rattles decorated the table along with a catered meal.

A massive amount of food covered several side tables as colorfully wrapped gift boxes and bags were piled high on another. Dena added her gift to the growing pile then greeted Villamina as soon as she returned from the bathroom. They chatted a few minutes until a few other workers approached, then Dena headed to the buffet table.

Up close, the spread was mind-boggling. There was every imaginable food from Texas-style baby back ribs to lobster and seafood salad to Mexican tacos and fajitas to Chinese egg rolls.

She walked up beside two coworkers, Jessica and Wanda, standing at the buffet talking and adding food to their already mounded plates.

"Hey, ladies," Dena said as she picked up a plate.

"Hey, girl. Where have you been all day?" Wanda asked.

"Busy, last-minute crash course on everything," Dena said, "but I think I got it all covered."

"I heard that," Jessica said. "Mattie's and Willamina's job is insane. I don't know how they do it, but they do. Now it's on you. I'm not trying to make you nervous or anything but you got some serious work to keep up with."

Wanda, older and apparently wiser, nudged Jessica's shoulder. "Don't be saying that. You'll have Dena running out of here yelling and screaming her head off. Don't pay any attention to her, Dena." Wanda consoled Dena. "It's not that bad."

"All I'm saying is that with all these jobs going on at one time in different phases of completion, it's hard to keep up. Personnel, budgets, materials, locations, it's just whacked," Jessica mumbled.

"Again, don't listen to her, she panics when the phone rings twice."

Dena smiled, Wanda chuckled and Jessica laughed full-out. "Come on and get some food," Wanda said.

"Good idea," Dena said.

"I love it when this company throws a party. They seriousl go all out. This is my first baby shower but I was here for farewell party. The food is always insane," Jessica said leaning over to whisper into Dena's ear.

"You can say that again, this is unbelievable," Dena said "but why so many different things?"

"Darius always asks the guest of honor exactly what the want. But if it's a baby shower he just gets everything on th menu, taking into account the food urges of pregnancy. guess he figures that he should cover all the bases and jus order everything," Wanda said, heaping another huge pile c seafood salad on her plate.

"I don't even know where to start," Dena said as sh looked over the assortment of food beautifully displaye on the table.

"My suggestion, lobster salad, it's to die for," Jessica sai adding another large spoonful to her plate.

When Jessica walked away Dena added a small scoop c salad and other edible creations to her plate. She followe Jessica and Wanda down the rest of the buffet line and the back to the far side of the conference room and sat down.

A few minutes later Julian and Jordan walked in. The went directly to Willamina then made a point of stopping t talk with everyone there. Dena laughed and joked with Jorda as Julian listened to Jessica talk about her recent vacation t Jamaica. Darius entered a few minutes later carrying a larg box and placed it on the gift table then began his greetings

Julian took the opportunity to glance over to Dena. Sh looked up in time to see his smile. In veiled silence they co nected and the memory of moments earlier swept throug ıem. The innocent interaction, unnoticed by the rousing aiety around them, brought a lifted brow to Jordan.

After another twenty minutes of socializing with employees, enneth entered the room and caught Julian's eye, he otioned his attention. They left the room, Darius and Jordan llowed just as attention was turned to Willamina as she egan opening her gifts.

One of the women nearest her wrote down what everyone id for a party game later and another wrote down the gifts ıd givers. Just when Willamina picked up another gift the oor opened and a woman entered. All eyes turned. A hushed lence settled then just as suddenly everything went back to ormal as Willamina opened a gift bag and held up a yellow-ıd-green-knit baby jumper with attached hood and booties.

Although the room returned to its former joviality, eyes ill glanced at the woman standing by the door looking ound.

Glamorous and refined, she looked like she'd just stepped f a Parisian runway. Obviously not an employee or client; veral people began whispering among themselves, includ-g those sitting with Dena.

"Wow, who is that?" Jessica whispered into the general oup of women around her.

"Oh, my goodness, I can't believe she has the nerve to ow her face after what she did," Wanda hissed.

"You know her?" Jessica asked quickly. "Who is she? 'hat did she do?"

Her name is Stephanie. She's the former Mrs. Julian amilton," Wanda answered.

"Get out," Jessica said.

Wanda nodded. "It's true."

Dena was suddenly very interested as a large gulp of ai caught in her throat making breathing difficult. To cover he surprise she took a large swallow of punch and let it slowl drift down her throat. Thankfully it eased and she didn' choke out loud, drawing interest. She turned her attentio back to the mutterings around her.

"I didn't know Julian was married," Jessica said.

Dena, for once, was pleased that Jessica was so boldl open and didn't mind saying exactly what she thought an asking questions.

"That was years ago, many, many years ago," Wanda con tinued. "I guess it's been about five years now, just afte James Hamilton died and about a month after I got here."

"Who's James Hamilton?" Jessica asked. "Anothe brother? I never heard of him."

"No," Wanda said. "You know who James Hamilton i: he's their father."

"Oh, that's right. I completely forgot, my bad."

"So is she back now?" Dena said, trying to get the conver sation back on track to the woman still standing at the door

"Um-hum, apparently, and heaven help us." Wand groaned, still staring across the room at Stephanie who ha begun speaking to a few people closest to her.

"Probably wants something. She looks like the type th: always wants something." Other women began talking, whis pering openly beside Wanda.

"I remember when she came around a few years bacl The place was in a ruckus for two weeks. She's a piece c work. She's trouble, you can bet on that." Wanda continue watching her walk around the room obviously looking fc someone.

"She has a way of…" another woman began then stopped s she walked by. The sudden silence had to be telling yet the voman angled her firm chin upward and kept going.

"She ain't all that," Jessica quickly surmised after seeing er up close.

"I don't know what he saw in her," Wanda said.

"Sex," Jessica answered. "What do they all see in her? ook at these men in here, their tongues are hanging out and heir eyes are bulging out along with their…"

"Ooh, stop it, girl, but you ain't lying," Wanda said, aughing along with several other women as the conversation uickly changed to the battle of the sexes.

Dena smiled cordially at Jessica's remark but afterward sat ilent just as she always did at the Graham Manor when there vas an interesting buzz. The woman, still strolling around the rowded room, reminded her too much of a younger version f Adel, and that gave her a sudden chill. Adel always got xactly what she wanted, no matter what it was. And if Steph-nie wanted Julian back, chances were she'd have him.

Suddenly thoughts of earlier in his office sent a quick burn rough her body. It was obvious his celibacy was waning and e attraction she felt for him was mutual. But competing for ulian was out of the question. She'd done that before. Using very trick she knew and then some, she'd still lost Forester the end.

But this wasn't about love or marriage or trust. This was bout a physical action that they both wanted. So why was he hesitating?

Stephanie Hall Hamilton Gray was no fool. She knew she eeded to do a damn good job to convince Julian that she'd

changed and that she wanted him back. The truth was she di
want him back, or rather, she needed him back. Her life wa
falling apart and the man she'd thought would be there wit
her forever had just walked out.

He'd turned his back on her and their child and refused t
pay child support just because of one tiny indiscretion. So th
only thing left to do was to come here to Julian. He'd love
her at one time and there was no reason why he couldn't lov
her again. They'd had problems but nothing they couldn'
work out. She was even willing to live here.

Luckily for her she'd kept an eye on his life. He'd give
up his position as a doctor to go into business with his brother
and in the process he'd made at least triple the money an
gained ten times the recognition. The Hamilton Developme
Corporation was huge and it was everywhere. Being his wif
again would be well worth it. All she had to do was t
convince him that she'd made a terrible mistake and that sh
still loved him.

That's why she needed to do as she did. He needed to se
her. A phone conversation just wouldn't work. She'd pur
chased a special outfit for the occasion. It was his favorit
color on her, tight but not too tight, short, but stylish, accente
with the perfect accessories: diamonds.

Instead of calling, she'd walked into the office and foun
herself in the middle of an office party, a baby shower. Dresse
in a stylish wrap dress that accentuated her slim form and he
well-endowed bosom, she drew every eye in the room as soo
as she arrived. The men stared, of course, she had it going o
and the women, mostly homely and plain, were green wit
envy. If this was her competition she'd have no problem. Smilin
happily, she could already feel herself back in Julian's life.

"Excuse me," she said to a man who'd been mentally wrapping his tongue around her body. "I'm looking for Julian Hamilton."

"He's not here," he said.

"Yes, I realize that," she said, then mentally called him a moron and an idiot.

"Uh-huh." He paused, looked down at her cleavage.

"Do you know where he is?"

"Uh, no," he said.

"Do you know where I can find his office?"

"Uh, no," he repeated, then looked around the room spotting several people staring at him. He smiled proudly, having been chosen. "But I'm here, maybe we can…"

"Thanks. Down, boy. I'll find him myself," Stephanie said, her smile restraining the impulse to rattle his brains or lack thereof. She walked away knowing of course that he'd be eyeing her tight ass. Not particularly impressed by the employee's social skills, she decided to step outside and call Julian on the cell phone. He answered on the third ring. "Hi, Julian, I'm here." Hearing his hesitation, she frowned. "Is there a problem?"

"I'll meet you out front."

"Actually, I'm in the building. I'm at the office party."

"I'll be right there."

A few minutes later Julian arrived. Stephanie watched him as he walked toward her. He was even more attractive than she remembered. As he approached, she raised her arms to caress him, he backed away. "This way," he said, turning.

They walked to his office. Stephanie smiled. This was perfect. His office was just the place to seduce him into taking her back.

Inside Stephanie was stunned to see Kenneth waiting for

them. "Hello, Mrs. Gray," Kenneth said, holding a folder of papers and smiling.

"Nice to see you again, Mr. Fields," she said, then turned to Julian. "An attorney is not necessary. What we have to talk about is between us."

"On the contrary," Kenneth said as Julian walked over and sat at his desk. "I've informed your attorney of your arrival."

"Good afternoon, Stephanie," the bodiless voice announced into the room. Stephanie looked around then glared at Julian as he motioned to the speakerphone on his desk.

"This doesn't concern you," she said simply to the room, directing her eyes toward the machine.

"Actually it does," Kenneth said, unfolding and holding up the papers for her to see.

"What's this?" she asked.

"It's a copy of the signed divorce decree with the approved amendment and attachment forbidding any additional contact or encroachment from either party," her attorney said through the speaker.

"I believe when you arranged this meeting, Mr. Hamilton asked you to wait outside off the property," Kenneth added.

"Yes, so what?"

"It is in the divorce decree, you can't have anything to do with Mr. Hamilton, Hamilton Development Corporation or any person so stated. In other words, Stephanie, your being here on the property is in violation of the decree."

"Julian…"

"Please direct all comments to me," Kenneth said as Julian looked on silently.

"So this is how it is? You gonna do me like this?"

"This is a court order requesting that you, Mrs. Stephanie Gray, refrain from contacting my client in person or through any electronic device or written media." Kenneth held another copy of the papers out to her. "Your attorney also has a copy."

"What about…?"

"I contacted a firm in Boston, it appears that a legal injunction was filed after Jamison Gray filed divorce proceedings. He, according to documentation you supplied, is the legal biological father of your child, which has subsequently been confirmed by DNA testing. He is solely responsible now for the welfare of your child. I suggest you contact his attorneys."

"Julian…"

"Please direct all comments to me," Kenneth repeated.

She ignored him and rushed over to the desk, leaning down, tipping her chest forward. "Julian, I flew all the way here to tell you that I still love you, that nothing will change that. We can be together again like it was before. We don't need these suits to come between us."

"Please direct all comments to me," Kenneth said again.

"Julian…" Stephanie said, then smiled, seeing a reaction in his eyes.

Julian stood and walked around to shake Kenneth's hand. They nodded and he walked out, leaving Stephanie with the lawyers.

Stephanie shook her head, astonished. She obviously needed a new plan.

Dena watched as Julian led the woman down the hall to his office. The sight was hurtful. It reminded her of the day Forester died and the way he'd paraded his mistress in front of her. Granted the situation was different, but the hurt was the same.

Gloria was her name and she was four months' pregnant when they'd met. At the time Dena'd had no idea that she was pregnant or that they each carried the same man's child. Adel told her. That's when she'd run out. Approved by his mother, fidelity had become a passing consideration as far as Forester was concerned. The insult was too deep. Forester followed, they'd argued as he got into the driver's seat and they sped away. Adel sent her husband and son to bring Forester back. No one returned that night or any other night. Dena walked away. Enough was enough.

Chapter 12

The evening was quiet.

"Dena, is that you?" Ellen called.

"Yes, it's me. Hi, Aunt Ellen. The baby shower was wonderful. Willamina received great gifts and the food was incredible," she said just as Dillon rammed into her legs at full speed, excited about something. He talked a mile a minute, which made it almost impossible to understand a word he was saying. She picked him up and hugged him desperately. There was something about holding him that always made everything seem all right.

Still carrying him, she rounded the kitchen and continued onto the back porch, seeing her aunt sitting talking with an old friend. Dena smiled warmly and slid Dillon down to his feet. "Hi, Mamma Lou," she said, hugging and kissing the matriarch. "It's been forever."

"Hello, Dena, how are you?" Louise asked.

"I'm fine. You look great."

"Aren't you sweet," Louise said. "And you're right, it has been a long time. When are you going to come visit me?"

"I'd love to. Crescent Island is one of my favorite places to go. Maybe I can steal some time and get up there before the end of summer."

"I'm going to hold you to that."

"Can I go, can I go, can I go, please, please, please?" Dillon asked earnestly, hopping up and down, drawing the last word out like gooey-stringy-cheesy mozzarella pizza.

"Go where?" Dena asked.

"To the fair," Dillon said.

Dena looked at her aunt questioningly. "What fair?"

"The county fair," Ellen said. "Louise and I are heading over this evening and we'd love for Dillon to join us."

Dena smiled. "That's awfully nice but Dillon…"

"…will be a well-behaved darling, just as he always is when we go out," Ellen said, already knowing the objection before Dena even finished speaking.

"I'll be good, I promise," Dillon added, standing perfectly still, smiling up at her.

"Don't you ladies want to stroll around and check out the plants and flowers?"

"We'll do that and we'll also stop and see the animals and eat some county fair food and maybe even go on a few rides," Ellen said.

"I'm sure there's going to be pony rides available," Louise added, winking at Dillon, whose eyes lit up like rockets though he didn't move or offer a single peep.

"I hear there'll be fireworks later," Ellen added.

Dena looked down at Dillon; he was obviously ready to burst with joy. The anticipation of her next words had him teetering on the brink of a major explosion. She took a deep breath and sighed, completely outnumbered.

"Okay," she began as an uproar of three laughed and giggled happily. "But you, young man, must be on your best behavior and listen to Aunt Ellen and Mamma Lou."

"I promise, I promise," he said, then flung himself at Ellen then Mamma Lou for a big hug and kiss. "I'll go pack." He dashed off at light speed.

"Pack?" Dena asked.

"The fair is in Henderson County so we thought we'd stay overnight in a hotel nearby. It's only a fifty-mile drive but after the fireworks, the lateness of the hour and all that walking, we'll probably be too exhausted to want to drive home. I hope that's okay?"

"I'll be happy to be the designated driver," Dena offered, realizing that Louise was eighty years old and her great-aunt was near seventy. Although Ellen was still an excellent driver the roads at night were often completely dark and deserted.

"No, that's okay," Ellen said.

"Don't trouble yourself," Louise said just after.

"We'll be fine, it'll be an adventure for all of us. Tomorrow we plan to get up early and really do the fair properly, see everything, do everything, probably not get home until late afternoon."

Dena paused. The reasoning sounded plausible enough but her gut was telling her that there was something else going on. "Okay, if you're sure." They both nodded agreeably. "Then I'd better go see what Dillon intends to pack. Knowing him, you'll wind up bringing home a naked three-year-old with only a red cape and construction hat on."

As soon as Dena went upstairs Ellen and Louise smiled. That was almost too easy. Ellen grabbed the cordless phone from off the small table beside her and dialed a number.

An hour later the three excited travelers were buckled in and driving off. Dena stood in the driveway waving until they were well out of sight. It wasn't until she climbed the front steps and went back inside that she realized just how alone she was. She went into the kitchen and made herself a cup of tea then stared out the window, remembering.

Julian came to mind. This was where she'd first laid eyes on him. Her body still reacted. "If only…" she considered out loud.

Then an imaginative thought occurred to her. She looked at the clock. It was already after seven. She had just enough time. "No, I couldn't," she said. "Could I?" Five minutes later she was in the shower. Suddenly finding herself alone and free for the evening, Dena followed her heart.

Julian was in his garage, as usual. It was Friday night and while his brothers had done everything in their power to try to talk him into coming with them to the beach house, he'd chosen instead to work on his car. The phone had rung several times but he'd ignored it. He figured that it was Stephanie and the last thing he wanted was another face-to-face with her.

Tonight all he wanted to do was to chill out and relax. The toil of the day and the aggravation of his ex-wife's arrival had him totally stressed.

Tonight's assignment was to figure out what was going on with the manual transmission. He'd already installed a new clutch but for some reason the car's gears were still off. Having raised the car up in the specialized jack, he slid underneath and began his evening's undertaking.

It was a booty call and the thrill of actually doing what she was doing, going where she was going, to a man's house this late at night, excited her. The last time she did something this bold and audacious, her parents grounded her for a month. At sixteen she'd snuck out of the house to go to a party with friends, then had to call her parents from a police station to pick her up. They were furious and grounded her. It was a punishment that never happened; they were killed on the way to the station.

The bold, brazen behavior ended with that incident. Ever since then she'd played it safe at all times, taking the tried-and-true path without causing waves. That behavior continued even into her marriage.

When Forester stayed out late or went on clandestine business trips, she said nothing. When it was no longer doubtful that he was playing around, she looked the other direction. It wasn't until the day he died that she reached her limit.

"Okay, Lynn, here's to your advice," Dena muttered.

Her heart pounded as she stood at the front door, ringing the bell several times. There was no answer. A few seconds later she pressed the button again. Eventually she climbed down the steps to return to her car, then heard music being played. Curious, she followed the sound around to the side of the house.

Now off the brick-covered path she walked awkwardly on the stone gravel then onto the newly trimmed grass. Her ankle-strapped, spiked-heel sandals seeped deep as she continued on tiptoe. Peering around the corner, the music grew louder. She stopped, seeing an open garage door a few feet behind, detached from the house.

The gaping hole of light brightened like a sunrise against the dimness of surrounding trees. She moved toward the light, still hearing music playing. At the large open doors, she peered inside. No one was there.

"Hello?" she called after knocking gently on the wooden doors.

Julian, too annoyed for words, dropped his head back onto the cushioned rolling platform. This had long since gotten ridiculous. The calls, the showing up in person and now, stalking. How far was his ex-wife going to take this? He heard the female voice call out again.

"Julian, hello?"

"We had this conversation already. There's nothing between us and nothing you have to say that I want to hear," Julian said from beneath the car. "I suggest you follow your attorney's advice and go home."

"Oh, I didn't mean—I mean, excuse me, I apparently misunderstood," Dena said, obviously flustered.

Julian was surprised, the immediate confession and withdrawal was too good to be true. He kicked his foot and quickly slid from beneath the car. He looked up, expecting Stephanie but instead saw Dena standing over him, her expression was of shock. His breath caught. "Dena." He said, "Wait. No, no, not you."

"I'm sorry I thought…" she said. "Obviously this wasn't such a good idea, I just—" She turned quickly then continued talking and walking. "Sorry, my mistake."

"No, wait, don't go," Julian said, scrambling to stand and

catch up with her before she left. "I thought you were someone else."

"I am—" she turned, half smiling "—someone else."

He stood in front of her, holding his hand up to stop her from walking away. "Wait, I thought you were my ex-wife."

"The woman at the baby shower?" she asked.

He nodded then grabbed an already soiled cloth and began wiping his hands. He shook his head. "That's a long story and apparently getting longer."

"Most of them are," she agreed.

He smiled, helplessly staring into her glistening eyes, then traveling slowly down her body. "You look like a breath of fresh air."

Having changed her clothes several times and finally deciding to wear a wispy, silk V-neck summer wrap dress, she nodded at the compliment. "Thanks," she said appreciatively, knowing that the dress she'd chosen was pure seduction. She glanced down at his rough tattered attire. "You look pretty rugged-grungy, but I like it," she joked of his oil-stained T-shirt, soiled blue jeans and scuffed work boots. He grabbed a cleaner work cloth and wiped his dirty hands again.

"Thanks," he said, adding to the lightness of the mood. "So, Ms. Graham, how did you know where I live?" he asked.

"I'm the operational administrative assistant at Hamilton Development Corporation. I have a number of departmental records at my disposal. I looked you up."

"Is that procedure?"

"Probably not," she admitted, "but, since I changed my mind about dinner this evening…"

"I'm glad you came."

"Are you?" she said. He nodded. They stared at each other smiling shyly like two teenagers on the first date.

He looked down and around her. "Where's Dillon?"

"He's away until tomorrow," she said, smiling. "Looks like I'm interrupting. What are you doing out here?" she asked, peering over his shoulder into the garage.

He turned to follow her line of vision. "Working on my car."

"May I see?" she asked before walking over to get a better look at the open car.

"Sure." He stepped aside to allow her to pass. The near-flimsy white floral dress breezed past him, leaving a heavenly scent in its wake. Julian swallowed hard. This was going to be a very interesting evening.

Dena walked over, touched the smooth body and looked at her skewed face in the shiny chrome. She smiled, recognizing the car immediately. Looking inside she noted the leather bucket seats and the plush interior. It was in perfect condition. "A 1969 Ford Mustang?"

"Close, very close. It's a 1968. How did you know?"

"It was lucky guess," she said jokingly.

Julian looked at her slyly. There was obviously something she wasn't telling him. "Somehow I doubt that."

"I thought you didn't know anything about cars."

"I don't, not really. I have schematics," he said, pointing across the room to several thick open books on the worktable and a detailed illustration pinned to the wall.

She nodded and continued to walk around the exterior of the car. "You did a very impressive job."

"Thank you. I was just finishing up for the night, so how about staying for a late dinner with me?"

"I'd like that."

An hour and a half later, showered, cleaned up and dressed in clean jeans and a pullover shirt, Julian sat barefoot with Dena out on the deck having just eaten grilled steaks, baked potatoes and a green salad. For lack of celebratory champagne they sipped ginger ale and laughed and talked mainly about his brothers and his extended family.

"Question. Why law, of all possible occupations?"

She smiled, having asked herself that question a hundred times since she'd married into the Graham family of attorneys. "I get the feeling you're not particularly fond of members of my chosen profession."

"I've had my run-ins with members of your profession. Each time I barely escaped sane. For the most part they seem to represent blood-sucking parasites looking for a free payday at someone else's expense. No offense."

"None taken, I think."

"What is about some lawyers who think suing someone is as easy as signing your name?"

"Because it *is* just that easy," she agreed. "Frivolous lawsuits jam up the court systems while legitimate cases languish for months, even years sometimes. But that's the system," she said sadly, speaking mainly of her situation. "So what happened to you to taint a whole occupation?"

"My ex, Stephanie, countersued when I filed for divorce. Talk about a blood-sucking parasite looking for a free payday at someone else's expense, she asked the court to award her spousal support, all marital assets, half of my stake in the company and punitive damages of ten million dollars for mental anguish and desertion."

"Sounds brutal," she said, commiserating.

"It was, and after the judge dismissed the case and I was vindicated, her attorney took me to court for his fees."

Dena shook her head sadly, not at all surprised; she'd seen it done a hundred times before. Graham, Whitman & Morris made millions annually on just such cases.

"Then a year later I was served with a paternity suit," he added. "Litigation lasted months since the mother refused a paternity test. Kenneth, my attorney, thankfully took care of both cases, but never again."

"That sounds brutal, no wonder you despise attorneys."

"Not all attorneys, just the ones who file lawsuits that take money from people. It kind of leaves a bad taste in my mouth. I swore to myself that I'd never step foot in another courtroom for the rest of my life."

Dena's heart raced. She often thought about telling Julian about her legal battles over Forester's trust, but given his disdain there didn't seem to be any point.

"So after all that, why law?"

She shrugged. "I don't know. Law always fascinated me. As a teen I liked breaking rules, going up against the law. I guess it was only natural to become a lawyer."

"Were you always a legal aid?" he asked.

"No. I did family law for a time, but that was too much. So I did some corporate, but that didn't work out, either. I eventually went back to what I loved, the down-and-dirty freebies," she said, smiling. "That's what we used to call it in law school."

"Family law was too much?" he asked.

"I worked in the family court system primarily. That's where if you were lucky your day would only be crazy and insane. I dealt a lot with runaways, abused children, negligent parents, deadbeat dads." She paused and shook her head sadly. "I've seen and worked on cases that made me physically ill. I know what people do to each other in the name of family, it's not pretty. I couldn't stay."

Julian heard the thick tenseness in her voice and saw the strained look in her eyes. He didn't want to continue the conversation. "Tell me about your family," he said. "You said that your parents died awhile back, any other family other than Mrs. Peyton and her son?"

"Not really, Aunt Ellen is actually my great-aunt. She's my mother's aunt."

"She's something else," he said, smiling.

"She definitely is. She and a friend of hers, Mamma Lou, are in Henderson Country at the fairgrounds with Dillon this evening. They're staying overnight."

"He'll have a great time."

"I hope so," she said, then paused, smiling at him. "So, Julian Hamilton, modern renaissance man, you fix cars, tear down cement walls, build fire pits, rescue stranded women with oil leaks, run a multimillion-dollar company and cook a fantastic meal. What else do you do?"

He laughed. She joined in. "I'm glad you came tonight," he said as he reached over and took her hand, bringing it to his lips.

"I am, too," she said then paused. "But I have to confess, initially I came here with an ulterior motive."

"Really, what might that be?" he asked. Dena immediately blushed and shook her head. "Come on, tell me," he insisted.

"A Freudian booty call," she said.

Julian immediately started laughing and continued until tears glistened and threatened to fall. "A Freudian booty call,"

Julian finally repeated. "I've never heard of a Freudian booty call, but I guess I have now."

"It's true. Psyche 101, selfish, instinctive primal impulses demanding immediate satisfaction. My id came here with the sole intention to seduce you into making love to me," she said, boldly looking at him.

"Is that right?" he said, smiling broadly.

"Yeah, I know what you told me but… I find myself being purely selfish these days."

"So how exactly were you going to do this seducing?"

She smiled slyly. "I hadn't figured that part out yet. I just thought that it was getting a little too quiet without Aunt Ellen and Dillon in the house so I figured since you might be alone this evening and I was alone, that maybe we might…" She stopped just short of admission.

"…be alone together, so to speak," he finished for her.

"Yeah, something like that. Pretty sneaky, huh?" she said.

"No, not at all, I'm flattered."

"I'm sorry. It's been a long time for me, not since my husband, and I was just…" She paused, feeling more and more embarrassed. "I have no idea why I'm telling you all this but as I said, I was being purely selfish these days."

"And so what are your thoughts now?"

"Honestly I'm ashamed to have even considered it. I don't want to put you in that position. It was unfair of me. I kinda like having you as a friend, to hang out with, to joke around and talk and laugh with." He shook his head. "No?" she questioned, not understanding. "We're not friends?" she asked.

"Yes, we're friends, but I don't want us to just be friends. I want more."

Dena bit her lip as her heart thundered in her chest. "How

much more?" she asked, hoping he still wanted her as much as she wanted him.

"You know how much more, Dena." He stood, pulling her up with him. The soft music poured out around them from the inside speakers. Her, still in spiked high heels and him barefoot, they stood nearly eye to eye, with him having just a slight height advantage. The evening was perfect.

Chapter 13

In silence they danced, continuing to move together with ease. Dena closed her eyes and rested her head on his shoulder, snuggling deep. She sighed, feeling the heaviness of her world finally lighten. A second song played, then a third and then a fourth. By the fifth song the gentleness of movement had become tantalizing foreplay. He stroked her back and she toyed with his neck.

They moved gently in each other's arms as she glanced across the horizon. The last remnants of sun dipping low beyond the trees and woods, lighting the sky ablaze with vibrant color. The moon climbed high and the stars peered out, twinkling and sparkling bright. He leaned back and smiled at her.

The direction of the moment was clear.

"May I kiss you?" he asked.

"Are you sure that's a good idea?" she asked.

"Positive."

"Julian, I don't want to compromise your principles," she began, still leaning against him. "I haven't been with a man in a while and it's obvious that we're attracted to each other. I can leave now, no harm done. It was unfair and wrong of me to..."

He leaned back slightly, tilted her chin up with his finger and smiled. "This is the right time and right place for both of us," he said, looking deep into her eyes.

"I certainly hope so," she answered.

Without missing a beat Julian gathered her into his arms closer and kissed her hard and purposefully. Dena surrendered, opening up to him as the kiss branded her. The feel of his power and strength was divine. She wrapped her arms around his neck and tipped up to him, begging for more. The instant sensation shot right through her as she quivered in his arms. It felt good to finally be wanted and desired.

Julian lavished kisses on her like gifts from heaven. Unrestrained, he'd been starved for too long. She was his hunger, his rapture and his desire. The intensity of their passion was beyond reason. In a feverous tangle their arms and hands grasped everything, caressing and teasing until the promise of pleasure was all too real. Then they stopped.

He stroked her face lovingly, smiling. "Would you come upstairs with me?"

She smiled. "I thought you'd never ask."

He reached down and handed her the glass of ginger ale then picked up the bottle and his glass. Holding them in one hand, he took her free hand and led her through the kitchen, dining room and living room, upstairs to the master suite.

The double doors were ajar. The lights were dim but she could easily see the rustic decor surroundings. A big, dark-wood bed stood near the center of the room and large matching dark-wood furniture completed the details supplemented by thick carpet and a huge walled window.

She walked over and looked outside. The window showcased the wonder of the heavens and the magnificence of his view. "Your view is breathtaking," she whispered.

"You are breathtaking," he said, standing behind her.

She turned. "Thank you."

"You're welcome." He took the glass from her hand and set it down on the nearest flat surface. Seconds later he kissed her. Sweet and loving, the kiss reminded her of new love and possibilities of a future.

When the kiss ended she stepped back, untied the waist sash then unbuttoned the only button on the dress. The silky wrap dress loosened, revealing a hint of a promising treasure. She stepped around him and continued toward the bed. He turned, his eyes cemented to the sweet sexy sway of her body as she walked away.

Dena stood at the side of the bed with her back to Julian, then slowly opened her dress completely and dropped it off one shoulder. She heard a sudden rush of air behind her and turned to glance back over her shoulder. She smiled; Julian's expression was priceless.

The next shoulder went bare, then as slow and easy as snow flurries falling from the sky, the white floral dress eased lower and lower until it shimmered completely down her body. She turned completely around and smiled. Bra and panties, scant pieces of Lycra and lace were the only barriers to her treasure.

She sat down on the side of the bed. Her spiked stiletto

sandals were still wrapped around her ankles and tied securely. She crooked her finger, motioning for him to come to her.

The air vanished around Julian as he watched Dena perform her slow, sexy striptease. His mouth dried as the desire he felt was nearly overwhelming. Every inch of his body hardened and beckoned to her. Catching his breath, he didn't even realize that he'd stopped breathing.

Without hesitation he obeyed her, crossing the room, slowly exaggerating each step. When he stood in front of her she reached up and loosened his shirt from his pants. Her hands were steady and sure in the task as her eyes never broke focus from his. She undid his snap and unzipped his pants. They loosened. Her fingers brushed against him. He gasped and moaned her name as he caressed her face.

In an instant he took her hands and lurched her up against his hard body. The sudden motion startled her, making her gasp as he wrapped his arm around her body and held her secure. His mouth captured her and in a continuous onslaught of passion, he ravished her with rapturous delight. Hands pulled and tugged, removing and tossing his shirt to the floor as he stepped out of his pants. Now both standing nearly bare, her in bra and panties and him in boxer briefs, they continued unimpeded.

His mouth descended to her shoulder and chest then captured her lace-covered breast. The front snap popped and her breasts freed. The once-spirited kisses turned heartily vigorous. Sucking, kissing, licking and pulling, her nipple pebbled instantly as her moans of anticipation escaped. The swelled fullness of her breasts seemed to fascinate him as he gathered both between his hands then licked, kissed and caressed them. He dipped his face into her cleavage then groaned, holding her even tighter.

She felt his throbbing hardness press against her. She moistened. The long-awaited sensation intensified as the pleasure she felt increased. His kisses continued down her body to her stomach, her hips, her thighs. Her legs weakened and her vision blurred.

She gasped when his hands secured her rear then began peeling at her panties. She held firm to his shoulders as his mouth searched for her. Nearly swooning, she fell back, sitting again on the side of the bed.

She leaned back on her elbows and lifted her leg, crossed her hip in front of his body and placed the spiked heel of her shoe on his chest. She smiled even as the needle-like heel gently poked him. She twisted her leg to show the sandal's wrapped leather straps and small buckle.

Without words he understood that she wanted him to help her with the ankle strap. He didn't. Instead he ran his hand down the length of her bare leg toward her mid-thigh, placing her foot higher up on his shoulder. He reached for and placed her other leg on his other shoulder as she lay all the way back on the bed.

The inviting position made her vulnerable to almost anything yet there was no fear or trepidation. The only thing she felt was the burning need to have him inside her. The skill of his foreplay made her shudder in anticipation. This was really going to happen. "Julian…I have…downstairs—" Dena moaned between deep, raspy breaths "—I have some…my purse is downstairs…condoms." She slid her legs down around his arms to sit up again.

"I have condoms," he whispered as he sat beside her and kissed her lips and reached for the bedside table. He opened the drawer and clumsily fumbled with an unopened box. She reached to help, adding to the scramble. The box opened and they each found a condom. He opened his and covered himself, then turned to her. She smiled and reached out to him. "Yes," she whispered huskily, "now."

In an explosion of sudden fierceness he covered her. Raw passion eclipsed them as body on body melted into one. He reached down between them and felt the moisture of her readiness then without delay he entered her full and hard. She gasped and screamed her pleasure.

The exquisite pain of long-term abstinence burned through her. Julian was long, hard and thick, the fit was perfect, filling her completely. Then just as suddenly he withdrew then thrust and continued repeating the rapture over and over again. The throbbing heat of her passion equaled the fierceness of his movements. She met him each time, wanting more, holding tighter as he surged deeper.

The ignited fire blazed with each thrust. Power met purpose and their untamed passion peaked closer and closer. Dena's nails bit into his shoulders as she held on, arching her hips for more. The powerful rhythm of their bodies crashed together as their hearts pounded. In and out, closer and closer, they met until they finally burst.

She climaxed full and hard, straining and trembling beneath his body. Savage spasms of pleasure gripped her repeatedly. She'd never felt anything so intense. Breathless and panting she closed her eyes and held on tight, never wanting this moment to end as he collapsed. They lay motionless in their spent rapture.

"I guess this kind of ends the whole celibacy thing," she said through slow breathless gasps and pants.

Julian leaned up and rolled to the side, still holding on to her. He looked up at his bedroom's high ceiling and smiled, stroking her back tenderly. "Yeah, kind of."

"Is that a bad thing?" she asked, cuddling close.

"No, it's a very good thing."

They drifted into silence as each savored the moments past and the experience of their union.

Dena smiled in the muted darkness as she watched the last remnants of color drain from the sky. Darkness had descended and she knew she needed to leave soon. But the idea of going seemed almost foreign.

The closeness she felt with Julian was what she'd been looking for all her life. It was only sex, she knew that. A physical reaction to stimulus, no commitment, no love, just a physical attraction acted upon and mutually enjoyed, but still he made her feel special. Something Forester had never done.

Suddenly she realized that she'd wasted two years of her life with a man who selfishly cherished himself and used her first to get back at his family and then to accessorize his arm when needed. Sadness enveloped her equal to the selfish joy she now felt. "Thank you," she whispered before thinking first.

"For what?" he asked, still stroking her back.

Committed to an answer, she continued. "For making me feel wanted."

"You are most definitely wanted, Dena Hamilton. You're a sexy, sensually desirable woman and everything about you makes me hunger for more," he responded softly.

Dena closed her eyes, smiling. Even if weren't completely true at least it sounded genuine. Moments later she drifted to sleep feeling particularly good.

* * *

Adel picked up her glass and sipped her drink as she always did this time of night, little finger extended, ladylike and proper. She sat alone in the solarium of her home and drank to the future while marinating in her self-imposed bile stew of regret. The last four years had been a blinding blur of hatred. The death of her sons and husband still taunted her.

She'd seen it coming from the moment she laid eyes on her youngest son's bride. She begged him at first to annul the marriage and then later to divorce, but he wouldn't have any of it. He was stubborn just like his father.

As soon as he'd brought her home Adel knew it was a mistake. Dena had no family of note, no prospects of a future and as far as she was concerned she was useless. She brought nothing to the table except her body. And apparently that had quickly worn out, as well, since Forester had so easily turned to Gloria to satisfy his physical needs.

In that light, there was no way Dena's child was Forester's. But then, Gloria had sworn that her child was. It wasn't until the child needed blood that the truth finally came out. Gloria had lied to gain control of Forester's money. Her child wasn't his. And for nearly four years Adel had given that child everything for her son's sake only to learn that it wasn't even his.

Adel shook her head at the intentional fraud. Gloria had endeared herself and expected that she would continue to support her and the child. She was wrong. Now she had nothing of Forester. But if by some chance Dena's child was his, then there was only one thing to do. She had very definite plans.

She set her drink down on the table, turned out the light

and headed upstairs to bed. The days and nights, although blurred together, seemed long and endless. Each step she took drained her of her will to go on. She was tired but needed to continue to save the only thing she had left of her family, honor.

The doorbell rang. She turned and looked at the clock in the foyer, it was well after ten. No one with any sense would dare come to her home this late unannounced. She walked over to the security camera and pressed the button.

Gaylord's face looked up at her. He rang the doorbell again. She pressed the button to speak. "Not tonight, Gaylord."

"We need to talk Adel," he said quickly.

"It'll have to wait until morning, I'm tired."

"You're going to want to hear this tonight."

She pressed the button and released the security latch. The iron gates opened and she watched as Gaylord drove his late-model Benz through and up to the house. She opened the front door and waited. Gaylord got out of his car and approached. "What's so important?" she asked as she turned and headed to the living room.

"You need to see this," Gaylord said, following and pulling a fat file out of his briefcase and handing it out to her.

She didn't take it. Instead Adel walked over to the bar and poured herself another drink then sat down on the plush sofa. "What is it?"

"I did the standard background check on Dena again," he began.

"So what? You did that when she married my son."

"Yes and she was clear, no police record, no unusual hits."

"Is there a point to this?" Adel asked impatiently.

"Yes, after you left this morning I did another check, expecting to find exactly what I found before. But this time I got flagged."

"Flagged. What does that mean?"

"It means that Dena had contact with the police since her marriage."

"Get to the point, or is that it?"

"The point is Dena filed a police report after her marriage."

Adel turned with interest. "What kind of police report?"

"It appears that she was attacked in her home approximately forty weeks before her son was born. Forester…"

Adel smiled and laughed. "He knew about it, didn't he? That slut had an affair and she was trying to pass her bastard son off on my son as his."

"She was attacked and raped…" Gaylord continued.

"So she says," Adel said relentlessly, interrupting as she stood and headed back to the bar. "How perfect is this. Once this gets out, all her innocent victim petitions can finally end. She'll get nothing from the Graham estate, not the Graham trust and not Forester's personal insurance."

"Adel, she was attacked by her husband, by Forester," Gaylord said, then waited for the reaction he knew would come.

Adel swung around, her eyes blazing wild and furious. "What kind of lies are these?" She spat the words. "My son never touched that woman, at least not the last few months of their sham marriage."

"Adel, Forester voluntarily confessed to assault, he even called emergency services to take Dena to the hospital that night. There's a voice-match tape recording."

"What? That's impossible, it's all a lie."

Gaylord riffled through the file and found the paper he was

looking for. "Here, his written confession, signed by the detective, the assistant D.A. and his attorney."

"His attorney?" she asked.

"Nelson represented him," Gaylord said, offering her the paper.

"Why didn't I know about this?" she hissed, snatching it from his hands.

"Here's the full workup." He handed her the file again.

Adel snatched that, too, then tossed it down on the coffee table as she sat. "What does this mean? Get to the bottom line, Gaylord."

He sat down beside her. "Bottom line, Forester Graham confessed to assault and rape of his wife forty-one weeks before their child was born, a child obviously conceived that night."

Adel went stoic. "What happened to the charges?"

"Forester was arraigned then released on his own recognizance the next morning, then Dena dropped all charges a few days later. Apparently she and Forester decided to make a clean start. That was three days before the accident."

"This is impossible. I would have known."

"No one knew except..."

"No, I don't believe any of this," Adel said quietly.

"I'm still working on getting the photo and also a DNA sample of Dena's child, just in case." He stood and picked up his briefcase. "I'll be in touch." Adel nodded silently as he walked out. Her evening had just taken a desperately wrong turn.

Chapter 14

Knees bent, waist tucked, she fit perfectly into the concave f his body. Dena lazily opened her eyes and looked around. was still dark, so she relaxed and snuggled deeper. Waking p in a man's arms always felt good, waking up in Julian's rms felt like heaven. The dream of last night was still fresh her mind. They'd made love and then they'd made love gain. Hot and exciting, their appetites were ravenous; they ouldn't get enough of each other.

It seemed like both of them were making up for time lost nd opportunities missed. Whatever it was, it was good, eal good, but now the dawn would be approaching and she eeded to get back to her aunt's house. Sneaking in after a ight out was one thing, sneaking in after a night out to an udience of her aunt, Mamma Lou and Dillon was something else.

She had all intentions of getting up and leaving, but th comfortable bed begged her to stay and being wrapped i Julian's arms didn't hurt. But still she needed to go. It wa the morning after and she knew that the night before woul either be seen as a wonderful moment between two consent ing adults or a horrible mistake between coworkers. She ha no idea what to expect.

She felt his body stir behind her and tensed.

Both naked, he was hard and she instantly moistened.

He kissed her neck and her shoulder, and his hand rubbe her stomach and stroked down the length of her hip. "Hi," h whispered, nuzzling in her ear. She smiled, knowing this i how they started the second time they'd made love.

"Hi," she responded softly.

"Sleepy?" he asked.

"No," she said, feeling his hand travel up her body to he breasts.

"Thirsty?" he asked.

"No," she repeated.

"Hungry?"

"What do you have in mind?" she questioned.

"Roll over on your stomach," he requested, then sat up. Sh did, positioning her head on her folded arms. "Close you eyes," he added.

She did, not knowing what to expect.

He removed the sheet, leaned in and stroked the full lengt of her body. First her temple, then her neck, then her shou ders to her back, then over the bump of her rear and then dow her legs. The sensuous feel of his hands ignited a fire insid of her. He slowly reversed then his hand stroked the smudge bruise on her bottom. He remembered their first meetin smiled and kissed the hurt and continued touching, ending up back at the nape of her neck.

Dena moaned by the time his hands came to her neck. The soft gentle touch was too tantalizing. He ran his hands down her body again, following the same path he'd taken before but this time his touch was more enticingly intimate.

Her body responded when he paused on her rear again, drawing large circles over her buttocks then sweetly massaged her curves. He remembered the first time he'd seen these perfect cheeks. Half wrapped in a towel and soaking wet, he was instantly hooked then. All he'd dreamed about since that brief moment was touching her here and feeling the round fullness. So his hands continued to explore her, touching everywhere.

Dena moaned, reeling in the ecstasy of his touch.

"Does that feel good?" he asked softly.

"Mmm," she hummed. "Yes."

He continued stroking and caressing her body, then leaned in and kissed her temple, her neck, her shoulder, then moved lower repeating the action his hand had just taken. Dena shuddered inwardly when he got to her waist. Her body responded to his lips instantly.

She rolled to the side and smiled at him. He lay down beside her as their mouths connected. This kiss, unlike the last ones, was slow and measured, sweet and all-consuming. Unhurried and deliberate, they devoured each other as hands touched, teased and tantalized, converging in all directions.

She pushed up, reversing their positions. Within seconds she sat on top of him, her legs straddling his hips. Sitting up, she looked down onto her conquest. The magnificence of his broad muscular chest and detailed abs never ceased to amaze her.

She reached up to his neck then ran her hand down his body, feeling the hard outline of his form. He was rock-solid. She felt her way down his arms and to his hands, resting firmly on her waist then back up to his shoulders. He groaned, obviously pleased by her touch. She pressed her hands to his nipples and slowly circled them with her palms. The tiny studs pebbled. He moaned and held her waist tighter.

She leaned in and up, then kissed his shoulder then his arm and then bit, licked, kissed and sucked the pebbled studs. She felt his throbbing hardness pulsate, seeming to search for her entrance.

"Does that feel good?" she asked softly as she grabbed a condom from the nightstand.

"Mmm," he hummed, closing his eyes. "Yes."

"Open your eyes," she requested. He did. She tore open the plastic covering, eased up and back then slowly covered him. Feeling the hard length of him renewed her anticipation to nearly unbearable. She maneuvered up closer, hovering just inches from him. With ease she let gravity take over, and in a restrained measure she impaled herself onto him.

Completely engorged, she closed her eyes and sat still, reveling in the fullness of her body. Then she felt his hands come up to cover her breasts to encircle her back and bring her down to his mouth. His tongue licked her nipples to harden, then kissed and suckled each breast in turn.

A blazing fire burned through her as she sizzled, wiggled and moaned. She rolled up then down, filling and refilling her body with his hardness. Tight and rigid, wild and fierce, she began moving excitingly. Kisses pecked and prodded at every part of her body and the burn of his mouth on her was ecstasy. She closed her eyes, experiencing everything all at once.

She sat back as his hands came to her waist again, holding her balanced and in place. Rocking in and out, her body arched as he sat up and she wrapped her arms around his neck. Hugging close, she rose up as his lips delved into her neck, kissing her mindless.

His mouth descended lower, crossing her shoulders, down her arms then back up again. The taste of her was exhilarating. He lowered dipped and kissed her nipples, suckling each sweetness as she held on tight. Already taut and sensitive, she moaned as he ravaged the two perfect mounds. He brought her breasts together then dipped his mouth between the swell of cleavage. Dena gasped and arched back farther as hot passion shot through her each time she impaled herself on him. She closed her eyes, reveling in the sensuous feeling of his mouth and his hardness. The soft suckling pull turned to sweet kisses as she quickened the pace, eager to feel the surging climax.

In fervid bliss she rocked wild and hard, feeling her swell of pleasure come. She moaned and held tight each time she rose up and released. Thick, hard and throbbing, she sat on him and he refilled her until the pinnacle of orgasmic pleasure eclipsed and took her to rapturous ecstasy. They came together, holding tight as each climax repeated through shudders of passion.

He lay back, bringing her to lie on top of him. Both exhausted and satisfied, they lay there silent, catching their breath, feeling the last remnants of pleasure pass between their bodies. He reached over and grabbed the sheet to cover her body sprawled over his. Then a gentle sleep took them for a short time. She was the first to awaken as she moved off his body.

"Good morning," he muttered close to her ear while holding her tighter.

"Morning," she said, moving away slightly. "I'm gonna grab a quick shower."

"Okay, I'll put some coffee on."

Dena nodded, moved the sheet away and hurried to the bathroom. Once inside she closed the door and turned on the shower. Already naked she stepped inside and let the water pour down her body.

The urgency of their passion was exhilarating. She'd never before been with a man who was so attentive to her needs and her pleasure. Julian was the perfect lover. No woman in her right mind could walk away after spending a night with him.

After a cool shower she dried off then wrapped the towel around her body and went back into the bedroom. The room was dark and quiet. She could hear Julian's gentle breathing; he had apparently fallen back to sleep.

Hesitantly she began gathering her discarded clothing. She put on her panties and snapped her bra front. She slipped her arms into her dress and was just about to fasten it when she heard him behind her.

Julian stirred restlessly, then awoke when he reached out and Dena wasn't there. He leaned up, seeing her dress quickly. "So, do we need to talk?" he asked.

She turned, seeing him leaning up on his elbows in the rumpled bed they'd just shared. Half covered and draped in the white cotton sheet, he looked like the perfectly posed nude model.

"Talk about what?" she asked, walking back to the bed.

"I don't know, you tell me. You look like you are making a run for the door."

"Do I?" she asked.

"Yes, you do." She sat down beside him. He wrapped his

arms around her waist and dipped his chin to her shoulder. "Regrets?" he asked.

"No, you?" she asked.

He kissed her neck and shoulder while drawing his hand up and down her back. "Never," he whispered.

"This is going to be awkward, though, isn't it?" she asked.

"It doesn't have to be…" he began.

"At work, I mean. Maybe it wasn't such a good idea. Maybe I shouldn't have come here last night," she said.

"Maybe you should have come sooner," he answered.

She smiled; that was exactly what she needed to hear. He coaxed her to lie back as he wrapped his arms tighter. "I won't lie to you, Dena, I don't know where this is going, but I know that I want you in my life."

"Really?" She smiled happily.

"Definitely," he said, kissing her shoulder.

She'd heard her share of horizontal promises. Forester made dozens, hundreds. Like Julian, she wasn't sure what would happen next. All she knew was that living in the moment felt good and being here wrapped in Julian's arms felt right.

"I have to go, it's getting late." She paused and looked out the window. "Make that early."

"When are your aunt and Dillon coming home?" he asked.

"This afternoon," she said.

"Then stay with me this morning," he said as he pushed aside her opened dress and covered her breast. "I'll make you breakfast in bed," he whispered in her ear as he licked and sucked her earlobe. His fingers busily went to her bra, unsnapped the clasp then he tweaked her nipple to harden between his forefinger and thumb.

She shuddered as he leaned in to tickle her nipple with the tip of his tongue. A shocking sensation shot through her instantly. She gasped and giggled, moving away playfully. He held her in place right by his side. "Stay with me," he repeated.

Dena shook her head, smiling. "You are too tempting."

An hour later dawn had come and gone, breakfast had come and gone. It was time to leave, at least for appearance's sake. And if she didn't leave now she was sure they'd be making love for the fifth time.

A sudden heat swept over her. Julian was unreal. Every time he touched her she burned for him. Over breakfast he rubbed his hand over her rear and she nearly jumped on top of him. She'd never experienced such climaxes with spasms of ecstasy one right after another. He not only found her G-spot he'd claimed it as his own and she'd given it to him willingly.

Julian was still upstairs finishing getting dressed, so Dena decided to step out and get the newspaper tossed in the front driveway. She opened the front door and jerked back. Stephanie stood on the other side.

Woman to woman, the meeting was obvious, one leaving and one arriving. Stephanie was immediately insulted. "Who the hell are you?" she asked indignantly.

"Excuse me?" Dena asked.

"You're excused. Again, who the hell are you?"

Dena shook her head and walked away, then stopped when Stephanie called after her.

"Look, I don't know who you are and what you're doing with my husband, but his son and I don't want to see you here again."

"His son?" Dena asked, surprised to hear that Julian was a father.

"That's right, his son, and our child, or didn't you even bother to ask before you slept with him?"

Dena walked away.

Stephanie stood at the open door. She smiled.

"Stephanie," Julian said behind her.

She turned instantly and smiled, delighted to see him. "Good morning, Julian," she said, walking inside and closing the door soundly.

"What do you want, Stephanie?" he asked coldly, opening the door.

"I need to talk to you."

"I'm busy," he said, looking around outside for Dena. He spotted her walking to her car parked in the driveway.

Standing in the great foyer, she looked him up and down, licking her lips with pleasure. He was even better than she remembered. The calm medical doctor she once married was now a buff muscled-toned wealthy businessman.

"What about our child?"

"We don't have a child," he said, turning to face her. "You saw to that."

"He loves you. We're still a family."

"We were never a family and please don't use your child to further your cause."

"It was always you, Julian. I was just scared to change and move down here. But now everything is different. I'm ready to be the wife you want."

"I don't want a wife."

"Does the woman who just left know that?"

"She's none of your business," he said, feeling a pang of

agitation seeing that Dena walked out and left him without saying a word.

"Julian…"

He started laughing. "What do you want, Stephanie?"

"I need money, child support."

"You rescinded my adoption papers after I filed divorce papers and told me that since I wasn't the biological father I had no right to adopt him."

"That was a terrible mistake, I swear, it wasn't supposed to happen like that."

"How was it supposed to happen? The only reason you married me was because I was a doctor and you needed a father for your son."

"No, that's not how it happened."

"I was there, remember."

"That's not what I meant," she said, trying to recant.

"Go to Jamie, he's the father."

"I can't."

"Then it's not my problem," he said.

"What am I supposed to do?"

"Again, not my problem," he repeated.

Stephanie stewed, glaring at Julian as if to burn her eyes right through him. She noticed that the woman she'd seen earlier was now standing in the open doorway. She half smiled then broke out in crocodile tears. "I never thought you would be so cruel. What about our child?"

"Get out, Stephanie."

"Please, Julian, we need you, our child needs you. I don't know where else to turn."

"Stephanie, please leave and don't come back here." He turned seeing Dena was standing in the doorway with the rolled newspaper in her hand. Stephanie stiffened, her glare refocusing on Julian then on Dena's disgusted expression. She brushed past him, then Dena, and walked out.

Julian closed the door soundly after Dena walked back inside. "That was Stephanie," Julian said.

"So I gathered," she said as she looked around the living room and dining room for her purse. "I have to leave now."

Julian saw the change in her demeanor and followed. "Dena, she doesn't matter."

"Doesn't she? Obviously neither does anyone else."

"What does that mean?" he asked. "Dena…"

"I really need to leave now."

He stood in front of her. "Tell me, what's wrong?"

"I can't believe I'm so stupid."

"What?" he asked, following her to the kitchen.

"I actually thought you were different—" she continued to look around quickly "—but you're just like all the rest. You do whatever you want no matter who it hurts just as long as it pleases you."

"Dena, what is it?"

"What is it? You have a child out there and you just walked away? And then when the mother comes to you for help you just ignore her."

"Stephanie is…"

"Yeah, yeah, yeah, I get that part. She's a piece of work, but I'm not talking about her. How can you just turn your back on your son?"

"You have no idea what you're talking about."

"True, but I know what I heard. How can you just leave your child like that?"

"Let it go, Dena."

"Yeah, I think I'll do just that." She grabbed up her purse from the side counter and hurried to the front door. "Goodbye, Julian, thanks for a swell time."

Chapter 15

Dena went directly to her aunt's home, took a long, hot, soaking bubble bath, changed, then read and waited impatiently. Her mind unfortunately stayed on Julian and their night together. And no matter how hard she tried, she couldn't get him out of her mind.

She also couldn't get Stephanie out of her mind. She was everything Dena wasn't, but the one thing they had in common was their maternity, and Julian had coldly cut her off just as Adel had done to her. Granted, she didn't know the whole story but she heard him admit that his child with her was not his problem.

The icy coldness in his voice chilled her heart. But then she'd already heard about his ex-wife. She was definitely a piece of work. Still, to completely turn his back on his child was inexcusable. It just didn't seem like his character.

She grabbed her cell and dialed the one person who might know more about the relationship.

"Hello?"

"Willamina, hi, it's Dena. How are you doing?"

"Bloated, exhausted, fat, pick one," she answered honestly. They laughed and commiserated the physical limitations of third-trimester pregnancies.

"I just called to thank you again for including me in the baby shower celebration. I had a fantastic time."

"It was great, wasn't it? I tell you, when Darius throws a party, the man goes all out."

"I'm glad I finally got to meet some of the other employees. I see their names on the files so it's nice to match a face with the name and job description. I also saw Julian's ex at the party. Are the two of you close?"

"Girl, please credit me with some taste. I have no idea what that heifer is doing here. She lives in Boston but I bet she wants back in with Julian. She does this every now and then."

"So you knew them back then."

"Oh, yeah. I first worked with their father. Then when he died, Darius, Julian and Jordan moved back and took over, she came down then. They weren't divorced yet. Apparently she has a child from a previous relationship and Julian wanted to adopt but then she refused to move down here from Boston. He filed and she married a doctor friend of his a week after the divorce was final. Kind of makes you think she had that planned for a while, doesn't it?"

Dena's heart sank. She felt like a fool.

"Yeah, sounds like she was stepping out while he was down here."

"Yep. Anyway the divorce went through, she remarried, but whenever she gets into trouble she comes running to Julian dangling her child as leverage. I just hope she's not doing that again."

"So the child isn't even Julian's?"

"No way. As far as I know her current husband is the biological father. It's a shame how she uses people. It's a cute kid, lives with her mother. Julian sends gifts signed 'Uncle Julian' all the time."

Dena felt even worse. She'd lit into Julian because he turned his back on his child, a child that wasn't even his and was already well taken care of, and he apparently still cared for.

"Listen, the twins wanted to know if Dillon can come over and hang out with us this afternoon. We're going to the movies then out to dinner."

"That sounds like fun but Dillon is out until later this afternoon."

"Oh bummer, maybe next time," Willamina said.

"Definitely. Anyway I'd better let you go. Thanks again for inviting me to the shower."

"Anytime, wow, it's gonna be hard not going into work Monday morning. Maybe I'll stop in for a little…"

"Don't you dare even think about it," Dena chastised firmly. "You once ordered me to take time off and relax, well, right back at you." They laughed.

"Okay, okay, but if you need anything, call me."

"I will, and same here."

They hung up. Dena smiled. She liked having Willamina as a friend. She was a wealth of information; unfortunately what she told her about Julian and Stephanie was no way near what she accused him of. She was wrong. Just as she put her cell back into her purse the house phone rang.

"Hi, Mom," Dillon said happily.

"Dillon, hi, honey. How are you? Are you having fun?" Dena asked.

"Uh-huh, we went on some rides and I played with a chicken and a duck and I ride on a horse and then we saw some fireworks and a parade and had my picture took and then I hurt my hair and then we went to eat and big place that had more horses." Dillon spoke nonstop making the whoosh of conversation barely discernable.

"Oh, my, sounds like you're having a wonderful time."

"Can I stay again?" he asked.

"Well, honey, I think it's about time…"

"Dena," Ellen said, taking the phone from Dillon. "Hi."

"Hi, Aunt Ellen. How are you?"

"Fine, just fine, we're having a blast. Dillon is really enjoying himself."

"I'm glad to hear that. When are you coming home?"

"About that, we were wondering if you'd mind Dillon staying another night. There's this farm we stopped at and it's wonderful, they're having a huge end of fair celebration there tomorrow morning. Dillon has his heart set on going."

"What about you and Mamma Lou, don't you need to get back here?"

"Another day won't make much difference one way or the other, and Dillon is having so much fun I hate for him to miss the ending."

Dena hesitated then yielded. "All right, if you don't mind. Thank you. Dillon sounds like he's having so much fun."

"He is, we all are. How's it going there?"

"Quiet."

"I bet. Anyway, sweets, our brunch just arrived. We're going shopping for new clothes this afternoon then going on a water ride and a tour of the local winery."

"Sounds like you three are having a great time," Dena said.

"Sure are, hope you are, too," Ellen said.

"I am," Dena replied, remembering the night before.

"See you tomorrow around three or four." She paused. There was conversation in the background. "Dena, Louise said that if Otis Wheeler gets there before we get back just have him cool his heels."

"Otis Wheeler?"

"Colonel Wheeler. You've heard me mention him with Louise, they drove down together."

"Oh, right, sure…oh, and, Aunt Ellen, one thing. Dillon said that he hurt himself?" she queried.

"Yes, but he's just fine, he was getting his picture taken and tried on a hat. The inside clip pulled his hair. It was a great picture but funny thing someone had taken it by mistake by the time we went to pick it up."

"That's odd that someone would take the picture by mistake, they had to see it wasn't theirs," Dena said offhandedly.

"We took another one and that one came out even better."

"Okay, have a good time, 'bye."

"'Bye, Mom," Dillon quickly said in the background.

"'Bye, honey," Dena said, then listened as the phone disconnected. She sat thinking a moment after hanging up.

A few minutes later she changed clothes again then tossed a few things into an overnight bag. She got into the car and drove back to Julian's house. She rang the bell then knocked on the door. There was no answer. She walked around to the back of the house where he was the night before. The garage door was closed and locked. She peered in the smoked window. The car was exactly as they'd left it the night before.

It was obvious he was gone.

She drove back to her aunt's house slightly despondent. She'd lost her faith and her trust. Thanks to everything she was going through she believed only what she saw and heard, and it seemed that quite often that was skewed and doubtful.

Feeling melancholy she sat out on the back porch overlooking the yard. The sprinkles had turned off and a light misting rain had begun to fall.

The past few weeks since her arrival had changed her life so much. For three years she'd barricaded herself in her house refusing to let anyone near her or her son. Now everything was different. She wanted to get back out into the world and she wanted Julian there with her.

Change was harder than she thought.

Adel hated being summoned to the law firm. It always seemed like they were in charge and not her.

"So it's true."

"Yes, I believe it is," Gaylord confirmed.

Adel held the photo up and stared. Her eyes, wide with astonishment and pain, welled with emotion. The question of paternity wasn't even an issue as far as she was concerned. The child was the exact image of his father, her son, Forester. There was no denying it.

"We'll have the DNA test results complete in a few days. You'll be able to establish paternity then."

"I don't need DNA to see that this is Forester's son," Adel said, touching the small face lovingly.

Gaylord hovered over her shoulder. "The results will establish irrefutable biological paternity."

"Forget that. How do I get him?"

"How do you get who?"

"My grandchild, of course," she said, looking up at him.

"What do you mean, you want visitation rights?"

"I don't want visitation rights, I want my child."

"Adel, you just spent the last four years denying that Dena's child was Forester's. You even went as far as to offer the Graham inheritance to Gloria and her child."

"But her child wasn't Forester's."

"Exactly, the DNA proved that and she finally admitted it. I think you should move very cautiously at this point. This could be another disappointment. Dena has been trying to get the Graham inheritance since her child was born. You don't want to make another mistake."

"I didn't make the last one. Your investigators failed to uncover that Gloria was having affairs with half the men in this town. Forester isn't the father of her child any more than you are. Her child didn't even look like him. But this one, what's his name?"

Gaylord reached across the desk and opened a file. "Dillon Leigh Graham."

"Dillon, what kind of a name is that for a Graham?

"I believe that the boy is named after her father and mother."

"Well, that will be the first thing we change. He's young, he'll adapt easily enough. How old is he again?"

"He'll be four next month."

"Four, that's impossible," she surmised. "Forester was killed almost five years ago. Then I was right, Forester isn't the father."

"It appears she might have gotten pregnant just before Forester died, possibly even the same night he attacked her."

Adel glared at him. The idea that her son was accused of attacking his own wife still didn't sit well with her, nor did the fact that Nelson helped cover it up. She shook her head.

"The medical records only mention early stage first-trimester pregnancy and that was just weeks after the accident, so it's very possible given the nine month period."

"He lied to me."

"Who?"

"Forester, he told me that he and Dena weren't physically active. He said that he didn't want children with her. But this is his child, there's no denying that. He's the spitting image of Forester as a child."

"The DNA tests will soon confirm one way or the other. The tests are ninety-nine point nine percent accurate. There'll be no mistake, I assure you."

"Petition the court, I want full sole custody."

"What? Excuse me?"

"You heard me. This is my grandchild, the only thing I have left of my life. My husband is gone, my two sons are gone, the least I can have is this child. She owes me that much. Get him for me."

"Adel, you can't just take a child away from its mother. This isn't 1860. It's illegal, not to mention immoral."

"Find a way. I want him at Graham Manor for his fourth birthday," she said, standing to leave.

"Adel, be reasonable, this is America, kidnapping is against the law. We've done everything you've asked regarding this situation. We've destroyed evidence and planted and created questionable leads and documentation. Any one of these offenses can put us behind bars, but to steal a child..."

"I didn't say steal the child, get him legally."

"How? His mother is alive and well."

"She's unfit."

"We could never prove that."

"Then you'd better find a way, hadn't you?"

"Adel, please, be reasonable," Gaylord said.

"I am being reasonable, if you can't do this I'll find someone who will, although..."

"Adel, please..."

"...I'd rather not, but I will if I have to. Just do it."

The elevator doors closed and Gaylord stood there shaking his head. This situation was getting out of hand. For the last four years Adel denied the biological paternity of this child, now she wanted to reverse everything.

Gaylord went back into his office and sat down at his desk. Adel's unreasonable requests were getting outrageous and putting the firm in considerable danger. She had nothing to lose, of course. She wasn't even an attorney. But going before the legal review board with the possibility of expulsion or loss of license was too much of a risk for him. So whatever he came up with had to be more than plausible.

He opened the Dena Graham file and began going through her papers. All of which he'd seen a thousand times before, he'd even manufactured a few. There was nothing he could use to take away her child.

He flipped through her medical profile. She was physically healthy, no help there. He read through her psychological review. Of course the documentation had been exaggerated. He'd hired a professional psychiatrist to evaluate her years ago just after the accident. At the time she had been on standard suicide watch because of the horrific tragedy she'd witnessed.

The report stated that she was mentally fragile due to fatigue and mental exhaustion, she'd stopped eating and sleeping. She was prescribed sleeping pills and antidepressants. On one occasion she'd taken too many, got sick and was rushed to the hospital. They cautioned it as possible overdose, then changed the diagnosis after taking tests. That's when she learned of her pregnancy. Since then there was nothing.

Gaylord read through the psychological study again.

At the time they used that as a way of providing incompetence and denying her access to several of Forester's family insurance policies. The deception was found out and thrown out of court but maybe now he could use it to his advantage.

This time he needed to be more careful.

He needed to show that she was unstable and unable to care for her child. His livelihood and his career depended on it. He picked up the phone and made a call. He had less than a month to put something together.

Chapter 16

"Whoa, check it out. Look what the storm dragged in. What are you doing here?" Jordan said, carrying several shopping bags and putting them down on the kitchen counter. He saw Julian sitting out back on the covered deck with his feet up on the rail.

The light rain he'd driven through was now pouring hard and a swift breeze swirled around him as he sat out overlooking the coastline. The boat he and his brothers bought a few years ago was secured and tied up, moored in its slip at the end of the dock. "Last I heard, I'm part owner," Julian said over his shoulder.

"Yeah, and the last time you were here was—" Jordan turned to Darius as he entered "—when was the last time he was here?"

"You got me," Darius said, following, carrying another two shopping bags and setting them on the counter, too.

"Well, I'm here now," Julian said.

"The question is why, what happened?" Jordan asked.

"Nothing happened."

"It's woman trouble, that much is a given. I know it's not Stephanie. So who is it, Dena?" Darius said.

"Do you ever stop speculating?"

"I was a stockbroker in another life, that's what I do. I calculate the odds and reach a logical conclusion."

"My money's on Dena, too. I really like her," Jordan said.

"You don't even know her."

"I know you slept with her." Jordan shot out, purely joking. But Julian's shocked reaction confirmed it. Both Jordan and Darius began applauding.

"So what'd you do?" Darius asked, handing Jordan a hundred-dollar bill.

"I didn't do anything. She just went off on me."

"Ha," Jordan laughed once as he put his winnings into his jeans' pocket. "Stephanie, yes, definitely, I could see that, she's volatile. But Dena, no, she's too good-natured. Nope, you had to have done something."

"Yeah, whatever," Julian said, walking into the kitchen and seeing the bags lined up on the counter. "What's all this?"

"We're giving a party this evening," Jordan said.

"A what?"

"You remember what a party is, food, drinks, fun, laughter, talking, women," Jordan added sarcastically.

"Yeah, I know what a party is. But why tonight?"

"Because we planned it for tonight," Darius said.

"Come on, I came down for a little quiet solitude."

"Damn, it's worse than I thought," Jordan joked.

"Have the party on the boat," Julian offered.

"Can't, note the weather, the boat will be a bit rocky, mind you, that's not necessarily a bad thing at times," Darius said.

"Particularly when you have the perfect woman there with you and she'd got—" Jordan started.

"Do you ever stop talking about women?" Julian interrupted them.

"Hey, just because you've landlocked yourself doesn't mean the rest of us have to put our sails away and go home, particularly when there's a lot of ocean out there," Jordan said seriously.

"What the hell was that?" Darius asked Jordan, laughing.

Jordan joined his laughter. "I have no idea, but you get the point."

"What point?" Darius asked, still laughing. "I have no idea if what you said even makes sense."

Julian couldn't help but laugh and for the next few minutes the three brothers laughed hard and long, and it felt good.

A few hours later the party was just as expected. It appeared that half the cove had shown up. Music and laughter flowed as continuously as the food and drinks. Everyone was having a great time. Julian enjoyed himself for the most part but he was still thinking about Dena.

He sipped his drink and leaned on the rail. The peace he'd come expecting had yet to materialize. He'd spent the afternoon doing paperwork he'd brought with him and the early evening on the phone and Internet. Curiously he typed in Dena's name. Nothing of note appeared. Then he remembered that Jordan mentioned a law firm. He typed in a general law firm search then narrowed it to the immediate area. He scanned several.

When the firm Graham, Whitman & Morris came up, he

paused remembering Jordan wondering if the Graham might be related to Dena. He clicked on the site then visited several links. He didn't find anything interesting and was ready to click to another law firm when he saw and clicked on the founder's page. Three portrait-like figures appeared with an extended bio beneath each.

All three deceased, Julian focused on Nelson Graham. Having recently passed, there was still a memorial dedicated to his life and his family. He was married to Adel and had two sons, Kirkland and Forester. Nelson and his two sons had died in a car accident just over four years ago.

The coincidence interested him. Maybe Kirkland or Forester was Dena's husband. Then he saw her name listed under a brief bio of Forester but there was no mention of a son named Dillon. Then it hit him. Dillon had said that he would be celebrating his fourth birthday soon. That made it impossible for Forester to be Dillon's father and Dena's claim that she hadn't been with anyone since her husband was mathematically impossible.

Julian wasn't sure what bothered him more, the fact that Dena lied to him or the fact that she was trying to pass another man's child off on her dead husband. Either way, he didn't like it. It hit too close to home.

He exited the site and turned off the computer, realizing that he was more tired than he thought and he'd had enough drama for one day. The morning with Dena, then Stephanie and then the long drive to the beach had drained him. He lay down on his bed and closed his eyes. Sleep came almost immediately.

A few hours later he awoke to loud music and laughter. Confused at first he looked around then realized the party must have started. He grabbed a quick shower, changed then went downstairs.

"Well it's about time you showed up," Jordan said, handing him a drink. "Did you call Dena yet and apologize?"

"What's this?" Julian asked, looking into the plastic cup, ignoring Jordan's question about Dena.

"Ginger ale, Darius and I make it a practice never to drink alcohol when we're hosting a party. Something about having a clear head in case anything jumps off."

Julian looked around at the mass of humanity around him. "Yeah, I can see how that could happen. Who are all these people?" He nearly shouted to be heard over the music blaring through the system.

"Beach friends, neighbors, whatever," Jordan said, waving to a few people who'd just arrived. "Most of them rent houses on the beach and come down on the weekends only."

Julian shook his head, amazed by the turnout. "How did they find out about the party? I thought you and Darius only decided to have this party this morning."

"Yeah, that's right, but word of mouth travels fast in the cove," Jordan said just as a woman shimmied up to him and began pulling him to dance with her in the center of the great room. "Hey, enjoy," Jordan said as he followed obediently.

Julian laughed, seeing Jordan doing his hip-hop moves. He looked around for Darius, finding him on the side speaking with a few older people. He nodded when Darius turned to him. They each raised their cups up in a silent toast.

After about twenty minutes the party had begun to wear thin with Julian. There were too many people so he stepped outside onto the back deck. Several people were also scattered around outside but they seemed to be just talking quietly between themselves.

"Hi."

Julian turned, seeing a beautiful too young woman dressed in a scant bikini top and low-slung sarong. Her long hair flowed easily in the breeze. "Hi," he said.

"So, I hear you're Darius and Jordan's brother." She smiled with genuine interest.

"Yes, I am."

"Older or younger?" she asked.

"Both. I'm somewhere in the middle."

She smiled brighter. "So Darius is the serious one and Jordan is the fun one. What does that make you?"

"Both, somewhere in the middle," he repeated.

She laughed too loud and too hard. "I'm Toni," she said happily.

"Hi, Toni. I'm Julian," he answered briefly.

"I'm staying at the beach house a few doors down. I'm here with my office mates, we have the place for the next few weeks. How come I've never seen you down here before?"

"I've been busy."

"Too busy to come to the beach and relax."

"Yeah," Julian said.

She inched close, allowing her small breasts to brush his arm, then looked out toward the dock pretending to be unaware of her close proximity. "That's a shame. Well, since you're here now why don't you show me your boat over there."

Julian turned with his back to the rail. "I have a better idea why don't I get you another drink?"

Toni smiled brightly. "Yeah, okay," she said, handing him her empty plastic cup.

"What are you drinking?"

"Diet soda, I don't do the alcohol thing."

"Good for you," Julian said as he took the cup and went back inside.

"Toni, huh?" Darius said, seeing Julian toss the cup in the trash, then get another one and fill it with a diet beverage. They both turned and looked outside, seeing her refresh her lip gloss in a small mirror.

"I don't think so," Julian said.

Darius nodded his agreement. "I'm glad to hear it. She's a bit young and needy. You, dear brother, need to be with someone more mature with a brain. Speaking of which, how's Dena, did you call her yet?"

"Why exactly are you and Jordan so worried about my love life, another bet?"

"Nah, we need a hobby. You're it."

"Thanks, I'm truly honored," he said dryly, then looked around the large great room. Half the women looked like they'd just come for a rap video taping and the other half looked like they were on their way to one. Skimpy outfits, fake hair, long nails, tons of makeup, it all seemed overdone. "I don't think I'll find the type of woman I'm looking for anytime soon."

"You never know," Darius said as he walked away.

His cell phone rang. He flipped it open to answer just as a young man walked by. Julian handed him the cup and pointed to the woman waiting outside on the deck. He took the cup, nodded and smiled.

"Hello?" he said.

"Julian?"

"Yeah. Hold on, I can't hear you."

"Julian."

"Hold on," he repeated, barely hearing the other person's

reply. The noise from the party and the bad connection made it impossible to tell who was calling. He walked away from the main area and went out the front door. The reception was even worse there. The line went dead.

He looked at the incoming number. It was Mrs. Payne's home phone number. "Dena." He called back immediately.

She picked up. "Hello?"

"Dena, you called me."

"Yes, I wanted to…" she began.

"Wait, I can barely hear you." He quickly walked around to the back of the house then headed down the dock toward the water's edge. He usually got great reception there. "Okay, Dena, are you still there?"

"Thanks for the drink, baby," a woman said behind him.

"Dena," he called. She didn't answer. "Dena, hello?" The connection was lost.

"I don't appreciate being pawned off on someone else. If I wanted a pimp I'm sure I could find one for myself."

Julian turned around, seeing Toni standing on the dock behind him. "That wasn't my intention, I assure you." He was slightly aggravated by not reconnecting with Dena and now Toni was back after he'd tried to discreetly brush her off. "Excuse me," he said, turning his back and taking a few steps away to redial. He waited, there was no answer. He closed the phone and turned. Toni hadn't moved an inch.

"I get lousy reception sometimes because of the weather," she said, "plus there's another storm headed this way, everything's probably off." He nodded and looked away, thinking of Dena. "Thanks for the drink, but you picked the one guy in this place I'm trying to avoid to bring it to me. He and I had a thing a few weeks back but I had to let him go."

"Sorry to hear that."

"Yeah, well, it happens. Anyway, I expected you to bring me my drink."

"I got busy."

"You get busy a lot, don't you?" He didn't answer. She smiled easily again. "Okay, you're forgiven. So this is yours, huh?" she said, looking over at the large boat in the slip beside them.

"My brothers and I own it, yes."

"And the beach house, too, right?" He nodded. "One of my girls was telling me that you three own some kind of big company." He nodded again. "Damn, you must have some serious deep pockets," she said openly, nudging closer to him.

"I work hard."

"I'm in school to be a medical assistant."

"Good for you."

"But, really, I'm a dancer. I've been in a few videos, maybe you seen me." She went on to name a few videos he hadn't heard of.

"No, I'm afraid not, but then I don't get a chance to see a lot of videos. I'm usually…"

"…busy," they both said in unison. She laughed again.

"So what do you do exactly, Julian?" Toni asked.

"Construction," he said, simplifying his occupation as he always did.

"Oh, so that's why your body is so fine," she said, cooing sweetly. Then she boldly reached out and began rubbing her hands over his chest and stomach, then continued lower.

"Toni," he said, quickly taking her hands of his body. "I'm not interested."

"Why not, baby?" she asked, stupefied by his objections.

"I have someone else in mind."

"Is she here tonight?"

"No," he replied, wishing she was.

"But I am," Toni said.

"It doesn't work like that."

"Why doesn't it? I'm here with you and she isn't. She obviously had something better to do. So she's out of the picture as far as I'm concerned," she said, sounding like an impertinent child.

"But not as far as I'm concerned and that's what counts."

Toni looked him up and down then smiled up at him. "Is it serious, this thing with her?"

"I don't know yet," he answered.

"You gonna marry her."

"It's too soon to tell."

"So what's the big deal, then? She's not here. She's obviously out with someone else having her fun. Why shouldn't we have ours?" she said, then reached up and untied her bikini top, letting the scant material fall down the front of her. Her small perky breasts beckoned him proud and bold. "Baby, men don't just walk away from this," she said, striking a seductive pose.

Julian smiled, shaking his head at her boldness. He felt nothing seeing her expose herself to him. "I'm afraid I'm going to have to."

She eased closer, rubbing her bare breast up and down his arm. "I can do tricks with my tongue that most women would be ashamed to even think about."

"Exactly, and I'm not surprised. But still, no thanks."

"What's wrong with you?" she asked, wrinkling her nose.

"That's a good question."

"Fine, then forget you."

Now totally pissed, she replaced her top, mumbled a few strong expletives then stomped away, heading back to the party still going on.

Julian shook his head. When a woman wholeheartedly offers her body to a man, history dictates his gleeful acceptance. But there was no way he could even think about another woman. And Toni could have stripped down to nothing and he'd still not want her. He didn't want anyone except Dena.

He walked back toward the boat, climbed onboard. He stood portside and looked out at the darkness of the water. The overcast sky shed about as much light as he had when Toni asked him questions and his plans with Dena.

Was it serious? Did he want it to be? And as far as marriage was concerned, he was completely lost. His relationships never ended well. He'd been burned too many times to just do the fall-in-love thing again. But a part of him knew that it was already too late.

He turned and walked down the few steps to the cabin below. Without turning on the lights he lay down on the oversize bunk bed and let the slow sway of the troubled water rock him to sleep. Dreams of Dena came just as he expected. They were in the greenhouse surrounded by plants and flowers. A monstrous storm raged outside. But they lay in each other's arms just after making love. A calm serenity surrounded them even as the elements battled outside. The peace warmed him.

Thanks for the drink, baby. What was that?

Dena hung up the phone, her mouth still wide open. Apparently their night together was just what he needed to get back in the game. She was just about to go on a roll when she stopped herself. Wait. Yes, there was a party going on and, yes, there was a woman's voice in the background, but jumping to conclusions had gotten her before. She remembered well.

It was the last holiday party at her in-laws' home. She and Forester arrived late because they had talked all night. He had committed himself to their marriage and together they intended to start anew. He was going to leave the law firm and she was going to find them a new place to live as far away from outside influences as possible.

They'd walked in hand-in-hand. He went to talk to his father about quitting, leaving her to mingle with the guests. Adel walked up with Forester's old girlfriend, Gloria, in tow. She was obviously pregnant. Since they had never been formally introduced, Adel had done the honors. She still shuddered hearing her voice as if it were just moments earlier.

"Dena," Adel had begun, smiling haughtily as she approached. "I don't think you've met Gloria. She's an old friend of the family. She and Forester were boyfriend and girlfriend all through middle school and high school."

"Hi," she'd said, extending her hand to shake.

Gloria had held out her weak fishlike hand then winced when Dena shook it gently. "Hi," Gloria'd said, holding her other hand on her stomach.

"Oh, yes," Adel had continued. "I almost overlooked the guest of honor, this is my soon-to-be-grandchild."

Dena's heart had trembled and she'd begun to physically shake. "What?"

"Yes, it appears that you and Gloria have something

very real in common. She's carrying Forester's child and you're not."

Dena had fainted. When she'd opened her eyes she was lying on the sofa and there was a crowd standing around her. Forster was at her side, holding her. Gloria was standing at his side and Nelson and Adel were arguing about something.

She'd gotten up off the sofa, grabbed her coat and hurried out. Forester had grabbed her arm to have her wait for him but she didn't. Another argument between Adel Forester and Nelson began as she'd closed the door behind her. Seconds after she got in the car to drive off, Forester had jumped in the passenger seat.

Snow and ice covered the ground but still she floored the accelerator. Driving down the curvy hill she and Forster argued that he was not the father of Gloria's child but that they had had an affair. He'd begged her to turn the car around so they could confront both Adel and Gloria, but she'd kept driving and crying.

He'd grabbed the steering wheel and pulled, the car went into a spin. She had been thrown from the car after it hit the tree and could only watch as the car continued its descent.

Just then a second car had appeared, driving down the hill just as fast. Before she could scream, it hit that same patch of ice and slammed into Forester. The car ignited into flames. Several other cars followed, but were able to stop.

She'd run to Forester and reached for him through the broken windshield. She'd held his hand as he'd died and even now the pain of seeing him lying there broken and crushed tore at her heart.

A slow-moving tear slipped down her face. She looked out at the rain still pouring heavily and let the tears release and the pain come. She was anguished of the lost lives, Forster, Nelson and Kirkland, three dead because of Adel's selfishness, Gloria's lies and her lack of trust.

Chapter 17

Keeping busy seemed to be the order of the day. Dena cleaned, vacuumed, dusted, washed, folded, shopped and cooked, all with Julian hovering somewhere in her thoughts. When the doorbell rang just after one o'clock she excitedly went to answer, hoping it was Julian.

It wasn't.

An older gentleman with a ratty old hat, dressed in weathered jeans and a long-sleeved plaid shirt, stood on the other side of the screen door and smiled down at her. "Hi, there. You must be Dena," the man said happily.

He was tall and broad with a smile that was contagious. "May I help you?" Dena asked, having no idea how he knew her name. The first thing she thought was something from Adel.

"You're just as pretty as they said," he added.

"I sorry…" she said, leery of him.

"Wheeler. Otis Wheeler. I'm looking for Louise or Ellen."

"Oh, right, you must be Mr. Wheeler, Mamma Lou's friend from Crescent Island."

"Colonel Wheeler, front and center," he said, snapping to attention.

"Come in, come in," she said, holding the door open for him. "No one's here right now, but I expect them soon. Mamma Lou asked me to tell you to cool your heels."

He laughed loud and hard. "That sounds about right."

It seemed that not only was his smile contagious, his laughter made you smile, too. "Can I get you a drink or maybe something to eat?"

"I'd take a nice cold drink if it's not too much bother. Been fishing all weekend without a single bite." He shook his head. "If I didn't know any better I'd say I lost my touch."

"I'm sure it's not that. What would you like to drink?" She headed to the kitchen, he followed.

"Iced tea, lemonade, water, anything cold is fine."

Dena opened the refrigerator as Colonel Wheeler took a seat at the counter. She poured him a tall, ice-filled glass of sweetened iced tea. He took a long sip then she refilled his glass. "So where did you go fishing?" she asked as she poured herself a glass of tea.

"A few miles west of here. A place in Henderson County called Buckeye Lake, supposed to be great fishing."

"That's funny, Aunt Ellen and Mamma Lou are in Henderson County, too. There's a fair there this weekend."

"Ah, that explains all the traffic on the way here, must be breaking up today." He shook his head, "A fair, huh? That means a dozen or so new plants, bulbs and flowers."

"Yea, I'm pretty sure that's exactly what it means," she

said. They chuckled, commiserating Louise's and Ellen's zeal for plants. "They took my son, Dillon, with them and stayed over Friday night then called and said that they were staying over again last night."

"You have a child, you look like a kid yourself."

"You are a charmer, aren't you?"

He winked then laughed. "That'll be our little secret."

"Dillon's three and a half, and a handful. They'll probably be completely worn out by the time they get back here."

"Louise will love that. Her grandson Tony and his wife Madison just had twins and she's spoiling them already, and they're barely out of the hospital."

"She's such a sweet lady."

"Yes, she is that, and then some," he assured her. "Now don't let me disturb you."

"I was on my way over to the greenhouse to check on the sprinklers. Feel like taking a walk?"

"After sitting and driving for the last hour and a half, that sounds perfect. Lead the way."

In the ease of the afternoon sun they strolled down the garden path, talking easily about the weather and the construction on the patio. Then the conversation lapsed.

They started walking around, checking the system. Dena pointed out several prized flowers while Colonel Wheeler talked about his home on Crescent Island. All of a sudden Dena remembered a dream she'd had the other night. She suddenly looked sad. "Are you okay, Dena?"

"Yes," she said quickly, then shook her head. "No."

"Do you want to tell me about it or is this something you want to talk to your aunt or Louise about?"

"I messed up," she said softly.

"We all do, it's called being human."

"I met this guy, actually we kind of work together now. He's nice, kind, funny, understanding, he likes me and he likes my son."

"Sounds like a winner," Colonel Wheeler said, nodding approvingly.

"He is, at least he was, his ex-wife came into the picture."

"Ah, that sounds like trouble."

"No, not really. I don't think there's anything between them anymore, not from his perspective anyway."

"So what's the problem?" he asked as he opened the door and they headed back to the house.

"I overheard them talking yesterday and she made it seem that he was neglecting their child. I got upset. If you only knew the drama I'm going through with my son's grand-mother…anyway I walked out on him. Then I found out later that he's not even the father and that he still keeps in contact with her child and she doesn't know it."

"Sounds like a good guy," Colonel Wheeler said as they walked back to the house.

"He is, but as I said, I walked out on him."

"You were overly sensitive for a mother's plight."

"You make it sound almost noble."

"Talk to him."

"I tried. Last night I called him, but we got disconnected. I don't think he was in town anymore. But even then, I don't think I'd even know what to say to him."

"Tell him how you feel."

"That's just it. It's confusing. I don't know how I feel."

"Doesn't sound like you're confused to me," he said. "Sounds like you really care for him." She nodded. "Then tell him that. If he's half the man you just described, then he'll step up."

"You think so?" she asked.

"I know so," he said.

"Thanks, Colonel Wheeler," she said as they reached the kitchen again. "Wow, I can't believe I told you all that, bet you had no idea that you'd be playing shrink this afternoon."

He squeezed her hand gently. "God puts people exactly where he needs them to be at exactly the right time. Right now this is where I need to be."

She nodded and exhaled the sadness away. "Sure I can't get you something to eat," she said as she turned to the refrigerator and pulled out some large crusty rolls and a few croissants she'd purchased earlier. "It's nothing fancy, I just finished cutting up some leftover roasted chicken for a chicken salad and I hate eating alone."

Colonel Wheeler smiled and nodded. "Don't mind if I do. Let me wash up and I'll give you a hand."

Dena pointed to the first-floor bathroom then she began pulling salad fixings from the refrigerator. By the time Colonel Wheeler returned a delicious-looking roast chicken salad was mixed and ready to serve. Dena had also piled a bowl high with crispy potato chips, had a side dish of assorted cheeses, grapes, melon and crackers. Colonel Wheeler slapped and rubbed his hands together and smiled. "Now that's what I call a lunch spread."

She handed him a plate and he scooped up a large spoon of chicken salad then grabbed a roll, some chips and cheese. Dena slit open a croissant and filled it with chicken salad then added lettuce, sliced tomato and cheese to her plate.

As they finished eating they laughed and talked about flower obsessions, the military, law and family. Dena listened and laughed, thoroughly enjoying herself. Colonel Wheeler was a treasure. He had an answer to everything and enough wisdom to have his own following.

"Mo-ommm, I'm ho-omme." Dillon called.

"Let me guess, Dillon," Colonel Wheeler said, chuckling.

Dena nodded then shook her head. One of these days she would have to teach him to calm down. "In here," she said, and stood just as he came barreling around the dining room into the kitchen. He slammed into her, grabbing her legs and holding tight.

"I had so much fun. I saw a horse and I rode on a pony and we played in some dirt and then we ate to funny-el cake, I don't think I like that again," he added firmly, then finally slowed down to take a breath. He looked at Colonel Wheeler and smiled. "Who are you?"

"Well, hello there, young man, and what might your name be?" Colonel Wheeler asked, holding out his hand to shake. Dillon looked at his mother, she nodded, then he reached out and shook hands.

"Dillon. I went to a fair with Aunt Ellen and Grandmamma Lou. See?" He held up a photo book of fair activities already completely colored in with crayon.

"My goodness, that must have been a lot of fun."

Dillon shook his head animatedly.

"Colonel Wheeler, this is my son, Dillon. Dillon, this is Colonel Wheeler."

"Colonel Wheeler?" Dillon said. Colonel Wheeler nodded. "Like in the army Colonel Wheeler?" He nodded again. "Where's your tank?"

"I put it away, it was kind of big."

"I know," Dillon said, obviously commiserating, then leaned in to whisper, "my mom makes me put my toys away, too."

Colonel Wheeler burst with laughter just as Louise and Ellen joined them in the kitchen. "Well, hello there," Louise said as she walked up to the center island counter and hugged Dena then leaned over and kissed Otis on the cheek. Ellen followed and greeted Dena and Otis. Dillon walked over and stood between the two older women, holding both their hands.

"You're here early. I didn't expect to see you for another few hours."

"The fish weren't biting." Colonel Wheeler said.

"Fish bite?" Dillon asked, looking up at Colonel Wheeler. "With teeth?"

"Not exactly. I'll tell you what, why don't we go in the living room and I'll tell you all about fishing and you can tell me all about the fair."

"'Kay," Dillon said, happily beginning instantly. "First we drove in the car a real, real long time and I went to sleep an' then we had a big dinner then we saw some flowers and then we talked to a fireman, but he didn't have his fire engine..." Dillon continued as he and Colonel Wheeler headed to the living room leaving Dena, Louise and Ellen in the kitchen.

"You hungry? I made some chicken salad for lunch."

"No thanks," Ellen said.

"We just ate," Louise added, exhaling happily.

"We stopped at a pancake house and ate just about everything on the menu. I couldn't eat another bite. So how was your weekend? Do anything special?" Ellen asked curiously.

"No, nothing special. I just hung around the house, did a little shopping this morning, no big deal," she said as she began covering and putting the leftover food in the refrigerator.

"You had the whole weekend to yourself and you didn't do anything?" Ellen asked.

She shrugged. "It was quiet," she said, wiping the counter off with a dishcloth.

"Huh. I tried calling you late Friday evening to let you know we'd arrived safely. There was no answer."

Dena froze midwipe. Her eyes widened as she blushed bright crimson-red. She looked guilty as sin without even opening her mouth. "Oh, um, I went out for a while, to dinner, with a friend." Ellen smiled at Louise. Dena caught the brief interaction between the two. "What was that?" she asked.

"What?" both Louise and Ellen asked.

"That look," Dena said, pointing to their now innocent faces.

"What look?" they responded in unison again.

Dena scanned her aunt's face then looked at Louise. Somehow they knew. She sighed heavily, surrendering. "Okay, fine, I went over to Julian's house Friday after you left." Ellen and Louise started nodding, waiting impatiently for more. "And we—I stayed the night," Dena added hesitantly.

Ellen and Louise squealed then burst with laughter. Dena stood, realizing that she'd just confessed to something they'd apparently already surmised. "You knew, didn't you? You planned it?"

"Let's just say I hoped and offered an available opportunity," Ellen said, taking Dena's hand as Louise nodded sweetly.

"Did you have a good time?" Ellen asked.

Her indignation dissolved instantly. "Yeah, I did," Dena

said as her face brightened by the thought of her night of passion with Julian. "I had a great time."

"I hope you're going to see him again?" Ellen said hopefully, nodding her head as she asked.

Dena stopped smiling. "I don't know, maybe, maybe not. I guess it was what it was."

"What kind of answer is that, 'it was what it was'?" Ellen asked, honestly having no idea what it meant.

"The only kind I can give you."

"Dena..." Ellen began.

"Aunt Ellen, I know you want the best for me and that you want to see me happy. I am. And if every now and then someone passes through my life for a moment then fine, wonderful, I can't expect more than that."

"Dena," Louise began, "you have to expect more than that. Love comes into our lives in so many different ways, through family and friends and the precious jewels in a child's eyes. But love between a man and a woman is not to be brushed off like crumbs on a dinner table. It's precious. You deserve precious.

"Heaven knows I've had men pass through my life. Some I've loved and some I've loved to distraction. Each time I value myself to expect more. I deserved it. You need to value yourself and know that you're worthy to be loved and much, much more."

Dena nodded her understanding. "We didn't end well, so can we please change the subject? Tell me all about the fair," Dena said, avoiding the current topic.

Seeing her pain Ellen and Louise changed the subject and began telling her the highlights of the county fair. Soon laughter and joy returned as they described Dillon's reaction to the baby chicks and how he chased them around in an attempt to catch one.

A half hour later, when the conversation lapsed, Dena stood. "Thanks again for taking Dillon with you, he's going to be talking about his trip for the next two weeks. I'd better go and take care of his overnight bag." She picked up the construction worker backpack and headed up the back stairs.

Ellen looked at Louise then shook her head. "Pity, all that for nothing," she said miserably.

"No, not necessarily," Louise said, smiling. "I've seen this before, many times, my son, my grandsons, even his in-laws. Love can be tricky, you just have to give it a chance to grow. And just like the seedlings we plant, they need encouragement and just a bit of fertilizer." Louise winked.

"Okay, now you lost me. Fertilizer?" Ellen said, then paused and smiled. "Wait a minute, I get it. I need to get Julian back over here, don't I?"

Louise nodded. "But first give them a little time, some breathing room. Maybe they can get it together without us."

Ellen nodded her agreement. "How would you like a little company this weekend?" she asked.

"I'd love it, sounds perfect."

Chapter 18

First thing Monday morning Dena turned the corner and ran right into Julian. She'd been looking for him, she just didn't expect to be run over by him. "Hey," she said.

"Hey," he responded, then stepped aside.

"Uh, I'd like to speak with you if you have a few minutes," she said before he walked away.

"Business?" he asked.

"Not exactly," she said.

"I'm on my way out. Can it wait?"

She nodded. "Sure, I'll see you when you get back."

Julian didn't get back to the office for another three days. Off-site, he arrived early and left detailed business messages then came in late after she'd already gone. It was obvious he was avoiding her, which was fine because she wasn't sure what to say to him other than, "I'm sorry I misjudged you." So, they danced around each other for the next few days.

Finally, Dena stewed for as long as she could take it. It had been almost five days since they'd actually spoken to each other. Meanwhile she heard through the ever-present office grapevine that he and his brothers had thrown a massive party at their beach house over the weekend. As expected, photos circulated on cell phones all week. She even saw a couple herself.

Nothing radical or outrageous, it seemed to be a simple house party at a very nice beach house. That of course made her feel better. She even talked to Jordan about it when she ran into him in the hall. He cordially invited her down for the weekend and asked her to feel free to bring Dillon, as well, since he'd heard so much about him from Julian and a few other men working at her aunt's house.

That's when he told her that Julian had missed most of the party, first by working and then by hanging out on their boat. She wasn't sure why he divulged the information but she was glad he did.

By Friday afternoon Dena zombie-walked through the rest of the day. Then as soon as five o'clock came she got ready to leave for the day. Totally unlike her, she usually stayed until at least six or six-thirty. But tonight, with her aunt leaving to visit friends, she needed to put as much distance between her and Hamilton Development Corporation as possible.

She'd obviously made a fool of herself. Tainted by her own insecurities and anxieties, she'd immediately chosen to see Stephanie's side of an issue that wasn't even her business. She'd accused Julian then turned her back and walked out when he'd wanted to talk. Could she be any more insane?

He was obviously not the man Forester was, but still she clumped him right there.

Thankfully Julian was out of the office most of the week and the one time he stopped by to meet with his brothers in the evening she was off-site. But today, nearly a week later, she knew he was in his office. Tired of avoidance she decided to bite the bullet and just talk to him.

Saying she was sorry was the only thing she could think to say. She'd messed up big-time. When Stephanie stood there and told her about her son and Julian seemed not to care, she'd been stunned but she should have known better. Not every man is deceitful and not every mother maternal.

Dena knocked on Julian's open office door and waited. He looked up from an unrolled blueprint and removed his glasses. He looked so sexy sitting there, her first instinct was to vault over his desk and jump on top of him. But she didn't move. They just stared at each other a moment then he dropped his pen on the desk and stood.

"May I come in?" she asked.

"Come," he said, walking over to the door and closing it as soon as she entered.

"What is it, Dena?" he asked, walking back to his desk.

"I came to talk," she said.

"About?" He sat, picked up and rerolled the blueprint he'd been scanning.

"About us."

"I believe we did that already," he said, then pocketed his glasses.

"Okay, fair enough. Then I want to talk about what happened, what I said, what I thought."

"What's done is done. You had your say. I got that."

"No, you didn't. I was wrong. I know that now and I'm sorry. When I overheard the last of your conversation with Stephanie I was shocked and hurt. I couldn't believe what I was hearing. All I could think about was what I'm going through just to get recognition for my son. I underestimated you and that was a mistake."

"Yes, you did."

She nodded agreeably. "I haven't known you long, obviously, but I do know you could never be the man she described." He nodded. "And I just wanted to let you know that and that I'm sorry for even thinking you could be." She stood waiting for his acceptance. It didn't come.

"What's your game, Dena?"

"What do you mean? I don't understand."

"Yes, you do. First you're hot then you're cold. Then you want me then you don't. What exactly do you want?"

"I just want to say that I was wrong. I'm sorry."

"No, not good enough," he said stiffly.

Dena frowned and braced herself, she had expected him to accept her apology then move on, but he obviously wasn't going to. "Okay, I understand." She nodded and shrugged, then turned on her heels and headed to the closed door. She stopped. "I guess you were right from the start. This was a bad idea. But it was nice while it lasted." As soon as she reached for the doorknob, Julian spoke up.

"Dena, wait," he said, moving closer.

She sighed and half chuckled. "So much for my classy exit." She smirked jokingly.

He stood right behind her. "I would never intentionally hurt you, or Dillon, I hope you know that."

"I do and I'm sorry. And yes, I know that an apology won't

fix this." She turned to face him. "I overreacted and said horrible things, making a bad situation worse. I didn't mean to hurt you," she said.

"Didn't you?" he asked.

She went silent, looking away, feeling the pain in his eyes. "So where do we go from here?"

"To tell you the truth, I don't know."

Dena nodded sadly then backed up, turned and walked out. Moments later she grabbed her purse from her office and left for the day.

It was already after five-thirty and she had planned to spend the evening with Dillon. Ellen had gone to visit her friend, Mamma Lou, and after his weekend at the fair and her putting in extra hours at work she was looking forward to spending time with Dillon and having their traditional cookie night.

After a celebratory dinner of fish sticks, fries, coleslaw and ketchup, Dena and Dillon made cookies and sat in front of the television watching one of his favorite movies. Later they went into the yard to build the first fire in the new pit.

Surrounded by an almost-completed patio, the construction of the granite barbecue grill and outdoor stove was complete. An arbor-covered area had been built to accommodate seating for ten. The crew was still working on the large stone walkway leading around back, then to the greenhouse and the landscaping surrounding the outdoor living area.

Unfinished as it was, it was still beautifully done. The material used blended in perfectly with the surroundings. It looked as if a living and dining room had been picked up and placed outside.

Dena and Dillon gathered and piled several logs and smaller saplings into the pit, then stood back as the fire ignited. The open flame blazed, leaping and dancing against the dark evening. Dillon, after roasting and eating two marshmallows, was fascinated as he sat comfortably cuddled together on Dena's lap, his eyes glued to the wondrous blaze.

They sat and talked and sang and whispered secrets and looked up at the stars. She told him stories about growing up with the grandparents he'd never meet. "So they went away like my dad went away, right?" he asked.

"Yes, they did."

"And they're not coming back, right?"

"Yes, that's right, they're not coming back."

"And I won't never see them, right?"

"Yes, that's right."

"So can I have a puppy then, right?"

"No, you may not have a puppy. Nice try, buddy."

"Aw, Mom, I saw a puppy at the fair and he had a hat on and he could dance and he was funny and I want one of those for my birfday."

"No puppies until you're old enough to take care of them."

"When I'm four, right?"

"Try when you're fourteen."

Dillon scrunched his face to pout then crossed his arms in front of his chest. "No fair."

Dena smiled. "Okay, when you're thirteen then."

"Yea," he said, then yawned slowly.

"Dillon, do you remember when we talked about moving away right after your birthday party?" He nodded. "Good, is that still okay with you?" she asked. He nodded again. "Good, California is beautiful. They have warm weather, and Disneyland, and mountains and lots and lots of beaches with tons of sand." He nodded again.

"Can we go to California now?"

Dena smiled, thankful and encouraged that he so eagerly wanted to go. "Not just yet, but right after your birthday party we're going to pack up our things and go, okay."

He nodded. "'Kay." Then moments later, he yawned and lay back, tucked against her shoulder. A few moments after that he drifted off to sleep. Not wanting the moment to end, she continued to sit out and enjoy the dimming fire and the warm summer night, holding him tight.

She relaxed back in the chair and listened to the crickets, watched the fireflies and gazed up at the stars. It was a perfect evening and a perfect night. The only thing missing was someone to share it with. She looked down at Dillon in her arms. Her little boy was her joy but having someone around, someone like Julian, would be…

"Dena."

Her heart jumped as she turned quickly, recognizing Julian's voice and seeing him standing behind her in the darkness. It seemed as if she'd conjured him from her thoughts. "Julian?"

"Yes, it's me," he said, stepping closer.

"Hi," she whispered.

"Hi," he said as he moved closer to her. "I went to your office after we talked, you left early today."

"Yes I did. I had…"

"Cookie night, I remember," he said. "How was it?"

"Good, we came, we saw, we ate too many oatmeal raisin with nuts."

"Um, sounds good and looks like it knocked the little fellow out."

Dena looked down at Dillon still comfortably asleep in her arms. "He had fun," she said then paused. "I didn't know you were coming here tonight."

"Neither did I," he answered. "Your aunt left an urgent message at my house that there was something wrong with the fire pit."

"Aunt Ellen isn't here."

He walked over, seeing the last embers crackling in the bottom. He knelt down and looked it over carefully. "Looks okay to me."

Dena instantly recognized Mamma Lou and her aunt's interference. "Actually, I think it's probably fine now."

"Still, I'd like to check it to make sure."

"Seriously, I wouldn't worry about it," she said.

"If there's a problem I'd rather I take care of it than your aunt, I've seen her workmanship. Quite frankly, it scares me."

Dena smiled at his humor. "Ordinarily I'd agree but I think my aunt and her friend Mamma Lou were doing a bit of matchmaking by getting you over here tonight."

"Matchmaking," he repeated.

"They took Dillon to the fair last week in hopes that I use the opportunity to go out and..." She paused, searching for the right word.

"And you did, we did," he said, nodding and finishing her sentence. "But what about tonight?"

"I told them that things didn't exactly end well with us. So this might be their way of planting seeds to rectify matters."

"I see," Julian said. "Where is Mrs. Peyton? I rang the front doorbell and no one answered. That's when I came back here."

"Aunt Ellen is in Virginia visiting a friend on Crescent

Island. She'll be back next week. She must have called you before she left, knowing that you'd come over tonight."

Julian smiled. "So she's taken up matchmaking instead of house remodeling, I guess the trade-off is worth it."

"Speak for yourself. I don't like being manipulated."

"She just wants the best for you."

"And she seems to think the best is you."

"Is that so bad?" he asked as he walked over and sat in the seat beside her. He looked down, seeing Dillon asleep in her arms. He smiled. "He looks so peaceful lying there."

Still not responding to his last question, Dena leaned in and kissed his forehead. "Yes, he does."

"So how did he enjoy the fair?" he asked.

"He had a great time. It's already on our schedule for next year."

"Maybe I can tag along, too."

She looked at him in the muted darkness. "Maybe it would be best if we keep our relationship purely business."

"Dena, about this afternoon," he began. "I guess I'm a little gun-shy when it comes to apologies. They never really make things right. Most times they're just words spoken to cover up lies and deceit."

"Wow, that was harsh."

"Yeah, I guess it is. Stephanie isn't my only mistake. After we divorced I got engaged a year later. That was disaster number two. Then I started seeing a nice woman who turned out to be the second bride of Chucky."

Dena laughed, taken off guard by his humorous comparison. Julian looked at her oddly.

"I'm sorry," she said, realizing that her laughter was probably inappropriate.

"No. You have a nice laugh, you should do it more often."

"I wasn't laughing at you really, it just sounds so…" Sh paused and sighed. "Heartbreaking."

"Yeah, tell me about it."

She smiled. "Look at us, a couple of heartbroken misfits." H smiled and nodded. "So that's when you did the celibate thing."

"Yeah. And it worked until you came along." He looke off, shaking his head. "I don't know, there's something abou you, about us together that…I don't know."

"Yeah, I agree. We do seem to have that chemistry."

"Not a bad thing, though," he said, turning back to her.

"No, not at all."

"So maybe we can get past this," he said. She nodded. " like you a lot, way too much."

"Me, too, way too much," she said. Dillon stirred in he arms. He woke up and smiled at her.

"Hi, Mom," he muttered.

"Hi, sweetie. Ready to go to bed?"

"No," he said, yawning then looking around, seeing tha they were outside and that Julian was there. He smiled.

"Hey, buddy, how you doing?"

"'Kay," Dillon said.

"Looks like you're sleepy." Dillon nodded. "Come on, I'l give you a ride upstairs." Dillon unraveled his arms fron Dena's neck and reached out to Julian. "Uh—" Julian grunte "—you're getting heavy."

Dillon nodded and wrapped his arms around Julian's nec and held tight. Dena stood and walked over to the back door She opened it and allowed them to pass. Julian continue through the basement to the kitchen then up the back stairs She followed, then pointed out Dillon's bedroom.

She pulled his pajamas from the dresser while Julian laid him down on the bed. Dena helped Dillon remove his shirt and then took off his sneakers and socks. She started to continue then stopped. "Mom, I'm a big boy now. I can do it by myself."

"You're right, I forgot." She straightened up and stepped away. Dillon grabbed his pajamas and went into the bathroom.

She picked up his shirt and socks and dropped them in the hamper then she pulled his covers back and took the teddy bear from the shelf and laid it on the bed. When she finished, she looked up at Julian who was standing by the window looking at her.

"You're a really good mom."

"I like to think so," she said, walking over to him.

He reached out his arms to draw her close, she tucked into the strength of his body with ease. Being there felt like coming home. "Mmm," she hummed quietly, "this feels good."

"Yes, it does," Julian said as he looked out the window. "Nice view," he said, seeing an unobstructed view of the barbecue grill in the backyard.

"Yeah, at times it's even better than nice." They both knew she was talking about the first time they'd met.

"I wondered what upstairs window you were looking through. I thought it might have been your bedroom."

"Nah, the oak tree is in the way. I tried."

They chuckled as he held her tighter and stayed pressed together like that until Dillon returned a few minutes later. He got down on his knees and said his prayers then climbed into bed.

"You all set, sweetie?"

"Yeah, I'm all set," Dillon said, yawning.

"Okay, pleasant dreams. I love you."

"I love you, too, Mom."

She kissed his forehead and he snuggled down, then she helped him with his teddy bear. She leaned up and looked at Julian then nodded. He walked over to the bed.

"Good night, little buddy," he said.

"Good night. I love you, too, Toolyian Hamydon."

Julian stopped cold. He didn't expect to be so affected by the simple words from an almost-four-year-old. "I love you, too," he whispered softly, then followed Dena out.

She stopped in the hall, her back was to him. "Julian, I know how hard it is to trust," she said completely out of the blue, "I guess I'm just not good at the one-night-stand thing."

He rested his hands on her shoulders then dipped his mouth to her ear. "Who says we were a one-night stand?" They each went still and quiet. "Is that okay?" he asked.

She nodded. "Yeah, that's more than okay."

"Good, so now that we got that straight, what are you going to do to make it up to me?"

She smiled. "I don't know. What do I have to do?" she asked, still without turning around.

"You'll think of something."

She turned, wrapped her arms around his neck and kissed him passionately. He put his arms around her waist and pulled her close, bracing her between the wall and his body. She rubbed into him as their lower bodies met. He reached up and began caressing her breasts, teasing her nipples between his fingers.

Dena closed her eyes, feeling the tantalizing sensation of his hands on her body again. He felt so good, too good.

Moments later they stopped almost simultaneously, panting hard to catch their breath. Both knowing that her bedroom was just down the hall but that Dillon was in the next room. He stepped back, took her hand and together, wordlessly, they went back outside and sat beneath the stars.

Chapter 19

"Good morning, Adel. I'm putting you on speakerphone, this is on the record," Gaylord said.

"I hope this is good news," Adel said impatiently. "It's been over a week, I've already had the room remodeled and a new wardrobe designed and ordered. I've hired a nanny and enrolled him in several character-building classes."

"I preface this as a warning, Adel. What you've requested is highly uncommon and could seriously backfire in our faces. And when I say 'our faces,' I mean your face. This maneuver could be devastating to the firm if it fails. We'll look like kid-nappers if this goes public, which I'm certain it would since we'll be filing this motion in family court and there is no such thing as a sealed motion in some chambers. I need to make sure you're aware of all this. The other partners will not tolerate this much longer, particularly if it goes public."

"You forget, Gaylord, I run the other partners. They tolerate what I tell them to," she said.

"Adel, you have no legitimate standing if they decide to force the issue. Having said that, I believe we might have something," Gaylord reported. "Dena Graham never went back for her final psychiatric examination as required by the courts. In addition to that she still has her sleeping pill prescription refilled regularly and her unusual behavior as witness in our conference room might suggest possible latent mental problems, more serious than we first expected."

"Excellent, build on that," Adel said.

"Well, since this condition has presumably gone untreated for almost four years, we can file that we're highly suspicious of her maternal abilities given her current deteriorating mental condition."

"Perfect." She smiled and nodded.

"I'm still waiting on a more up-to-date report of her medication usage." He opened and read from his file. "I have a record of antidepressants for clinical depression and sleeping pills for frequent insomnia. I've already attained information from our therapist regarding suspected abusive tendencies."

"Yes, that will work."

"Added to that, we've already recorded her great-aunt's tendency for emergency police and fire activity at the house where the child stays. This could be a safety issue, putting him in mortal danger. You'd be saving his life. In our opinion, the boy, Dillon Graham, is better off with his paternal grandmother for the time being."

"What do you mean, for the time being?" Adel questioned.

"We'll start off asking for temporary custody then file for sole permanent custody in a few months."

"I want sole custody now."

"It doesn't work like that, Adel."

"Make it work like that."

"There's nothing I can do. This maneuver is already risky The success of you actually getting temporary, let alone full custody, of a child you never met and adamantly denied his entire life, is remote at best."

"I don't want to hear that, Gaylord."

"I'm sorry but you need to. As your legal representative I suggest that if you want a lasting relationship with your grandchild you need to work out something with his mother. That means you and Dena need to reconcile and come to some reasonable resolve."

"I told you to do one thing, get my grandson…"

"I can't work miracles, even for you, Adel. This is family court and family law, Dena's backyard. She owns the play-ground here."

"Well then buy the damn school, I don't care. Just get my grandson."

"We'll file as soon as the information we requested comes in."

She went silent, not at all pleased with the situation. "Fine file the paperwork as soon as you can, just see that I get sole custody by his birthday."

"I can't promise that, Adel."

"I'm guessing you can," she said. "I want this finished."

"I'll keep you apprised of the situation."

"See that you do," she insisted.

"Adel, as I have stated on numerous occasions, we need to cut our losses and bring Dena Graham into the fold. She's an attorney, we can at least make her a junior partner with full voting rights, bonuses and ample pro bono work would be an excellent offering. That combined with everything else she's entitled to as Nelson's sole surviving daughter-in-law and Forester's widow is considerable."

"You know how I feel about that, Gaylord. I don't want her anywhere near my law firm."

"Of course, as always, just a legal suggestion offered for your protection," he said stiffly.

"Oh, one more thing, how many men has she seen and been involved with since Forester was killed?"

Gaylord flipped through the notes he'd received earlier. "According to this file, she hasn't seen or been physically involved with anyone, not for years, although it looks like there's currently a relationship with a construction worker, Julian Hamilton."

"Tsk." She sucked her teeth. "A construction worker. Good, then he's of no consequence but then how typically pathetic. She goes from my Forester to a common house painter. Has the relationship progressed to be serious?"

"The file doesn't say."

"I don't want my grandson raised under those circumstances. Keep me informed." She hung up, smiling. In less than three weeks she was going to get her life back. She picked up the phone and called a party planner she'd chosen for the birthday and coming home celebration. She detailed exactly what she wanted, a nice proper gathering of twenty or so children from the best families with a sweet Disney-type theme.

She walked down the hall to his bedroom. It was Forester's old room. It would be perfect. She opened the door and stepped inside, marveling at the remarkable job she'd done. She had already had it redesigned and remodeled. The bed was Forester's, a four-poster oak with brand-new designer sheets and down comforter. The bookcases were lined with books she wanted him to read, none of the trash literature for him. He would be the perfect gentleman, just like Forester and Kirkland. This time she would get it right. He would listen to her and do exactly what she said. She nodded her approval; everything was ready for her grandson.

Gaylord hung up and pushed the stop button on the phone recorder. He opened and pulled out the small tape. Of late, he taped most conversations with Adel. Being prudent in the face of adversity was just smart business. Physical proof and credible witnesses were a litigator's best offense and defense. If and when Adel went down, he had no intention of going down with her.

He looked at the three men seated at the table and nodded. Three senior law partners of Graham, Whitman & Morris returned his gesture. "I'll have transcripts by Monday morning."

"Thank you for bringing this to our attention and for your assistance in this matter," one of the men said.

"Do what she wants for the time being," another one of the partners said, "but first and foremost, we must protect this firm."

"Understood, any suggestions?" one of the partners offered.

"Actually, sir, yes. Perhaps we might head this off, just in case," Gaylord said as he handed out a proposal. "I've taken the liberty of drawing these up."

The three partners looked the paper over. Each nodded in turn. "Agreed."

The three men looked to Gaylord. He nodded. "I understand, I'll make the call," Gaylord said.

"Your loyalty in this matter will not be forgotten."

"Thank you, sir."

They stood and left. Gaylord sat and smiled, feeling no ense of remorse. As a nonvoting partner he was given Adel s his sole client to placate because she was the widow of the ast founding partner and therefore acquired full veto and oting status and a large enough block of shares to carry the oard. He served her well, bowing to every whim and doing very menial job she deemed necessary with regard to her velfare.

But, as well, he'd warned Adel repeatedly that her single-ocused behavior would be her downfall. He placed the small ape in an envelope, sealed it and placed it in his in-bin. His ecretary would transcribe it into transcript form first thing Monday morning.

As always, the voting partners would each receive a copy nd proceed accordingly. That would be the end of Adel raham's four-year tyrannical reign of Graham, Whitman & Morris.

The construction site of the Kellerman Building was wesome.

Dillon was on cloud nine. Having not told him what they were oing or where they were going, he was beside himself with joy s they met up with Julian in front of an ongoing project.

The site was enormous and even though it was near midday aturday there were several workers there. Julian handed ena a hard hat then bent down to fit Dillon's brand-new hard at to his head. After a few adjustments, Dillon slapped his at several times then nodded his approval.

Dena adjusted her hard hat and put on her shatter-proof

protective eyewear. "Thank you for this," she said after ad justing Dillon's eyewear. "You're incredible."

He winked. "I get that a lot."

"I bet you do."

Loud chuckling laughter interrupted them. They looke down then across the quad, seeing a huge dump truck empt its load into a metal bin. There was a loud crash then a dee crunch and a moaning-type roar. Dillon laughed again.

"Not exactly a warm and fuzzy Disney kind of guy i he," he said.

"No, not nearly enough action for him," she said.

They each took a hand, putting Dillon between them, an headed to the building under construction and the grate elevator on the side. "I know we're not going up there," she said

"We are," Julian informed her.

"No way," she insisted.

"Mom, please, please, pretty please," Dillon said.

Dena looked at Julian; he chuckled as he steered he toward the elevators. She was obviously outnumbered.

"Wow, look at that," Dillon said, pulling at Julian's han to get his attention. While on the grated elevator they watche a huge crane pick up and lift a large load of material to a upper level platform then continue to an upper floor. "Did yo see that? Wow," Dillon said breathlessly, excited. "Wow."

He had one small finger intertwined in the grate an giggled and laughed each time the elevator stopped at an as cending floor. Dena looked out and down cautiously. "Aren we up here kind of high?"

"This is our floor," Julian said as the elevator stopped. H opened the roll gateway and lifted and shifted the bracing gat He swung the door open then closed it when they stepped ou

"Wow," Dillon whispered continuously.

They walked down a half skeletal-like hall into a partially applied drywall room then continued to another open area. Completely enclosed, there were large windows across the back half of the room.

"Are you sure it's okay for us to be here?" Dena asked.

"It's okay," Julian said as Dillon half dragged them across he open space to the windows.

"Look down there," he said, excitedly pointing to the small cars and people on the street. Completely engrossed, he giggled and laughed full-out.

Julian looked at Dena. She looked at him. She couldn't turn away even if she wanted to. The man who had come into her life when she needed him had just stolen her heart.

She watched as he took her free hand and lifted it to his ips then kissed her. She smiled as his eyes stayed locked nd unwavering. She had no idea what follows love but the enderness and heartfelt joy she experienced with him made her wonder.

"Mom, look at that," Dillon said, getting her attention. he looked away to follow where he pointed.

Julian didn't. Every minute with her was too precious to e denied. For so long he had searched for a woman to fill im completely and all he'd ever found were selfish, self-entered spoiled brats looking out for only one person, them-elves.

Dena was different. She was nurturing and kind, a loving nother, a devoted niece and the woman he wanted in his life. And she was sexy as hell. The night they'd spent together consumed him from the start. Her confession to coming over o seduce him without knowing how was just that, the seduc-

tion. She'd had him captivated with desire from the momen
she'd walked in the garage.

"This is incredible," Dena said, agreeing with Dillon.

"Come on, this way." He took her hand and Dillon's hand
and led them through another open space. As soon as Den
entered, she stopped and smiled. "Aw, wow, this is beautiful."

"You like it?"

"Yes, very much." She started laughing. Dillon looked u
at her strangely. Then back to the picnic lunch spread out o
the makeshift picnic table. He didn't get the joke.

"Tell me, little buddy," Julian began happily as they sa
down, "what's your all-time favorite food in the world?"

"Pizza, yea," he squealed, clapping his hands.

"After pizza," Julian said.

"Hot dogs, yea," Dillon called, clapping his hands again

"Uh, after hot dogs," Julian stammered slowly.

"Fish sticks, yea," he cheered again while clapping his hands

Dena began laughing. The conversation between the two o
them had become comical. Julian shot a quick glance at her. Sh
shrugged, shaking her head innocently. "Okay, I'll tell you wha
how about hamburgers and fries?" he said, finally relenting.

"Hamburgers and fries, yea," Dillon cheered again an
clapped his hands as Julian opened the picnic basket besid
him and pulled out a clear plastic container with a hambur
ger and fries inside. "Hamburgers and fries, yea." He ap
plauded again.

Julian opened the container and placed the burger and frie
on Dillon's plate. He offered to cut it up for him to make i
easier to handle but Dillon declined. They bowed their head
briefly then he dug in, taking a huge bite while using his thi
fries as building sticks.

"He's easy to please, hope his mom is."

"You know she is," she said sexy and low.

Julian looked at her in a way that made her blood instantly boil. He licked his lips and a flash of excitement shuddered through him as thoughts of his kisses on her body swirled in her mind. Forgetting to breathe she exhaled slowly.

"Is that a seduction?" he asked quietly.

"Let's say it's an open invitation."

"I will be taking you up on that."

"I'll look forward to it."

He nodded and reached down to get two more plastic containers, each containing hamburgers and fries. He opened a small container of chocolate milk and gave it to Dillon then opened a liter of ginger ale and poured Dena and himself a glass. "Cheers." They clinked plastic cups and a small party of three on the twenty-second floor of the Kellerman Building downtown began.

An hour later they gathered the trash and picnic basket and headed back down to the ground level. They took a short tour of the site-planning trailer then Julian followed Dena back to her aunt's house. She parked her car as Julian got out and said goodbye.

"Thank you, Julian, for everything, it was a wonderful day, we really enjoyed ourselves."

"Thank you," Dillon chimed.

"So maybe we can do this again?"

"Yes, I'd like that a lot, I think we both would."

Chapter 20

A week of madding mornings and hectic afternoons blurred by in a rapid succession of activity. It wasn't until the evenings that Dena truly appreciated the blessing of her life. She and Julian went out, stayed in or joined with Dillon or sometimes not; they reveled in the delight of being together. Movies in front of the television or on the big screen, dinners out, dinners in, dancing beneath the stars in the park or in the yard or playground, the three of them were inseparable.

Dena's desk was piled high with paperwork, invoices and requisition forms. She needed to assign duties, verify materials, order supplies and check the job sites. She spent most of the morning on the phone and was delighted when Julian stopped by midafternoon to say hi. He literally made her day.

"What are you doing this evening?" he asked, poking his head in her office.

"Nothing, why?" she asked.

He walked in and closed the door behind him. "I have three tickets to the local minor-league baseball game this evening."

"Wow, really." He nodded, pulling the tickets from his pocket and fanning them out. "Are you asking us out?"

"Yes I am, interested?" He came around to sit, then leaned back against her desk.

"Yes," she said happily. "What time?"

"Wait," he said. "Didn't you tell me that your aunt was out of town this week? Who's watching Dillon while you're here at work?"

"The same person who has been watching him since we got here a few months ago," she said. "There's a nice-size day-care center around the corner from Aunt Ellen's house. We were passing one day and Dillon saw the kids out and wanted to stop and play. I arranged for him to go in the mornings for a few hours. So when I got this job, I simply extended his time there. He loves it and he needs to be with other kids socially."

"Not bad," he said, nodding.

"Glad you approve. So what time?"

"Right after work, around five-thirty or so," he said. "We'll get to the ballpark early, let Dillon meet some of the players then grab something to eat before the game starts."

"Sounds like fun, I'm looking forward to it."

He reached out, grabbed her hand and pulled her up to his body. He wrapped his arms around her and held her securely against the desk. The kiss was expected but the instant passion was a surprise to both of them. When the kiss finally ended, they looked at each as if they were about to rip clothes off. "Probably not a good idea, huh," he said, rasping after the wild embrace.

"Exciting, yes, definitely, but no, probably not," she answered breathlessly.

"Pity, I'd like to try that with you one day," he said as he leisurely ran his forefinger down the front of her blouse, ending right between the crevice of her breasts.

"An afternoon tryst, why, Mr. Hamilton, that would compromise my genteel sensibilities."

"Mmm." Deep and low, he moaned in her ear then whispered, "I like that, and I'd like to compromise a few other genteel senses, as well." She giggled as he leaned in, bending her back onto the desk and lying on top of her. "Right here, right now," he added, nibbling her earlobe.

She melted, closing her eyes and wrapping her arms around his neck, holding him tight. A sudden flow of adrenaline surged through her body.

The offer was more than tempting self-indulgence. The risk, the thrill, the danger, the idea of a forbidden rendezvous behind closed doors excited her. But knowing, of course, that neither one would dare compromise the office, they laughed heartily as he helped her up from the desk.

"What am I going to do with you?" she questioned.

"Fall in love with me of course," he said poetically.

"Too late, I'm already there," she said offhandedly, then froze realizing what she'd just confessed. They looked at each other as the fun exciting moment passed and the seriousness of her words penetrated deep. "Julian…" she started, shaking her head from side to side.

"No," he said, shaking his head, "don't say anything."

She closed her eyes, miserably knowing that what she'd said was in fact what she was feeling. She was in love with Julian, that much was undeniably true. But she didn't want to be. Her life was shattered and out of control. How could she possibly have time for love?

"Dena..."

"Julian, wait before you say anything..." she began as her phone started ringing. They both looked at the annoyance then back at each other.

"We'll talk tonight," he said, then kissed her tenderly and let her go.

As soon as he left the office Dena sat down in slow motion. The phone had stopped ringing, denoting that her automatic answering machine had picked up.

Was she nuts? She'd just confessed to being in love with her boss. It was bad enough that they had a physical relationship and now a relationship that included her son, but now she tells him that she loves him.

But it was the truth. She did love him.

She sat pondering the reality of her feelings when her phone rang again. She picked up. "Dena Graham."

"Dena, there's someone here to see you. She doesn't have an appointment but she says that you might be expecting her. Her name is Lynn Brice."

"Lynn. Sure, I'll be right down."

Dena cleared her desk and immediately took the escalator to the front lobby. Lynn stood talking intently on her cell phone. The flash of anger in her eyes gave Dena a chill. She nodded but kept talking on the cell. Dena motioned for her to follow, she did. By the time they got to Dena's office, Lynn was off the phone.

"I know trouble when I see it," Dena said.

"We have trouble," Lynn said.

"What happened?" Dena asked.

"Can we go someplace to talk privately?"

"Lynn, just tell me."

"In a nutshell—" she pulled out a legal document and handed it to Dena but summed up its contents "—on behalf of Adel Graham, Graham, Whitman & Morris has filed for protective custody of the minor Dillon Graham."

"What?" Dena said, unfolding the papers.

"I'm sorry, Dena. Adel has petitioned the court for temporary custody of Dillon. But don't worry, I got this."

"What? How can she do that?" Dena said as a swell of air left her body. She staggered, stepped back then stopped breathing.

"We have a hearing in a few days."

Dena put her hand to her chest, trying desperately to hear the words coming out of Lynn's mouth. "No, wait a minute, she can't do that. How, on what grounds?" she asked.

"Dena, breathe, calm down, this is just another one of her games. We'll beat this, okay," Lynn said, standing and moving to her side.

"She's gone too far this time. She had Forester and Kirkland and Nelson, and now she wants my son. No, not this time," she said.

"Good, that's what I want to hear. Get pissed, we can use it. We're going to need that determination. And we're gonna win this once and for all. So stay focused, you know I've got your back. Do nothing until you hear from me. I have a few ideas I'm working through."

Dena nodded. Lynn was the perfect person. She was just as angry. As Dillon's godmother there was no way she would let anything happen to him.

"Now I need to do some planning. As I said, I already have

somethings lined up. I can come by your aunt's house this evening. We can talk then."

"Okay," Dena said, nodding.

"Besides, I haven't seen my little fellow in weeks. How is the little Dill-weed doing?"

"He's still on cloud nine after spending the day with Julian at the construction site last weekend, then hanging out all week…"

"Whoa, whoa, back up. You and Julian? Mr. You-know-what?"

Dena half smiled. "I took your advice. All of it."

"Now that's what I'm talking about. That's the Dena I remember, bold and audacious. You want it, go get it. That's exactly what we're gonna need up against Adel. So listen, I seriously want more details later, but in the meantime, I need to go and check some things." She stood and headed to the door.

"I'll walk you out."

Julian and Darius walked toward the building just as Lynn and Dena exited. "There she is," Darius said, seeing Lynn with Dena.

"There who is?" Julian questioned, then looked over to see what drew his brother's attention.

"Ladies," Darius said smoothly, "good afternoon."

"Hello," Lynn said, brightening instantly. Dena half smiled then nodded her greeting to both.

"Nice to see you again, Mrs. Brice," Darius said.

"That's Ms. Brice, but please call me Lynn."

"Lynn, it is. This is my brother, Julian. Julian, Lynn Brice."

Julian, distracted by Dena's morose expression realized

he'd been introduced then quickly greeted and shook Lynn's hand. "Nice to meet you, Lynn," he said.

"A real pleasure," she responded, smiling, knowing far more about him than he would possibly imagine.

"So, Lynn, what brings you this way? I thought you worked in the city," Darius said, turning his full attention to her.

"I do. I was in the area and just popped out to see Dena."

"So you two have known each other for a while?" Darius asked.

"Since college, then we went to law school together."

"You're a lawyer, too?" Darius questioned, smiling.

"Yes, I am."

"What a coincidence, I was just telling Julian that I'm looking for a good lawyer," Darius fabricated. Julian looked at him, having no idea what he was talking about. "May I have your card? I'd like to talk to you later, if you're free."

She reached into her briefcase and pulled out a business card and handed it to him. "Actually, Darius, I'm working a pretty tight caseload at the moment but I'll be glad to refer you elsewhere if you're in a hurry."

"No," Darius said quickly, reading the card, noting her cell phone number. "No hurry at all." He reached into his jacket pocket and pulled out his business card and gave it to her. She read the raised lettering, nodded and smiled at him. "I'll be in touch," he promised sincerely.

She nodded. "I look forward to hearing from you."

They smiled knowingly as Julian focused only on Dena who was completely distracted. She stood uncharacteristically silent as the conversation carried on around her.

"I need to get back to the office," Lynn said. "It was nice meeting you, Julian."

"Likewise," he said.

"And very nice seeing you again, Darius."

"My pleasure," he said.

Dena nodded silently and walked away. Lynn followed.

Darius watched Lynn and Julian observed Dena as they stood at her car talking. He knew there was something going on. Having just spoken to Dena moments earlier, her demeanor was like night and day. "Are we going in or do you want to make love to her right here in the parking lot?" Julian asked Darius, who was still eyeing Lynn.

"In time," Darius said, slowly backing up to walk away. Lynn glanced over just before he turned. They smiled in each other's direction, knowing that there would certainly be more to come. "I guess I could ask you the same question. So what'd you do this time?" Darius asked as he and Julian went into the building and took the escalator to the executive level.

"What are you talking about?" Julian questioned.

"To Dena, she looks shell-shocked. What's wrong?"

"I have no idea. I just spoke with her a few minutes ago, she was fine. We're going to a baseball game tonight with her son."

"Ah, yes, Dillon, I'm looking forward to meeting this little charmer."

Julian smiled. "He could probably teach you a thing or two about women."

"What do you mean?" Darius said.

"Could you be any more obvious outside?" Julian asked.

"I have no idea what you're talking about."

"Yeah, right," Julian said sarcastically as they entered the office.

"What's up?" Jordan said, looking up from his desk as Darius and Julian entered his office.

"Ask him," they both said.

"Never mind," Jordan said, preferring to stay neutral, "let's get started."

Darius and Julian nodded then took a seat across from Jordan's desk as he handed them each a folder. They opened it to find the preliminary proposal for the next major job. He outlined the basic ideas then turned his large-screen monitor to face them and continued with a shortened PowerPoint presentation. As Jordan continued discussing the details of progression for his intended presentation, Darius nodded, following and agreeing. Julian, on the other hand, only heard every other word he said.

Dena stayed on his mind. She'd told him that she loved him and he didn't respond, and it looked like that lack of response had hurt her. Remembering the expression on her face was distressing.

Fifteen minutes into the meeting Jordan stood and unrolled several blueprints.

"I need to step out for a minute," Julian said. "I'll be back in a few." He stood and walked out.

Jordan looked at Darius questioningly.

"Dena," Darius said.

Jordan shook his head, understanding. "I wish they'd get themselves together and stop dancing around. We all know where it's leading. That reminds me, I need to get my tux refitted."

"Ditto." That said, they continued with the meeting.

Chapter 21

Julian went directly to Dena's office. He knocked and waited, then knocked and entered. One quick look around confirmed that she hadn't yet returned. He checked his watch then walked over to the window and glanced out. The parking lot view of the visitors' section was obstructed. Slightly annoyed and frustrated, he sat down and waited.

His thoughts centered on Dena's lackluster demeanor and troubled expression. The easy, joking frivolity of just fifteen minutes earlier had completely vanished. As Lynn and Darius obviously flirted, she was miles away. Then it hit him, the last utterances was with regard to her feelings for him. She loved him. Certainly that had left each of them somewhat thoughtful but this was something different.

There may be a case that the two of them didn't know each other long, but he knew her well enough. And there was definitely something else wrong. He stood and paced the floor, pausing to look out at her window, anxiously expecting her return.

He loved her. He knew his heart was connected to hers and when she hurt, he hurt. Lynn, her attorney friend, obviously had something to do with her demeanor. Helpless for the moment, the only thing he could do was to wait.

Dena had gone numb by the time she got back to her office. She walked in without even seeing Julian standing there. She stood in the center of the room and just stared at the back of the picture frame.

Julian, standing at the window, turned as soon as she entered. "Dena," he said as he walked over to her and touched her hand.

She looked at him as if for the first time.

"Are you okay?" he asked.

"Not even close," she said in barely a whisper.

"Dena, about what you said earlier, that you love me. I can see how distressed you are and I just want to…"

"I can't do that now," she said.

"Yes, this isn't the place but we need to…"

"No, that's not the problem."

"What is it then?"

She shook her head.

"You don't have to be here, why don't you go home early, we'll manage okay and we can talk about this tonight."

"No, I need this. Lynn can handle everything else. I need the distraction of work. I just can't lose this time."

"Lose what this time?" he asked. Her telephone rang. She reached for it. "Let the machine get it," he said.

"No, I'll get it." She picked up; it was obviously work-related. She moved behind her desk and pressed a key on her keyboard, the computer and monitor came to life. She sat down and went to work.

Julian watched her, knowing that behind the tough fighter exterior was a melting heart. Whatever was going on had shaken her to the core. And if she wasn't going to tell him, then maybe Lynn would.

"I'll see you this evening," he said, and left.

Dena opened her mouth to cancel the evening's activities but Julian was already halfway out the door. She made a mental note to call him later and cancel. Not at all paying attention to the caller, Dena asked if she could get back to them then hung up.

Alone again in her office, she picked up and read the letter several times. Each time she got madder and madder. The audacity of Adel to set her sights on Dillon was monumental. Yet, given her vindictiveness, she should have seen this coming. It was a desperate ploy by a desperate woman.

Right now she needed to appear strong and in control. This was no longer just her life, this was her son's life and his future. And there was no way she was going to allow the law to just hand him over to Adel to raise.

She hugged her arms around her body, feeling the protectiveness of one. Her whole world was falling apart and she was alone in this.

There was Julian, but he wasn't part of this drama and she didn't want him to know what was going on. He was very explicit when he talked about his feelings on legal proceedings and lawyers. He'd been hoodwinked by a shyster lawyer then again with a false claim of paternity, the last thing she wanted to do was to drag him into her drama.

So the phantoms of her past continued to haunt her, to rape her new life and destroy any semblance of peace and happiness she might find. Adel concocting this new torture only proved that she was still a bitter, manipulative woman.

Dena looked at the clock. It was just four-thirty. She refused to leave early and allow Adel to win. So she reached over, picked up the phone and returned the earlier call then busied herself in front of the computer. Half an hour later she walked out of the building with the other employees. Granted it was still extremely early for her, but she needed to see her son now.

"I need Lynn's phone number," Julian said as soon as he walked in Jordan's office. He looked at Darius impatiently.

Darius looked at him as if he were crazy. The brothers had never in the past crossed each other when it came to women, so Julian's newfound interest in Lynn, knowing of Darius' interest, was unfounded. "Excuse me?" Darius said.

"I need Lynn Brice's phone number now. Something's going on with Dena and I need to know what."

"Out of luck there, bro," Jordan said, "she's not going to tell you anything, girlfriends never betray a trust."

"She's also an attorney," Darius added.

"Well, in that case, you're doubly out of luck."

"She'll tell me, every lawyer has a price."

"Not all attorneys are the same, haven't you learned that yet," Darius said, handing over Lynn's business card.

Julian punched the numbers into his cell phone and waited for her to pick up. She didn't, an answering service did. He left a message that he needed to talk to her as soon as possible. Then hung up and handed Darius the card.

"Why don't you just ask Dena what's up?" Jordan asked.

"She won't tell me. The only thing she said was that she didn't want to lose him."

"Who's the him she doesn't want to lose?"

"I have no idea," Julian said.

"Doesn't she have a son?" Jordan asked.

"Dillon," Julian and Darius said.

Julian's eyes widened as he dashed out of the office.

"That's a man in serious love," Darius said.

"I couldn't agree more," Jordan replied as he handed Darius a hundred-dollar bill.

"Aunt Ellen," Dena called as she hurried inside.

"Out here," Ellen hollered from the back porch.

Dena walked outside to her aunt. "Would you watch Dillon this evening please?" she said.

"Sure, of course. Truth be told, I missed that little charmer while I was away, and Louise fell head over heels in love with him. She's already talking about matchmaking with her great-granddaughter," she said happily. "Is Julian taking you out?" She looked up from her planting, seeing Dena's desperate expression for the first time. "Dena, what wrong? What happened?"

"Lynn came by the office earlier. She gave me a letter from Graham, Whitman & Morris. Adel wants temporary custody of Dillon."

"She wants what?" Ellen asked, not sure what she heard.

"She's decided that I'm an unfit mother and that she's better suited to raise my son."

"Oh, my goodness, she really is insane," Ellen concluded.

"She wants to corrupt and control him like she did her own sons and her husband. Nelson was completely whipped,

Kirkland was an alcoholic and Forester was both. But she's not doing that to my son. She'll have to kill me first," Dena said. By the time she finished talking tears were streaming down her face.

"She'll have to kill the two of us," Ellen said, hurrying to her niece's side. Dena breathed hard and fast as she looked around like a rabbit in a foxhole. "Sit down, child, you're about to jump out of your skin."

"She can't have him."

"She won't," Ellen whispered gently. "She's alone, marinating in her own hatred and self-pity, and she's desperate."

"Yes, she is. But that doesn't mean she won't win or at the very least tie this up in court for years. The state laws are clear. Dillon would be sent to foster care. And that's not happening."

Ellen sat down, suddenly finding her legs weak. "What did Lynn say to do?"

"She told me not to do anything until I hear from her, but she doesn't know Adel like I do, she's dangerous. I can't just sit back and do nothing while Dillon's life is in jeopardy. I need to go to the house and take care of some business. I have books there with legal precedence, I need to look some things up, then I'm going to visit my mother-in-law."

"You're what? Is that wise?"

"I don't have a choice. She's not taking my child."

"Dena…" Ellen began.

"I don't know how long I'll be, probably late."

"Then stay overnight, Dillon and I will be fine."

"Thanks, Aunt Ellen, I better go now. Dillon's in the kitchen eating a snack. I'll be back as soon as I can. Call me if you need me." She turned and went back inside.

Ellen followed her into the house and watched as she

wiped Dillon's milk mustache and cleared the peanut butter and jelly spill on the kitchen table.

"Hi, Aunt Ellen, you're home again," he said. "Guess what? I went to a construction building and got on a elevator and went all the way to the top. Mom was scared," he said, then laughed out loud.

"Don't talk with your mouth full, sweetie," Dena said, and she tucked another napkin under his chin.

He took another bite from his sandwich, swung his legs quicker, then continued to work on a construction site puzzle Julian had given him earlier that week.

"Aunt Ellen, I'm sorry, I completely forgot. Welcome home. How was Crescent Island and Mamma Lou?"

"I had a good time. Louise and the island are fantastic as usual. But truth be told, looks like you could use a trip there for some R and R when all this is over."

"That sounds perfect, I just might do that. Thanks again for watching Dillon this evening."

"Go, do what you have to do."

She nodded then knelt down to Dillon. "Hey, sweetie, I need to dash out for a bit this evening."

"To California?" he asked.

"No, sweetie, not that far. That's *after* your birthday, remember? You gonna be a good boy for Aunt Ellen?" He nodded, his mouth full and stuck together with peanut butter. "Good, I'll see you later, be good now. I love you." She kissed his forehead and tickled his ear. He giggled. She stood and nodded to Ellen then left.

Moments later Dena headed home, to her real home.

She charged in and went directly to her office right off the family room. She turned on the light, grabbed and piled books by her side from the bookcases, then went to work studying up on every bit of information she could find on negligence, child endangerment and custody battles. If Adel wanted war, she intended to arm herself to the hilt.

Julian knocked on the door and waited. Ellen opened and smiled. "Perfect timing. I have a sink that's backed up and I need…"

"I'll send someone over first thing in the morning. Is Dena here?" he asked abruptly.

"No, she's not."

"Is Dillon here or with her?"

"Dillon's here with me," Ellen said.

A wash of relief flowed through him. He was wrong, Dillon was fine and safe. "What's going on, Ms. Ellen?"

"Come on in, you and I need to talk."

Julian walked in and headed to the kitchen. "No, in here," Ellen said as she walked into the living room and sat down. Julian sat beside her and waited impatiently.

"Ms. Ellen, I know something's going on with Dena. She mentioned something about not losing him. I thought it had something to do with Dillon but since he's here with you I…"

"If I'm not mistaken I think it's about time you called me Aunt Ellen." He nodded. She began, "Dena has a friend, Lynn…"

"Brice. Lynn Brice. Yes, I met her this afternoon."

Ellen nodded. "They're not just friends. Lynn is representing Dena in a four-year lawsuit against her former mother-in-law, Adel Graham, and the law firm Graham, Whitman & Morris."

"She's suing them for money," Julian said, obviously disappointed.

"No, she's suing them for Dillon. She doesn't need their money, or anyone's money for that matter, in case you have any lamebrain ideas. Her parents' life insurance policy hasn't been touched. Over the years it's grown considerably, believe me, she's just fine financially."

"Then why the lawsuit?" he asked.

Ellen began at the beginning and laid out the saga of Dena's legal battles. She briefly mentioned her niece's marriage then Dillon's birth and finally the latest accounts as per the letter Lynn brought to the office. Julian asked questions, most Ellen answered without elaboration, others she left for Dena to fill in the blanks.

When all was said and done Julian got up and walked to the fireplace. He stood, stoically looking at a photograph of Dena and Dillon smiling in happier days.

"What can I do?"

"Nothing, wait until it all plays out," Ellen said.

"No, not good enough," he insisted, still with his back turned. A fire in his eyes began burning hot and fierce. This was more than personal. "No one's taking Dillon away from Dena. This Adel has no idea who she's dealing with."

"I'm impressed," Ellen said, smiling.

Julian turned back to face her. "Now to answer your earlier 'lamebrain ideas' comment of me, I love Dena and I never assumed she wanted me for my money." Ellen nodded her approval. "Just so we're clear."

"Have you told her you love her?" she asked him.

"No, we were scheduled to talk about it this evening but…"

"Wait a minute, you mean to tell me that you two scheduled a talk about your feelings for each other?"

"I know it sounds crazy, but yes, we did."

Ellen shook her head in pity. "You young people have no idea what to do with yourselves. She's about to run away and the best you can do is schedule a talk."

"What do you mean, she's about to run away."

Ellen continued shaking her head. "That's something you two need to discuss." Julian looked at her oddly. Apparently there was something more going on that he and Dena needed to talk about. "Well, what are you still sitting here talking to me for? Go before it's too late, tell her that you love her, do what you have to do to keep her here."

"Where is she?"

"She's at home," Ellen said, standing.

"But, you said she wasn't here."

"Not here in my home, her home." Ellen quickly gave him the address and basic directions but he insisted that he'd use his GPS shortly before he bolted out the door.

Forty-three minutes later into an hour-and-a-half drive, he pulled up in front of a huge house with a For Sale sign in the front yard. Dena's car was parked in the driveway. He pulled up next to hers and got out. He walked the path to the front door and rang the bell. Dena opened the door.

"What are you doing here, Julian? How did you find me?"

"We had a date, remember," he said. "May I come in?"

"No, I'm sorry, I'm busy," she said, closing the door in his face. "You have to leave now."

"A few minutes, I drove all this way…"

"I'm sorry, Julian, not now."

"Dena, I talked to Ellen, she told me about Adel."

The door stopped then slowly opened completely. Dena turned her back and marched through the huge open foyer through the massive living room back to her office. Julian followed. She sat back down at her desk.

"Nice house," he commented.

"Want to buy it?"

"Yeah," he said offhandedly, "sure."

She slammed shut a book she'd been studying then grabbed another and continued her reading and note-taking. "What do you want, Julian? I don't have time for this anymore. I lost my focus and now I need to deal with the consequences. So just get to the point and go."

"The point is, I know about the lawsuit."

"So, Aunt Ellen told you that I'm a blood-sucking parasite looking for a free payday on someone else's expense. No offense," she said cockily.

With his words slammed back in his face, Julian didn't even flinch. "None taken. Nice shot," he said simply, clearly unaffected by her tirade. He knew she was furious and that she needed to lash out. He could take it and on some level he deserved that shot. He remained standing and began looking around the large room. Bookshelves lined most of the back wall.

He pulled a book, read the cover, flipped through a few pages then put it back. She continued with her nose in the book. "You and I were supposed to have a serious conversation tonight."

"That was before all this."

"All this doesn't change anything."

"You have no idea what I'm dealing with."

"I know that for some reason you want to deal with this alone. Why? I'm here for you. I love you and nothing changes that fact."

"Love is transitory, it'll pass."

"No," he said, taking her hand and pulling her into his

arms. "Don't shut me out. I love you and all this only makes me love you more. This woman, Adel, will *not* take Dillon know that."

"It's not about the money," she said, her voice thick with emotion. "He's my baby, I'm supposed to protect him."

"I know, we will."

She collapsed into his strength and felt his strong arms wrap around her, holding on to her, protecting her. She broke down and the tears flowed and he was there to catch and console her. Moments later her cell phone rang. She nearly panicked. Staring at it, she finally reached over to pick it up on the second ring. "Hello?"

"What are you doing there?" Lynn asked.

Dena sighed. "Looking for a precedence."

"I told you to hold tight, I had something working."

"I know, but I couldn't just do nothing."

"I know. I half expected as much. Okay, this is where we are—good news. I need to speak with you in person as soon as possible."

"Where are you?" Dena asked.

"I'm at home," Lynn said.

"Okay, I can be there in thirty minutes."

"Good, see you in a few. Oh and by the way, Kenneth Fields of Fields and Associates, do you know him?"

Dena paused to think. "The name sounds vaguely familiar but my brain is just too fried."

"He's a big-time defense attorney here in town. His name is always in the papers having set some new precedence and won some unwinnable case. He's a legend, the man is beyond good, he's brilliant."

"What about him?"

"He called, offering his services, stating that as an employee of Hamilton Development Corporation his office and staff are at my disposal."

"Did he?" Dena said, turning to Julian, suddenly remembering where she'd met Kenneth Fields. "I'll see you in a few." She closed her phone.

"What about this?" Julian said, holding a book up for her to see. "This passage might work."

She looked at the passage he suggested. "Yes, actually I already have that. Kenneth Fields just called Lynn."

Julian nodded. "I might have mentioned this to him on the way over."

"Anybody else happen to get notified?"

"Darius and Jordan, they're always in the loop."

She nodded and quickly began closing and putting books away. "We're done here."

"Dena," Julian said, guessing that she was still upset with him, "don't say that, please." He placed his hand on his heart then took her hand with the other. "I need you in my life and I need Dillon. Don't just say we're through and throw us away, please."

She smiled lovingly. "I meant that we're physically through here. I have to go to Lynn's house."

Julian smiled, pulled her to him and kissed her hard.

Twenty minutes later Lynn opened her door. She and Dena hugged then with Julian shook hands. Lynn led them into the living room where Darius, Jordan and Kenneth sat talking and drinking either beer or soda. They all three stood and greeted Dena and Julian. Dena asked Lynn away to speak privately.

"What the hell is all that in there?" Dena asked as soon as they entered her kitchen.

"That, little one, is four fine-behind brothers."

"Yeah, okay, granted, but what are they all doing here? Julian tagged along with me, but Darius, Jordan and Kenneth?"

"Don't get too upset. Darius called earlier then stopped by with pizza. While he was here I got an interesting phone call. So I called Aunt Ellen's house for you. She said that you were at the house and that Julian was on his way there. I assume Darius called Jordan and Kenneth, they came a few minutes before you got here. But that's not important right now." She smiled like a cat in a birdhouse. "I mentioned earlier that I had something working. Well, it came through, we're expecting a phone call in a few minutes."

"From who?" Dena asked.

"Gaylord Till."

"What does he want?"

"To settle out of court," Lynn said.

"What? Adel would never."

"Apparently there's about to be a coup going on over there." Dena's mouth dropped open. She was stunned. "Come on let's join the guys. Girl, you just gotta love this part."

As soon as they joined the others in the living room the phone rang. Lynn put it on speaker then introduced Dena as the men sat silent.

Gaylord laid out a very impressive case both protecting his firm and Adel. He made her out to be a helpless widow still grieving the loss of her beloved husband and sons. Toward the end he detailed Forester's full holdings.

"Due to recent in-house restructuring, we here at Graham, Whitman & Morris would like to offer you, Dena Graham, the following." He cleared his throat and began.

"We've recalculated Forster Graham's holdings, which

under law will be transferred and turned over to you, or if you'd prefer, this firm will be delighted to manage in perpetuity." He went on to extol his firm's perfect record and exceptional management skills and how they'd be honored to continue handling her account.

"Why the three-sixty turnaround?" Dena asked.

"Suffice to say the senior partnership would like to end this unfortunate misunderstanding as quickly as possible." He then continued to whitewash the firm and its partners.

"That's all very nice, Gaylord. Just tell us what you have on the table?" Lynn asked.

"Dena, we'll forward a final listing of your and your son's account to Ms. Brice's office tomorrow morning. But off the top of my head, Forester had a land trust from his grandfather, two insurance policies, one for his wife and the other for any legitimate offspring. Since we've checked and identified Dillon's DNA as a ninety-nine point ninety-nine percent match he will be listed in our formal records as Forster's sole heir and have all benefits befitting that status.

"In addition, Dillon as Forester's only son will have a permanent seat and voting powers on the board of directors here at Graham, Whitman & Morris. You, Dena, of course will be expected to take his position until he is of legal age. I believe that would be twenty-one. With that power comes bonuses and a number of very lucrative perks." He stopped.

"Is that it?" Lynn asked.

Gaylord chuckled. "Well, what more do you want, another pen?"

"Actually I was thinking something in the line of compensation of mental anguish."

"Ms. Brice, I don't have the power to grant something like that."

"But I'm sure someone there does," she said.

"I'll see what I can do," Gaylord said.

"You do that," she added.

"But I'd like to inform you that barring any other unforeseen acquisitions from the trust, this offer is worth a considerable amount. I'd say just south of five million," he said.

"That is before you add on the company shares and profits for the past four years." They heard him gasp. "Yeah, let's not forget that," Lynn said.

"Of course, that would bring your client's total to somewhere worth conservatively close to over eight million dollars."

"Let's make that fifteen million dollars," Lynn corrected.

"I'll have to recheck some numbers."

"By all means, we're not going anywhere. And to help, I'll send over one of my CPAs to give you a hand."

"That won't be necessary."

"No bother, I'll be happy to, I'm sure his auditing skills will come in handy."

"Dena, I sincerely hope that you hold no malice toward us. We here at Graham, Whitman & Morris hold you in the highest esteem and still, as always, consider you part of our family. That said, if there's nothing else?" Gaylord said, preparing to hang up.

Kenneth nodded to Lynn. "Actually there is…" She nonverbally granted Kenneth the floor to speak.

"Off the top of my head we'll also be looking for restitution and interest somewhere in the neighborhood north of eight million to atone for added grief, suffering and mental anguish due to your firm's lexical handling of this matter."

The sudden male voice took Gaylord by surprise. "Who's speaking, please?"

"That was attorney Kenneth Fields of Kenneth Fields and Associates, as a close personal friend of Dena's, he stopped by along with the owners of Hamilton Construction Corporation to give much needed emotional support. Didn't I mention that earlier?"

"No you didn't. Hello, Kenneth," Gaylord said tartly.

"Good evening, Gaylord," Kenneth said. "And good evening to the five senior partners standing there with you."

Five voices spoke up.

Gaylord cleared his throat. "One more thing, Ms. Brice. I believe you have a tape recorder that we would be interested in acquiring."

"I'm no longer in possession of that item."

"We filed an injunction."

"I'm sure you did."

"It can't be used in a court of law."

"As I said, I'm no longer in possession of that item. But if you'd like to negotiate further, I'll be happy to pass the offer on."

"We can discuss that at a later date."

"I'll be around," she said.

"If that's it…" Gaylord said.

"Not quite." Dena spoke for the first time. "We'll discuss how you got a DNA sample from my son without my permission also."

"Of course," Gaylord said, then hung up, obviously unhinged.

After one united deep breath, the room went into an uproar. Hugs and kisses came from every direction.

Chapter 22

After the evening had settled down and congratulations and champagne circulated throughout Lynn's condo, Dena called Ellen afterward and told her the news. She was ecstatic. Julian drove Dena back to her house. They walked inside and stood in the moonlit foyer.

He pulled her into his arms and kissed her. "Congratulations," he said, "you did it."

"I did it for Dillon. It's his victory and his birthright."

"He has no idea, does he?"

"No, at almost four the only thing that matters is pizza getting dirty and loud noises," she said.

"I'm proud of you. Dillon is a very lucky young man. He's blessed to have an incredibly loving mother."

"Thank you."

"So why exactly did you need to come back here?"

"I need to straighten up. This is the weekend, and poten-
ial buyers love weekends and open houses."

"I thought I was buying it," he said.

"Oh, that's right I forgot," Dena said jokingly. Julian miled, crossed his arms and waited, looking at her question-
ngly. "What, am I missing something?" she asked.

"I'd like a tour. If I'm gonna buy it, I'd like to know what 'm getting."

"You'll have to talk to the Realtor, she does that part."

"But it's your house, you know it better than anyone else, he cracks and creaks, you know them all," he offered.

Dena looked around, suddenly feeling the ghosts of her ast memories around her. She nodded. "Well, lets get tarted, shall we?"

"After you," he said.

"The house is a Tudor style built six years ago. This is the ving room, large picture window to show the sculpted land-
caping all around the grounds."

"Does the gas fireplace work?"

"Yes," she said, walking through to the formal dining oom. "This is the dining room, cathedral ceiling in both ooms. This is the kitchen and breakfast room."

"Are you a good cook?" he asked.

"Not really, but I get by."

"We'll have to change that. What's through here?"

"The garage. Open the door, the light's on the wall."

Julian opened the door and turned on the light and found classic 1969 Ford Mustang and a five-year-old Porsche lassic. He laughed loud, and hurried over, looking at the cars dmiringly. "So this is how you guessed the year of my car."

She nodded. He laughed again then he stopped and looked a her. "Forester's, I presume."

She nodded.

He walked over to her and took her hand. They wen back into the kitchen and she sat at the table overlookin the deck and yard. She looked out, seeing solar light shining bright in the darkness.

"Forester was a player who loved the ladies and the car and the money. He married me to get back at his mother, bu surprisingly we lasted almost two years. There were goo times and bad times and just plain times in between. W would have definitely divorced eventually."

"Maybe," Julian said.

"Definitely," she corrected. "When he died, I felt so guilty He'd had an affair with a woman, then Adel made a point o introducing us and telling me that this woman was carryin Forester's child. I believed her. After all, a woman woul know the father of their child, wouldn't she? I ran out Forester followed. I got in the car and drove, he jumped in It was icy and snowing, we got to the bottom of the hill an he reached over and grabbed the wheel. The rest is history."

"He would be so proud of Dillon and what you just di for his son."

"Yeah, I think so, too. Funny, on some level it feels lik he's sticking it to her, too."

"He is, through you."

"Come on, Mr. Hamilton, I'll show you the rest of th house."

Upstairs she showed him three guest bedrooms, the Dillon's bedroom. "I like it. It looks just like him," Julian saic picking up a child's construction hat and looking it over.

"Come on—" she reached out her hand to him "—I want to show you one last room." She led him to the last door at the end of the hallway.

"Your bedroom?" he asked.

"Yes." She grasped the knob, turned then opened the door and walked inside. He followed her, then moved to the center of the room. He stopped and looked around. It was like a showplace. Everything was perfectly styled.

"This is really nice," he said.

"Thanks," she said huskily as she walked up behind him and placed her hand on his rear. She started rubbing his back then around to the front of him. Her skillful hands roamed over his body like a sculptor's on clay. She rested her head on his back and just felt her way.

He turned to the side and half smiled. "Are you trying to influence my purchase?"

"Yes," she said playfully. "Is it working?" she asked, already knowing it was. She felt his body tremble and tense. Then as her hand drifted lower, she felt him harden.

"Julian, make love to me," she whispered just over his shoulder.

"Dena, you know that there's nothing I'd want more to do than to make love to you, but this may not be the appropriate place."

"But it is, trust me. You said earlier that there were a lot of memories here. You were right, some good memories and some not-so-good memories. I need a new memory in this room, a good memory, one of tenderness and love."

Feeling her way, she started unbuttoning his shirt from behind. When it was done, she opened and stroked the firm tightness of his six-pack. The tense steel pectoral and abdomen muscles flexed and tightened beneath her hands. She felt a sense of power that exhilarated her. He groaned, allowing her to have her way.

She lowered the open shirt from his shoulders and let it fall between them. Then she reached up onto his shoulders and ran her hands along the line, down his arms then back up to his neck. As he lowered his head she gently scratched down his back then leaned in and nibbled his arm. She kissed his body as her hands returned to his waist.

Feeling along the top of his jeans, she found the front button and stealthily opened the waistband. As she slowly pulled the zipper down, Julian's hands clamped onto hers. He reached around and pulled her to face him. The eagerness in her eyes moved him.

He took her face gently in his hands and stroked the smooth line along her cheek. He leaned in and kissed her briefly, sweetly, on the lips then leaned back and looked into her soulful and promising eyes. He saw his future. And his past, once troubled and unsettled, melted away like snow on cinders.

A flood of passion poured out to her. "You are so beautiful," he whispered as he raised her hand to kiss.

She tilted her head and smiled, moved by his words, then held his hand and touched his chest to guide him toward her bed. He sat as she stepped back and slowly unbuttoned her blouse then removed it. She undid her zipper then stepped out of her skirt. Now standing before him in lace bra and panties, she moved closer.

She smiled seductively as he reached out to touch her. His hands came to her hips, her waist, then her stomach, then he cupped her breasts. She gasped, then sighed deeply. She was in heaven. She arched back and, leaning in, felt him bury his face between the crevice of her breasts. He nipped at her nipple through the lace and it immediately pebbled taut. Pulling herself close, she sat straddling his hips, her arms at her sides. Looking down into his eyes she felt the fiery blaze of passion burn as the precarious position enthralled them both.

Eyes wide open, they stared hypnotically, mesmerized as passion surged. He reached between their bodies and unsnapped the front clasp of her bra. It fell away. And her breasts, swollen and full, perked up. Her nipples hardened, offered out to him. He accepted, opening his mouth but not touching. Instead he blew a whisper.

The hot breath burned her body. She squirmed and leaned back but his steady resolved kept her in place. He licked her, thick and full, letting the flat of his tongue rub, tickle and tease circles around the dark brown orbs. The feeling was sensually divine, sending quivers through her into her stomach and making her shudder. Watching the thrill of his action was just as intoxicating as feeling it.

Time dizzily slowed as he took his leisure pleasuring her body. His sultry kisses were intense yet passionate and serene with secret promises of fulfillment. Dena clung to him, urging his passion as she raked her nails over his back. She moaned as he devoured her with his mouth, scorching her body as he sucked and she moved with his rhythm.

She felt his body throbbing hard for her and it excited her more. Uttering incoherently, she moaned her rapturous pleasure anticipating as he eased her up and his mouth teased and tingled her stomach and waist. Slowly she rolled to the side as he removed the rest of his clothes, pulling a condom from his wallet. Covering himself, he came to her.

She reclined on the bed, watching him. Leaning over, he kissed her then slowly lavished her body as he removed the last remnants of clothing, tossing the lace panties to the floor. Touching her all over, his masterful hands spoke lovingly. Her breasts, then her stomach, then lower, until he reached the sensuous treasure. Pulsating and throbbing, he relished her body until her moans turned to shrieks and gasps turned to screams.

Seeing her lying there naked and breathless was his undoing. "Come inside," she whispered, then opened and welcomed him.

The intensity of their joining made her squeal with pleasure and an instant spasm of pleasure escaped. He filled her and she sizzled, inhaling deeply then holding her breath, releasing gasps of delight.

Yielding to his cadence she wrapped her legs around him and moved against his motion. Plunging deeper and deeper, he entered and reentered her, building on the arousal of their passion. Throbbing, thrusting strokes rocked them while her gasps and shrieks continued. The pace quickened then slowed, driving her body closer and closer to the pinnacle as together they culminated, surrendering to ecstasy.

Breathless and depleted, he rolled over, holding her to rest on top of him. Dena closed her eyes and smiled for the memory she would keep forever. After a while she moved to the side and snuggled beside him as his breathing and heart rate slowed to normal. Hours later she woke up in peace in a room that had given her so much pain. She was finally free.

She looked over, seeing Julian still asleep. She smiled. She loved him and spending the rest of her life with him was all she wanted, but to do that she knew she had one more thing to do

After a quick shower she dressed then went back into the bedroom. Julian was gone. Moments later she heard the shower turn off in the master suite's second bathroom and the door open. She turned, seeing Julian standing there with a white towel wrapped around his waist. His body, sweet chocolate, was still deliciously wet.

"Good morning," she said.

"Good morning," he said, his brow rising with sinful interest seeing her standing there.

"I have to go," she quickly said.

"Then wait a minute, I'll get dressed, we can have breakfast and I'll follow you back."

"No, take your time. I have something to take care of before I leave the city."

"Are you okay?" he asked, seeing the strained expression on her face.

"Yes. I just need to make a few stops before going back to Aunt Ellen's house.

"Dena..." Julian began.

She turned away quickly, ready to finally get this over with. "I'll talk to you later." Hurriedly heading down the steps, she was nearly at the front door when Julian called after her again.

"Dena," Julian said, leaning over the rail from the second floor.

"I'll talk to you later, promise," she called, then hurried out the front door.

Julian stood overhead seeing her dash out. He walked back to the bedroom and stood by the window looking out. Her car backed up and quickly drove away.

A sinking feeling pitted him.

* * *

Guilt propelled her.

Leaving Julian like that was unfair but she knew she needed to finish this once and for all.

Dena drove around the curved lane leading to the Graham Manor on the hill. It was the first time she'd been to the house since Forester died. As she drove by the tree and slowed, she felt her heart tremble. This was the place where it all ended and now it will begin.

She continued up the hill, around the bend toward the big house. The front gate was open. She pulled into the driveway and parked next to the Benz, the Porsche, the Cadillac and the little red sports car that belonged to Kirkland. All newly waxed and detailed, displayed like a shrine to the departed.

She rang the bell and waited for the door to open. Adel stood there, glaring. Her mouth tightly pinched and her eyes glazed with too much alcohol and too much pain. Dressed in a black silk jacket with pants and a pristine white silk blouse ruffled at the collar and cuff, she looked like the perfect socialite for *Town & Country* or one of the other magazines she always fanned out on her sitting room coffee table.

"Hello, Adel," Dena said, standing in place.

"To what do I owe this dubious pleasure?" She smirked slurring her words far too early in the day to be the proper lady she always professed to be.

"It's time we talked," Dena said, holding her chin upward to ward off any reflection of weakness.

"Speak with my attorneys."

"I did, last night."

Adel half smiled, cracking the stern victimized expression

she'd built up over the years. "That's right. You know about all that by now. They kicked me out," she said matter-of-factly, as if she'd just ordered a drink from the bar. "After everything I did for them and everything my husband did for them. Nelson founded that firm and I was right there beside him when he did. I gave them my life and that's how they treated me." She chuckled then stepped back. "Come in, you might as well. They probably gave you my home, as well."

"I don't want your home, Adel," Dena said, crossing the threshold to follow her into the solarium. Surrounded on three sides and above by lush greenery and tinted glass, Dena remembered that she'd always loved this room. It was the only place in this mammoth house that seemed even remotely alive.

Adel walked over to the bar and sloppily poured another drink into her empty glass. She leaned back and looked up at the new day above her. "It's all over, so if you've come for more you need to talk to the traitors."

"You still don't get it. I never wanted anything for myself. All this, everything I did over the years, I did for my son. Dillon has a right to his heritage."

"All that's moot. You're talking to the wrong person. Weren't you paying attention? I don't control any of the money anymore, the lawyers do, talk to them."

"No, this part is between you and me, woman to woman."

"How dare you set foot in this house after you murdered my sons and killed my husband then profess to be righteous."

"I'm not righteous, Adel, and I'm not your enemy."

"You were always my enemy. The moment I laid eyes on you I knew you'd be trouble. Forester was so smitten with you, but I could see through that facade of yours. You wanted his money, the family money."

"It was never about money, Adel, it was about control. You needed to control everyone and everything around you, and I wouldn't let you."

"You ruined everything. You poisoned his mind, so how dare you have the audacity to stand there and judge me. You kill everything you touch—your mother, your father and my sons and my husband. Five dead because of you. Haven't you done enough?"

"Adel, I haven't done anything."

"You ruined my life," she spat out.

"I'm sorry you feel that way."

"'I'm sorry you feel that way.' Is that all you have to say? You walk in here and destroy my family and all you can say is I'm sorry. Save your apologies for someone who cares. I don't."

"I didn't destroy your family, Adel, and I didn't come here about the past. I came to talk to you about the future, about Dillon."

"To rub it in, I assume. He should be with me. You don't deserve him."

"He's my son."

"You took my son," Adel spat out venomously as she completely broke down and cried, "You took his life."

"No, Adel, you're wrong. I gave him a life," she retorted firmly, "The spoiled, confused person who couldn't blow his nose without you learned to be a man on his own, and you couldn't handle it."

"You weren't good enough for him."

"As far as you were concerned nobody was good enough for him, but at least I made him happy."

"He hated you," Adel spit out.

Dena went quiet. "No, Adel, he loved me, and you couldn't stand it. I'm sorry for your hurt and I'm sorry that you can't get beyond it. I know the grief, the pain, of guilt. But I have a child to raise and the only reason I came here was to try and reconcile our differences for Forester's sake and ask you to be a part of my son's life. I see now that's not possible." Dena took a step backward, turned and walked out. She left Graham Manor and never looked back.

Chapter 23

"Aunt Ellen," Dena called as soon as she entered the greenhouse.

"Over here," Ellen said, elbow-deep in mixing soil, compost and vermiculite. "Welcome back," she said as she firmly packed the soil mix around transplanted seedlings in larger more decorative pots.

"Hi," she said, hugging her aunt. "It's good to be here," Dena added then looked around. "Where's Dillon?"

"Hi, Mom," Dillon said, and he came running up and hugged her waist. "Guess what? Aunt Ellen said that she's gonna buy me a real fishing pole and I could go fishing with Mr. Marshall on his farm."

"That sounds great, sweetie, but we'll see, okay?" Dena looked up at her aunt questioningly. "Mr. Marshall?"

"He's a real live fireman," Dillon said excitedly. "Can I ride on his fire truck please?"

"We'll see," Dena said, then glanced at her aunt who suspiciously busied herself with another plant.

"'Kay," he said, and hurried off to continue mixing his soil on the other side of the aisle.

"Reggie Marshall?" Dena queried with interest.

"Reggie stopped by last night after Julian left."

Dena was immediately concerned. "What happened?"

"Nothing happened, he just stopped by."

"For no reason?" Dena continued, knowing her aunt's love for remodeling and the fire department's frequent visits.

"For no reason," Ellen confirmed. "Just to say hello."

"And his farm?"

"Oh, didn't I mention it, we ran into Reggie at the county fair. His family farm was on the way. When he stopped by last night he invited us to come visit the farm again. He had a small pond out back. He told Dillon about going fishing last night."

"Wait a minute. 'Again,' as in, you went there before?"

"We might have stopped by while we were in the area," she said casually.

"Really," Dena said, smiling happily from ear to ear.

"Enough of that," Ellen said. "Newsflash, Willamina had another baby boy last night."

Dena smiled. "That's great. Is she okay? How's the baby?"

"Her husband called and said that both she and the baby are just fine. She's being released tomorrow."

"Good, I'm glad to hear that. We'll send flowers to her house this afternoon."

Ellen, seeing Dena's changed expression, reached out and

took her hand, comforting her. "It's really over," she assured her. Dena nodded and smiled. "Good, I'm glad."

"Me, too."

"Lynn called earlier. She said she'll be stopping by this afternoon with some paperwork for you to sign." Dena nodded. "Are you okay?" Ellen asked, lowering her voice so that Dillon wouldn't hear them.

"Yes, I'm fine," Dena said just as low. "Just tired, this day has been a long time coming."

"And now it's finally over."

"Yes, it is, finally."

"I'm proud of you, you did good."

"Thanks," Dena answered pensively, then picked up a spade and dug it into the trough of soil. After mixing it around a few times, she stopped. "I went to see Adel this morning."

Ellen looked up, surprised at hearing what Dena just said. "And?" she questioned openly.

"I guess I thought we would come to an understanding."

"But you didn't," Ellen surmised. Dena shook her head. "Adel is still angry and blaming you?" Dena nodded. "Then it's something that she's going to have to deal with."

"She said that my selfishness killed five people."

Ellen paused, realizing that Adel included Dena's parents in her attempts to hurt Dena. "And did you believe her?"

"Yes."

"Oh, Dena, baby."

"For a real long time I felt guilty. If I hadn't snuck out that night then Mom and Dad would still be alive."

"No, it was their time, nothing and nobody can change that."

"But I believed that it was my fault then when Nelson, Kirkland and Forester were killed..."

"It was an accident," Ellen said firmly.

Dena looked across the room to where Dillon was playing happily. She smiled. "I carried all that for so long."

"Dena, your parents' deaths, Forester, his brother and his father were all horrible accidents. And as for Adel, you did what you had to do for Dillon's future."

"I know that, too, it's just that she's still so sad and she has no one. I have Dillon and you."

"Yes, you do. I once heard that when a person is ready, love will come. When Adel is ready, she'll move on, or not. It's her choice. She'll miss many opportunities, but it's her decision to make."

Dena nodded, agreeing. She just wished Adel would find her peace.

"Is everything all set for the party tomorrow?" Ellen asked.

"Yep, the moon bounce will be delivered and blown up first thing. Balloons, decorations and cake will be here in the early afternoon."

"Perfect."

"The new patio and grill area look fantastic. When did they finish?"

"Yesterday afternoon."

"They did a beautiful job. Are you ready to break in the grill with hot dogs and hamburgers?"

"Definitely."

"Okay. After we finish here I'll go to the store and pick up the food." She turned to leave.

"Oh, before I forget," Ellen said. "Julian called about thirty minutes ago. He asked for you to call him when you got in."

Dena nodded. "Thanks." She went back to the house, knowing that he deserved an explanation since she all but ran out and left him in her house. But she wasn't ready to talk to him, not yet. She didn't know what to say.

Walking upstairs to change clothes, she found herself sitting on the side of the bed staring out her window at the oak tree. It was so simple before. She watched and he worked and the security of her heart was safely intact. But it was too late now for *I should haves.* She was already in love with Julian.

As soon as she climbed the back stairs, the front doorbell rang. She answered, knowing who it would be. "Hi, Julian."

"Hi." He walked in and stood. She closed the door and walked into the kitchen, he followed. "You want to tell me about this morning? You ran out like the house was on fire."

"I needed to take care of something personal."

He nodded, deciding not to press the issue. "Willamina had a baby boy last night."

"Yes, Aunt Ellen just told me. That's great news."

"Also, Mattie got the okay to return to work."

"Oh," Dena said, her expression completely changed.

"She's coming in Monday morning."

"That's wonderful. That means the office can go back to normal. I'm sure that will be a relief to everyone there." She turned away from him.

"Dena, this means…" he started.

"Julian, you don't have to, I understand. It was a temporary position. A few months at best, right? That was the original plan."

"We were thinking…" he began.

"You know what, Julian, I need to change and help Aunt Ellen out in the greenhouse. Then I still have a ton of things to do before Dillon's birthday party tomorrow."

"Dena, we need to talk."

She nodded, not sure she could speak anymore.

"Tonight," he offered.

She nodded.

For Julian, tonight never came. Dena purposely turned off her phone, took Ellen and Dillon out for dinner.

Chapter 24

By Sunday afternoon the Peyton household was alive with activity. Friends and family enjoyed as neighborhood children, playmates from the day-care center and children and grandchildren of friends ran around having a blast. Although the clowns, magician and moon bounce was a major success, it was the pony rides Julian, Jordan and Darius provided that made the day. The kids had a ball taking turns riding in large circles.

Dena was scattered, entertaining and hosting. Ellen and Louise sat chatting happily as Reggie and Colonel Wheeler manned the grill, serving burgers and hot dogs to the kids and more stable food to the adults. The new patio got rave reviews as Jordan and Darius continually handed out business cards.

"I've been thinking of doing a little renovating job at my place," Louise said, reading the business card Jordan handed her.

"That's great, just give us a call. I'll be happy to stop by and take a look and see what we can do," Jordan said eagerly.

"I most definitely will," Louise said, smiling and nodding happily. "My, my, my, you and your brother must stay extremely busy with everything you have going on. When do you find the time for family obligations?"

"We're both single," Darius said assuredly.

"Is that right?" Louise questioned.

"Yes, ma'am." He nodded confidently.

"Please call me Mamma Lou, everyone else does." Louise smiled as she just happened to glance across the open area to Colonel Wheeler. He shook his head and began laughing, knowing that she would never change and loving every minute.

Across the way Dena looked over, seeing Julian helping kids blow up balloons. She smiled and nodded, he returned her gesture.

"What'd you do now?" Jordan asked, seeing them.

"Nothing," Julian said.

"Doesn't look like nothing to me," Darius added. "If you want my opinion…"

"Isn't that Lynn Brice?" Julian asked.

Darius stopped talking immediately and turned around, seeing Lynn walk over to the patio area with someone else. Jordan started laughing, seeing Darius' overly delighted expression. Darius glared at Jordan. "Excuse me," he said, then walked away.

"Looks like it's just you and me, bro," Jordan said. "Now, if you want my opinion…"

"Looks like Lynn brought a girlfriend with her."

Jordan's neck turned so quickly he should have gotten whiplash. "I'll be right back."

Julian smiled. Knowing his brothers' weaknesses always came in handy. He looked over to where Dena was. She was busy handing out drinks. He turned his attention to Dillon. He was sitting on the side, looking very sad. He walked over.

"Hey, little buddy, how you doing?" Julian asked, holding his hand out for Dillon to halfheartedly hit.

"I don't want to be four anymore," Dillon said.

"Of course you do, being four years old is the best. You get to do so much more than you did when you were three. You'll see new things, go new places and meet new people."

"I know, but I don't want to anymore."

"You'll love it, trust me."

"No, I won't. I'm staying here."

Julian was confused. "What do you mean, staying here? Where else would you be going?" he asked, assuming that now that everything was over Dena might be considering moving back to her home in the city. If that were the case, he'd just buy someplace close by.

"California."

"What about California?" he asked as his heart began sinking.

"After my birthday we gotta go live in California, but I don't want to anymore."

"I see."

"If I have to go, can you move to California with us?"

Julian took a deep breath as his heart knotted tight. "I'll tell you what, why don't you let me talk to your mother, maybe I can change her mind." He looked up, seeing Dena walking toward them.

"Really?" Dillon said hopefully.

"Yes," Julian said just as Dena arrived.

"Hi, birthday boy. How are you doing, having fun?" she said just as Dillon looked at Julian, nodded, then ran off.

"Dillon?" Dena called as he ran away.

She took a step to go after him. "Dena," Julian said.

She whipped around anxiously. "What's wrong with him?"

"He doesn't want to be four anymore."

"What?" she asked.

"When were you going to tell me?"

"Tell you what?" she asked.

"That you're leaving," he said. She immediately looked regretful. "That you're packing up and walking out. Dillon just told me. Apparently being four means moving to California, and he doesn't want that. So the question remains, Dena, why didn't you tell me that you intended to leave all along?"

"Would it have made a difference?" she asked. He didn't speak. She shrugged. "I didn't think so." She turned to walk away.

"I remember you saying once that you loved me." She turned hard, her eyes blazed. "So, is that it? You just fell out of love with me, just like that."

"Don't you dare…don't you dare use my feeling against me. I love you and nothing can change that."

He smiled. The fire in her eyes was all he needed to see the truth. She did love him. "I love you, too, Dena. Don't leave me. I never asked that of any other woman, my mother, my ex-wife. But I'm asking you, Dena, please don't leave me. I love you too much to let you go."

"You really love me?" she asked as a warm glow began to burn inside her.

"Yes, I really love you," he repeated eagerly. "Stay."

"I'm not leaving," she whispered softly. He looked

confused. "I was, yes. But that was before you. All my life I wondered what followed love, now I know, it's you. How could I possibly leave you?" She reached up and touched his face gently.

Julian smiled and leaned down to kiss her gently. "That's exactly what I wanted to hear and to make sure you stay by my side—" he reached into his pocket and pulled out a beautiful diamond ring "—marry me. Be my wife."

"Julian," she said as her eyes welled full. "I…"

"Just say yes," he instructed.

She smiled. "Yes."

"Mom, is it okay to be four now?"

Dena looked down and smiled just as Julian swept Dillon up in his arms. "Yes, sweetie, it's okay to be four."

"Yea," Dillon said, then hugged Julian. "Good, 'cause it's time to eat cake and chocolate ice cream."

Julian set Dillon down and he immediately took off running. "What are we going to do with him?" she said.

"I thought I'd adopt him, then we could get to work on his little sister."

"Oh, really," she said, smiling from ear to ear.

"Yeah, really." He kissed her, then they headed around to the back of the house for cake and chocolate ice cream.

Epilogue

Dena walked on cloud nine for the next six months. Every day was like a dream come true. She'd never been so happy, and the recent news about her pregnancy added to her joy.

Her wedding was a delight and after a quick resolution in family court and her favorite judge, her new family was now complete. Julian had just signed off on adoption papers and although they hadn't quite finalized where they would live, for the time being shuttling between Julian's house and her house in the city was just fine with her, with, of course, frequent visits to her aunt Ellen's.

The busyness of their new life was exciting but exhausting. So after dropping Dillon off, the two of them took time for a nice long romantic weekend. Julian and Dena returned, expecting a quiet evening's visit with Ellen, then back home. Not exactly, since as soon as they drove up they knew something was going on.

"Mo-omm, Da-add, come see what we did today," Dillo
yelled from the gated front yard as soon as he saw their ca
drive up. Dressed in his perfectly fitted hard hat, work glove
and goggles Julian had given him, he grabbed each hand an
nearly dragged them around the side of the house to the patic
Dena and Julian looked at each other with concern, hearin
the start of a loud engine roar. They weren't sure if the
should be excited or scared to death.

"What in the world," Dena said, starting to panic.

As soon as they reached the backyard Dena looked arounc
seeing her aunt perched comfortably high on top of a backho
with the large shovel-like scoop in midair. The engine wa
running hard and she had just scooped up a huge patch o
earth. "Oh, no," Dena said as her heart sank and her mout
dropped open. She began waving to her aunt to stop.

Both she and Julian started toward Ellen but, Dillon, sti
holding on to their hands, held them back. "No, we can't g
over this line," he said, pointing to a powdered chalk lin
several yards away from the machine. "I'm in charge. Nobod
can cross, not even me."

The engine shut down as soon as Ellen saw them. "Hello,
she said, happily waving. "Perfect time for a short break."

"Aunt Ellen, what are you doing?" Julian asked.

"What do you mean?"

"You can't have this machine here and you can't just sta
digging massive holes in the yard like this," Dena said, con
cerned about buried cables and power lines.

"Of course I can," Ellen said as she climbed down off th
perch. "I think this is a great place for a swimming pool."

"A swimming pool?"

"Dillon needs to learn to swim, every child does."

"Aunt Ellen—" Dena began to say, way past panicked.

Julian interrupted calmly. "Aunt Ellen, you need certifications, zoning authorization, utility approval, about a dozen permits, not to mention a qualified professional," Julian said just as Reggie Marshall walked around from the other side of the machine with gloves, ear plugs, goggles and a hard hat on.

"All taken care of," Ellen said, walking over to them and pointing to the back window covered with permits. "How about some lemonade? I just made a fresh pitcher with some oatmeal-raisin cookies."

"Oatmeal-raisin cookies, yea," Dillon squealed, clapping his hands then hurrying over to the new patio area with the insulated juice container and covered plate of cookies.

"Hey," Reggie said, following Ellen over. "Welcome back, and congratulations again." He removed his gloves, shook hands with Julian and hugged Dena.

"Thanks," both Dena and Julian said, utterly relieved to see him. The two men began conferring on the new swimming pool site and design. Ellen added her opinion as everyone sat down at the picnic table for lemonade and cookies. Dena smiled, knowing that this was how her life would be from now on, Julian and Dillon at her side and completely surrounded by love.

KIMANI
ROMANCE

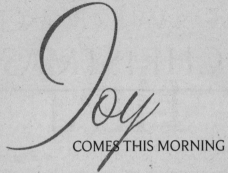